MR BAWMAN WANTS
TO TANGO

First published in 2010 by
Liberties Press
Guinness Enterprise Centre | Taylor's Lane | Dublin 8 | Ireland
www.libertiespress .com
info@libertiespress.com
+353 (1) 415 1224

Trade enquiries to CMD BookSource
55A Spruce Avenue | Stillorgan Industrial Park | Blackrock | County Dublin
Tel: +353 (1) 294 2560
Fax: +353 (1) 294 2564

Distributed in the United States by
DuFour Editions | PO Box 7 | Chester Springs | Pennsylvania | 19425
and in Australia by
InBooks | 3 Narabang Way | Belrose NSW 2085

Copyright © Mogue Doyle, 2010

The author has asserted his moral rights.

ISBN: 978–1–907593–03–1

2 4 6 8 10 9 7 5 3 1

A CIP record for this title is available from the British Library.

The publishers gratefully acknowledge financial support from the Arts Council.

Cover design by Sin É Design
Internal design by Liberties Press
Set in Garamond
Printed by Thomson Litho

Mr Bawman Wants to Tango

Mogue Doyle

You, four angels by my bed,
Stand this soul in all good stead;
See me safe right through the night;
Guard our house until daylight.
Amen. Please, amen, amen.
Mammy, Daddy, will you stay;
Make the *bawman* go away.

1

Button-eyed crows scan for scraps along early-morning pavements, balance in clusters on overhead wires, and spit their gruff jibes down on pedestrians' heads.

Having been around him now in one cluster or other for these donkey's years, I should know like the back of my hand the capers of one raven-haired J. V. Ryan – my old pal, Johnny Val. Our fellow scavenger here has a story to tell.

It's over to you now, Johnny, boy: open your beak and take it away.

When the clouds lift, this town can be seen for the lopsided way it straddles the river: how a lady of old would sit side-saddle on a palfrey, facing nearside with her all cocked over the off as she'd pig-jump through the morning fog. Morning fog; evening fog. What matter? Who cares? Well, it *does* matter: every last blessed thing that happens here concerns others, like the single twig which shakes on a tree to disturb the whole forest. And believe you me, as my father, the Gunner Ryan, used to say, there's a lot of shaking going on in this neck of the woods, all the time – yeah baby, all of the time. The early mist is a shapeless mass of cloud from the night before which clings to water like gum to the soles of your feet, as its grey arms swirl, ebb and slink from the lower ends of our narrow streets as much in dread of the sun as a thief in the night. Now, don't talk to me about the breed of haptic, happy-hearted crook we have hereabouts. But more anon, as they say in all the best circles. More anon, dear boy.

Though smaller by far, this side of town was here nearly before time was invented, as my old man used to put it. In the beginning, fellows wore animal skins the length of miniskirts, which were more than likely just about long enough to keep their privates from freezing over in winter, and with whiskers and selvedge tails blending, they cocked their bare bony asses to the east wind and gouged out furrows for the very first foundations, using oars that had batted their dodgy coracles upriver, while some master builder-cum-developer grunted and hopped off them with an even bigger cudgel. (What has changed?) The rocks they threw over the wickerwork at wild boar for amusement and recrimination during lunch break had only just cooled enough to be handled, having spurted from the middle of the earth a short while earlier. After frightening off all hairy pigs but still in want of diversion, they formed into two gangs and used the oars to hurl stones at each other, an activity which, when moderated slightly with some rules added, became so popular as to turn into a national pastime. Indeed, up to quite recently this side of town produced mighty slingers and hurlers.

This area is so old that the insides of buildings reek from the must-damp saga of times past, and the whang off backyards makes a body hold his nose till he gets so used to it he can't tell the difference between this and the musk bouquet from a ladies' cloakroom in a dance hall. But when it comes to commerce and trade – as in all matters of importance where the aged don't count for much, with the exception of dying – these old buildings are forgotten, abandoned here with other all-sorts getting on in years, each marked out by the same delicate beautiful whiff – and *beautiful* is the word, boy: pure fucken nirvana. And yet they betray a distinct feature of great age, a certain quality closely related to that which hoity-toity furniture restorers refer to in antiques as patina – well, how's your patina coming along, dear boy?

Built up round its centre, the far side of town on the west of the river happens to be where the thrifty women, as my old fellow used to call them, go shopping for their pennysworth, with their hair tied back in hard-rock buns to match the grip they have on their purse strings and twice-folded brown envelopes, as well as on their spouses' must-bags. It's where the merchant princes live – horse traders who'd tan their mothers' sagging hides to flog them at a knock-down price. Just look at their houses, each bigger and better than the next, monuments to their owners' stash and status, rather than homes in keeping with the lines of evenly stepped gables which sloping streets need for a uniform appearance – and who says looks don't count? That clique there beyond rules the roost like bantams in broiler coops with baggy wattles a-droop and luscious heads ripe for the pot, while the one thing they have mortal fear of, day and night, is a stray cock nearing the hen house. I know all about them. So, cockalorums over there on the hill, you pay heed now: for this little ol' rooster here is on the loose. Cock-a-doodle-doo, boy: Johnny Valentine Ryan, let me tell you, has the lowdown on every one of youse over there.

What's more, this town didn't always hang the same way. A time was when both sides had their fair share of trade, as coalcots sailed the fourteen-odd miles from the harbour. Stone wharfs and silent warehouses still there to the south are a testament to those days – maybe not that long ago, either. I remember the old galoots in my father's bar who had worked on the cots and gabbards, their faces so ingrained with dust, or patina, they were as black as any gaggle of kohl-eyed girls out on the town for a good night's tear. And they hawked up such an amount of phlegm that a barman's worst nightmare was having to sawdust and clean a sputum-gummed floor after closing time. They swore that a cot-man's chest can never be got rid of, and rum for relief was your only man.

'Give us another black Jamaican there, Gunner Ryan, like a good fellow', they barked at my father. 'It's the only thing to soften the cough. We'll sink the gabbard yet again, eh? Down the hatch, boys, down the hatch.'

But those same fellows who haunted Ryan's bar were no more than the remains of a kind, a dying breed, just like their womenfolk, who carried huckster baskets to the matches above in the park on Sundays – and the Widow Flynn has for a good while now been the huckster queen of this town.

'Bananas, apples, oranges and chocolates. Only the last few left now, three for a bit – a half-crown. Is that the smallest you have, love? Anyone for oranges, apples or chocolates? Get yourself a nice ripe banana there, son, to put colour in your face.'

The Widow Flynn carries the best apples and oranges, with more of everything bigger, better and sweeter in her basket; besides, you wouldn't want to buy from anyone else when she's around. Up and down between rows of terraces, on Sundays, she harries spectators into making purchases, mainly chocolate – a safer bet by far for cautious country lads: heaven knows whose hands the apples were in.

As if driven by tiny battery-operated motors, her occasional red earrings dangle and whirl against her mother's ancient black shawl, which partly covers her head but whose main purpose is to drape the basket. Completing the trader's costume, a dirndl skirt, red of course, sits in tight against her waist to be swooshed before eyes, otherwise fixated, in order to gain attention and prise from their owners' pockets as many harvest-bright pennies and shiny shillings as possible. You know from the whiff, though, as she comes close, that the widow has done more than her fair share of tromping in the sun for one afternoon. Still and all, while her pestering presence there sets thin-blooded old lads against her, most young whelps can't help but allow her to deflect their interest, as they feel their billies bulge hot – red and black on a dame will catch a man's eye as long as he has any kick at all left in him. And even the most keyed-up spectator will bite back impatience when she bellows him with an earful: 'Only the last few left now.'

'Missus, do you carry any Peggy's leg?' I once heard a fellow shout. 'This match is flipping useless; I'm tired of watching it. Be a sport, missus, and send me home with a smile.'

'There's no better one to put a smile on a chap's face going home to its mammy', she says. 'But you'd want to wash it first.'

'Go on, Nance, give us an old kiss.'

'Look at here, son–'

Though letting on to be too exasperated to get the rest of the words out, she couldn't hold back a look of satisfaction at having found just the right kind of foil needed for the pantomime that best advertised her basketful of wares, for there was nothing like a good putdown to entertain spectators at a bad match. Nancy stood back, raised her hems like a Romany lady about to dance, and revealed a black-stockinged limb.

'Do you see that?' says she. 'Would you know what to do with it?' After staring him down, she hissed: 'Son, you'd eat it first. Ask Mammy when you go home to loan you her instruction manual, and while you're at it, get her to feed you more porridge in the mornings. Would you like some chocolate in the meantime – a banana even, to help put meat on your bones?' Turning to face a growing audience, she nodded her *Huh* at the lad and whined: 'Like any healthy fun-loving woman, I do prefer to play ball with men rather than boys.'

After the cheer she got from the crowd, the Widow Flynn

walked away, but she was soon back with a full basket among that swath of spectators, where her pickings had taken such a surprising turn for the better.

*

Doesn't the river look a treat, though, this Sunday morning? The nicest feeling in the entire world is to wake up here under the dry arch of the bridge, unchained, free as a bird, with not a care in the world, and to gaze out on a sheet of clear shop-window glass. One section is in shade, with the other shining as she moves in from the dark north, coyly at first, but she spreads wide and loose at the last moment, like the Widow Flynn after two glasses of Blue Nun. Bless that woman; may her generosity never falter.

Such a grand entrance as she makes for us, the recipients of her bounty, to fill burghers' cisterns and flush out their pots – though in return she picks up a few odds and ends before reaching the rock factory and curving out of sight under the turret rocks; she then flows through the Beare meadows and past the asylum to maunder off towards wherever it is that all good rivers wind up. Keeps the place going, she does, like farmers' wives to town of a Friday – that bespectacled specimen of tightness who used to exact nearly a week's shopping from Ryan's bar and grocery on the strength of a dozen eggs and a few pounds of half-washed salty butter: pure fucken axle grease, it was. Give us instead a woman straight off the twice-weekly Kilkenny bus, who'd never pass off her addled eggs on a soul or do you for a halfpennyworth, yet there was nobody better for picking out real quality: Murphy's best-blend tea, the sweetest of our bacon factory's teat-rashers, and the usual noggin of Powers malt to tide her over the celibate nights and mountain chill.

This river has a more exotic personality than what is needed to service the dour wants of routine shopkeepers, and like every chick of a certain age, she is a beauty to behold. It's the same as waking up next to the most gorgeous dame with nothing on but her dark blue work-coat. Stop the lights at the thoughts of it – but more of that, too, anon.

Every once in a while on a balmy afternoon during the dog days, though avoiding the hour when there's a spark off the water that would cut the eye from your head, a fellow would want for nothing better to do than walk out the mill road there to gape at the river meandering into the valley's light-blue haze. With or without diamonds – what matter, who cares? – she swaggers a left buttock into the distance, a lot like the girl I once knew who swagged her curved tush – and such legs – from side to side through the cloisters. A time was when a falling star shot its arc across my dark firmament.

On quiet Sunday mornings like this, too, the river puts me in mind of the poem 'My Dark Rosaleen', which our English teacher, the Shed, drummed into us below in the college. (What a joint that was in which to be locked up for nearly four months at a time.) Going there was a pure waste of good youth; it was a place where a fellow would get only the odd glimpse of Rose Brien's fair legs, which were so well curved that a mitred bishop with any stir left in his crotch would have to stop and stare. I had serious designs on those pins in penny loafers as they strutted past, their owner balancing a glass of milk and two biscuits on a tray headed for the distant room of some unwell ecclesiastical student, while the eyes of every gawk in window embrasures along the cloisters leaped out on sticks and became glued to the lump of her rump. With horns on them like whelks, they would, if they could, rip that tight navy work-coat off her body stitch by stitch a thousand times over – if his lordship hadn't beaten them to it.

The further into our school term we went, the more enticing those curves of hers became, as week by week fellows grew demented to a tizzy, till, fortunately for all, the holidays arrived and a state of pure bedlam was just about avoided. For such was the effect of the joint that September's boniest knock-kneed domestic gradually altered to become by Christmas the most delectable dancing diva – and by which time even the kitchen's old Sister Spud had begun to look good, almost.

To this very day, I lament lost opportunities of having let that girl pass untouched beneath the bleeding-heart statue in the recess halfway down the main cloister. But whichever had the most hold over us – the terror of being expelled by the college president, or the horrors of eternal damnation that our spiritual director had injected through his sermons on the anguish of sin-ful flesh forever searing in sealed-off black pits – it helped us to keep our hands, if not our inclinations, off fair Rose Brien's legs. Such self-denial was purgatory, though, to a youth for whom the feel of Brylcreem buttressing his slick jet-black coiffure was all the spiritual nourishment he ever needed, and for whom the pungent sniff of Old Spice that titillated his pipes when patted on the chin was elation close to a divine mystery. Just as well, then, that the old bishop – whose palace was across the road from our institution – really knew nothing of such unhallowed fetishes, or else his piousness might have succumbed to wild hankerings after the good life. Come to think of it, though, it was Elvis, with his blue suede shoes and Graceland palace, who was my kind of prelate. *Uh-uh-uh, uh-uh-uh, uh-uh-huhuu.*

But as purgatory eventually leads to heaven, a boy's torment, too, led to bliss when he met fair Rose on one of the college's dormitories – '*Voulez-vous rendez-vous?*' says he. If the dean, Dr Quigley, had caught a student fraternising with a girl – or with any creature in Malaysian sarong or Hawaiian muu-muu that resembled a female – an emergency conference of the college authorities, in full-frock regalia, would have been called, and the lad expelled with enough high propriety to make a proper example of him. If the degenerate had, however, been found hopscotching in the arms of a domestic on the counterpane on top of some cubicle bed, he would scarcely have been given time to pack his suitcases – and likewise the girl.

Those things happened some fourteen years ago, when the slurped kisses and fumbled touching of a fifteen-year-old were even tastier than the capfuls of poteen I had snaffled from the Gunner's secret stash, which I replaced with equal amounts of whiskey – which, in turn, were eventually replaced with water, a ploy that worked well till the time my mother found me comatose inside the rasher counter two hours after closing time and had to get the doctor out of bed to come and make sure her son wasn't on the road out.

Right now though, here under the arch, I have to keep my wits about me. For there is one among us that I need to be wary of: Lousy Jim, whose vital fluid, due to the way he sidles up to you when he wants something, must come from the blue blood of the horseshoe crab, certainly not from that of nobility; or maybe it's green, like a worm's is green.

During the last half-hour, not as much as a snore, or a stir, has come from the farthest-over bundle on the ground – so he must be ready to intrude once more upon our little company. The creature will again impose on us the one must-dank tang of old buildings and backyard sewers, and we will be obliged to hold our noses till we get used to him. A strong breeze through the arch will help.

How in heaven's name did we ever let that go-by-the-wall of a fecking Louse break into our little coterie of dreamers? And we had been a company of such fine gentry before: blue-blooded nobility, you might say. Ah, well!

2

Crows need street savvy to forage and exist in a scaldy old town. This morn-
ing, I saw one fly a paper bag up to a rooftop, pin it against the ridge and
peck out the left-over chips. Johnny is a sharp operator, too, when he needs
to be.

There is far less of the usual rumble of traffic aloft this Sunday
morning: we can savour the burbling rush of water across stones
just beyond the arch and let it soothe our souls. But all of a sudden I feel my palpitations flutter as a flurried crunch of newspaper comes from that farthest-over bundle on the ground, with
the flap-swish of cardboard off its sides. One piece, glossier
than the others, flips against the butt of the bridge and stops
short of the water.

No doubt, most of us wish that a face, any face, other than
the one we expect, will appear and smile benevolently as much
as to say: hello, what a lovely day, good to be alive and isn't life
beautiful? But no such luck: out pops the weasel-faced head of
Lousy Jim from underneath a pile of rags and papers. As usual,
his humour is in keeping with his looks: tell me something new.
Lately, he has been sticking to us like sputum gummed to the
floors in a fellow's childhood, and every morning we wake to
find him still here in the *parlour*, impossible to shake off. But we
must be grateful for small mercies, and acknowledge that at least

one more of our kind, the true torch-holders of freedom, has made it through another night.

'Did you hear the racket last evening?' he shouts. 'Something should be done about that; never any cops on this side of town when they're wanted, especially on a Saturday. Quick enough they were, though, the other day to stop me and grab the bottle from my hands and empty the cider onto the ground, every last fucken drop, a pure sacrilege. The music man Guard – what's his name again? – held it at arm's length lest he might have caught the plague, and whistled '*Drink, drink, drink*' (from *The Student Prince*) as the precious stuff gurgled out. Anyway, those whores only pick on gormless mortals like me – easy targets – instead of chasing crooks. Has anyone the loan of a fag? Please, I'll give it back to him this evening, I swear.'

No answer; it's safer not to draw him on us; he's not called the Louse for nothing.

'Who knocked over my shaggen flagon?' The Louse scowls, starting to turn wicked once more. 'I tell you, if I catch who done it, I'll swing for him.'

A second sheet of cardboard is flung against the masonry. He'll swing for himself if needs be one of these days if he's not careful about whom he's accusing: I'll get my friend Sputnik here to deal with him. Ever more obstreperous as the days pass, the Louse must be back on the meths. He snatches the brown bottle and jerks it against his lips to suck the dregs. The tyke probably forgot to put the cap back on and knocked it over himself during a nightmare when the buzzing ghouls arrived to take over what was left inside his skull, while the snores groaned worse than the traffic overhead. The sooner the white-coats come to bring him away for drying out, the better; anyway, a spell in the asylum would crown him – and I ought to know. It's certainly not advisable to lie with your back to him.

Take the night I went into a fever and a certain lady came down here to look after me. The Louse kept groping at her till Sputnik caught him up and lobbed him wholesale, bags and rags, there in the drink. Seeing him splash, shriek and cool off must have been a circus; he was lucky, though, that the water was low at the time. The river can be a great solution sometimes, the way she cleans things up. We would all be lost without her.

That dark lady flows under five of the six arches – except when there's a flood, which washes right through our parlour for spite – that female, vengeful type. And the mention of arches reminds me of the bridge in the story 'The Vision of Mirzah', which had to be learned for the public exam back when the Shed taught us English. Some bloody bridge that was. It had 'three score and ten entire arches, with several broken arches'. Just like here on a bad morning, it had 'a black cloud hanging on each end of it' and 'there were innumerable trapdoors that lay concealed in the bridge', which several of the people 'no sooner trod upon but they fell through them and into the great tide that flowed underneath'.

That story used to put the wind up me; it still does, when I brood too much after a bad dose of loony-juice – and heaven knows what the Louse has poured into a bottle behind our backs. It seems as if the Louse himself might have dropped through a trapdoor hidden in our bridge. Well, in that case it was the wrong one: he ought to have landed in a current and been carried past the asylum, the Beare meadows and away to the sea; the sea is the spot for a louse.

It is said that a couple of Welshmen did the stonework on the arches. I hope they didn't starve; the merchants of this town wouldn't toss you a farthing to save your life – and I ought to know, seeing as how I was once part of their clique, that inner circle of toffs that says what goes hereabouts. Except that when the forebears of these same panjandrums landed in this town without so much as an arse in a trousers between them and knocked on Gunner Ryan's door, they weren't turned away empty-handed. No, they were brought in to be seated round his table as equals, where they licked his plates dry – a fact of history that has long since slipped the minds of their spawn. I could tell you stories about them.

While the beasts of the field recognise a hand that has been kind to them, there's not one of those sons of upstarts who wouldn't break his neck crossing the street to avoid me now. It's a long road though that has no turning; one of these days a fellow will get back on his feet and expose them for the jumped-up misbegotten sons of usurpers they really are. I swear.

*

On weekday mornings – not like today – the rumble breaking overhead marks the arrival of yet one more day of trade. At first come the milkmen, their jingle-jangle rings a bell of boarding-school routine. Next up, Earl's bread vans clatter across as if pneumatic tyres had never been invented; then the deliverymen; and lastly come the workers; while the noise steadily grows to an incessant drum roll as the snaking slave traffic has to crawl.

On weekends at least, it's peaceful – especially since work in the slaughterhouse was cut back and there are no pigs squealing or gulls shrieking over guts and red spill from the pipe into the river: I couldn't look at a sausage or rasher now if you paid me. Daytime you know for sure has arrived when Taw Lyons, in contempt, grates his shovel along the kerb and rattles his handcart down the quay as if the council was paying him to raise the dead rather than clean the streets. Shag off with yourself, Tawser boy.

Is that big Johnny Leary's voice? What's he doing out at this hour, and on a Sunday too? I thought he was a night-owl like me, instead of a lark. Well, at least I *used* to be one for the late nights, as anyone will vouch, but nowadays I prefer to retire earlier with a little something to send me to sleep. Has Johnny Leary, the carnival man, found a new woman or what, a clucking hen to shake him off the nest? But now I remember why: Duffy's circus is due in town, and it's his job to get out all the posters. It's what the man does; he's got talent for it. I'll set the Louse on him for the crack.

'Hey, Louse, Johnny Leary's giving away free tickets for the circus.'

The mention of 'giving away', or 'free', is enough to push a button. The Louse drops the empty flagon, and heaves the remaining lower end of his carcass from under the pile to clamber up the bank on all fours.

The Madagascan lemur has nothing on Lousy Jim. If he's not careful, he'll get nabbed by animal trainers and put in a cage. Except they wouldn't keep him for long: he'd cause a riot among the primates.

'Don't forget the rest of us,' I shout after the Louse.

'You're expecting too much, Boy,' Sputnik says. 'He's too mean to get us tickets, mean as ditch-water.'

But we also have to be wary of Sputnik, and watch his moods – even if he is my good mate. Until recently, when let down and disappointed, he was liable to throw a wobbly and become unaccountable for his actions – and he's as strong as an ox. These days, Sputnik is steadily improving, getting back control: he's nearly out again into the normal light of day. Not that normality was a condition we experienced much of over the last fifteen years. Be assured, though: there was a time before that episode in boarding school when my friend here was no moron among his peers.

'If he doesn't get us tickets,' I reply, 'I'll not give him any-thing when later an old girlfriend of mine drops me down the food parcel, and we'll see who will have the last laugh then. Be patient, Sputnik boy.'

There's a wistful look on his face, which over the last year has got less dreamy and more forlorn. But life does that to a person in this pile of dead wood where an ace up the sleeve is ever needed to stay on top. Although our spoils generally get divided after the forager has had a head start in sating his own appetite, each person must stay sharp to compete for his share in case viciousness breaks out amongst the tribe. This constant need to have an edge, along with the scrounging for food and hooch, not to mind the cold, would weary a shagging saint. But a fellow has to pull himself together if he is to hold on to his vision of inde-pendence and continue to shake the flag of freedom with fer-vour rather than join the slave traffic overhead. He knows what is needed to keep going with the only way of life that points up the dream. So I have no choice but to chafe my hands and laugh till echoes bounce off the underside of the bridge: that's real responsibility for you.

Sputnik picks up on the laughter, and the others fall in line with the chorus, till the arc of sound drops off. Right enough, the spirit is still there among us – a hopeful start to any new day.

'But, Johnny, he mightn't be able to get us tickets,' Sputnik says. 'Then what'll we do? We won't get to the circus and see the acrobat women with next to nothing on, showing us their all, and flying inside the top of the tent. I'd just love to see them in their little frillies, and gawp at them all day long. Don't you like looking at frillies, Johnny Boy?'

'You'll get to see Frilly Lily,' I say. 'We'll have tickets, don't worry.'

'The Frilly Lilies will come,' he calls out. 'Won't they, Johnny? The Frilly Lilies will come.'

To distract my friend from his growing fixation on the circus, I'll use an old ploy. The Widow Flynn story always gets him going; causes him to forget his obsessions.

*

Like her mother before her, Nance Flynn got supplies at a knock-down price off my father – mostly items past their sell-by date but still passable at the matches on Sundays, the parades and processions, and to peddle during the county show in the showgrounds. When I was old enough, and the delivery boy whom the Gunner had employed in the shop left for Camden Town, I got the job during the holidays of delivering Mrs Flynn's messages to her house up the hill.

Once, while going there during the summer that marked the end of my period in primary school, I was forced by the weight of my messenger-bike load in the sticky heat to walk the entire way uphill to her front door. She was then the fine broth of a newly married woman. I had already acquired a taste for skirt, having dated a few flighty good-lookers of my own age as well as goofy older pullets – all cheekbones and crockery while rubbing their crotches against your thigh enough to scorch any few sprouting curly pubes. When they had said that they liked my black wavy hair and ready smile, their remarks roused a coy awkwardness about next moves which had to be subdued, and yet most girls were afraid to swap tongues lest they conceive babies and have to take the cattle boat to England. The Widow Flynn, though, was hardly too pushed about the colour of a fellow's hair, and the fear of travel didn't put her off either.

'Leave them on the kitchen table, son,' says she, when I called. Eying me up and down, she stepped aside in the hallway to let me pass with the cardboard box, and smiled. 'Here, I'll bring in your bike just in case anyone makes off with it on you. We wouldn't want that now – steal the steam off your wee, they would, around here. You're the Gunner Ryan's son all right,' says she. 'Good-looking like him, and you have the same quick glint in your eye for devilment. Oh now, don't tell me different: I can tell. You're fond of the ladies, too, I'll bet.'

'The good-looking ones anyway,' says I.

'Of course, of course, the good-looking ones. And do you think I'm good-looking? Come here till I tell you,' she goes in a whisper. 'Do you know I'm just back off my honeymoon? I am that. Can't you tell? I'm supposed to have a big glow on my cheeks. Do you see a glow there?'

'There's colour in them right enough, Mrs Flynn.'

'"Mrs Flynn" he calls me. You're a codger to be addressing me as "Missus". My name is Nancy – or Nance if you prefer. Would you like me to call you "Mister"? Well good day, Mister Ryan – now how does that sound? Call me Nance, ah go on. I think you're wrong about the colour though: there isn't any there worth talking about, and personally speaking, I don't feel any different.'

'You don't?' says I. 'Where did you go to? Was it warm there?'

'Was it warm there?' she mimicked. 'Well aren't you the right nosey one though? Rome, if you want to know; I was in Rome, no less. And it wasn't that hot there – only when we went out-side. But we had lovely siestas – aye, during the afternoons. Will you help me put this stuff away? It's a lovely place; you should go there sometime. The Gunner himself might send you off on a wee holiday – it's not as if he can't afford it. You'd pick up a nice little Roman miss to sit on your lap on the steps of the Vatican. Were these yokes the best you could bring me? I'm going to have to put these few bits of fruit on the floor of the kitchen press to keep them cool; they look as if they won't last a day. I got married in Rome; what I saved by not inviting guests covered the expenses. Now you hand them here to me. I was disappointed, though, I didn't get to meet the Pope. Careful now, don't bruise them, or you won't get paid, mind. I'd have loved a holy shake of his old hand.'

There was nobody in the house save the two of us, and I ended up on my hunkers beside her, passing her each piece of fruit, which she twice wrapped in newspaper before placing it gently on the stone-cool floor of the press. The operation was taking forever, and we were little more than half-finished when she decided she wanted tea. She put a hand on my shoulder to get to her feet.

'Oh I'm parched,' says she. 'You'll take tea? Anyway, you've got to stay and help me finish the job, so you might as well have a cup with me, but first the kettle.'

Mrs Flynn reached for a kettle that showed more verdigris crust than copper, swiped it from the sideboard and, with her other hand, turned on the bib cock that clung for all it was worth to the pipe up the side of a deep enamel sink. Water gushed out as if from the hydrant on our street, and splatters bounced off hard gloss onto my cheeks. She had the gas switched on before a box of matches could be got, and surely a minute passed by the time a light was struck. I couldn't be sure how close to the burner she had managed to bring the flame when a light blue cloud burst out – *Boom!* And the two of us got flung back against the wall.

Shocks seldom come alone. For didn't she turn this way, fling her arms about my neck, and cling to me as if in mortal dread of another, even greater bang. 'Oh, I'm scared,' says she. And what was any strap of a lad supposed to do but be a man and comfort her. Swallowed up by triceps and biceps in a swelter round my jawbone, I let the moments pass for the sweaty boa to dislodge itself – and did it ever? She kept me in a clasp till I warmed up and began to relax, maybe too much. Not a stir from a mouse in the house; it felt as if there was no need for stirring, no need in the wide earthly world for movement ever again.

Yet something somewhere, a whelk of a thing that couldn't be helped, was twitching, and Nance was so close she had to have been aware. But it didn't bother her much, other than to cause a tightening of that grip. Although I didn't for a second forget that here was a grown woman, and married too, my embarrassment didn't amount to much: that this body was acting of its own accord hardly seemed to be my fault. I hoped she wouldn't mind. Mind! Did she what? Her hands came up slowly, deliberately, along the nape of my neck, fingertips quivering enough at hair-ends to turn a lad into a right porcupine, and then rested on the back of my head – an action that made my twitching in the nether regions so rife and rampant that this area got as tight as a drumstick knob.

Despite the lack of guilt over such carnal delights, something inside my head still went on about how unfair it was that a podgy young messenger boy's body was somehow being availed of here, and I felt mixed up. Nonetheless, I put my arms about a waist that was much greater in girth than that of any of the girls I had already met in quiet corners up the lane. Still her kisses were soft, with enough toned-down zest in them to suit my inexperience, and this sense of her reined-in lust only added to my disquiet that in this situation I was being confronted by a girl of bumper-sized voluptuousness with a powerhouse of dammed-up frenzied passion. But her hands soon left the back of my neck.

Her skirt hems tickled my legs as they got dragged up along my flannels. Next there was a downward tug of undergarments, before her hands unbuttoned my front, so slowly it ached. I felt an instant of cool relief before the moist heat of her deep soft folds made me quiver.

She stood back and led me inside the other room. I sensed how my body was exposed; a touch of unwanted uncovering; a mix of discomfort and mortification. We got down on the shaggy mat in there, rather than on that shabby chaise longue, and owing to the way the lace curtains trembled in a light breeze through the raised window sash, the light flickered down on us – about the only place in the entire town, probably, where a puff of air could be felt. Puff puff. The difference between our separate squirming was that her movements were controlled and powerful, while my body all too soon became a rigid torrent that in one final twist collapsed over the abyss of a roaring Niagara Falls – the one from the school atlas. Then all feeling was gone.

'Crikey, Johnny,' says she, 'that ended horrid quick. You wouldn't go far in a marathon. I must check to see if I can get you a book that explains things – you could do with a few tips.' As ever the businesswoman, Mrs Flynn asked: 'You have nothing else in that basket of yours? A packet of biscuits, or a bit of sweet cake, maybe? I'd love something sweet now. I hope I'm not in the club. You know what that means, don't you?'

'No,' I said.

'Well that's all right then, isn't it?' says she.

*

'Did you ever do her again?' Sputnik calls out. 'Nance Flynn was some frilly lily, wasn't she, Johnny Boy? I can't wait to get my hands on a ticket for the circus.'

'If the Louse doesn't bring us back tickets,' I assure him, 'I'll go after Johnny Leary and get them. Upon my word, you'll not miss that circus.'

'Will you be a good man,' says he, 'and tell us another story, Johnny, while we're waiting for the Louse? What was it like living in a public house, with the Gunner and the Doll for a mother and father? It must have been mighty. I wish I had grown up in a pub on the side of the street. It had to be as good as living in a circus, with all the frilly lilies stopping to look in at you. I'd never ever forget a perfect thing like that.'

To laugh would seem to be the only solution; so I start to guffaw and go on till the other friggen fossils join in and the whole darn racket resounds off the underside of the cavern – a cavern like where the Beatles started.

I have recognised from my early days that there is nothing like a full flash of the crockery to charm your way round and help get what you want from people. Mustn't forget to wangle a new comb from the girl in the chemist's; think she likes me. But first the story . . .

3

Nestling crows cower and tilt their heads to watch the horned-beaked elders of their flock practise quirks of survival, hard-learned from time immemorial. For the moment comes when each winged thing under the sun must take flight, and any fledgling allowed to flout the old customs or defecate in its nest is already a dodo.

In his day, when the notion took him, my old fellow was a bit of a charmer. An awful lot of pipe-dreaming went on beneath those deathly black tufts of eyebrows, even if he wouldn't have admitted it to save himself from the eight o'clock walk: he just had to be seen as businesslike. I can still picture the whites of those eyes against the brown of his delivery coat and the hair beginning to lighten at the temples, when he stopped outside Squire Maguire's gate and strutted round to open the back of the van. But before he could reach the mahogany door with the box of groceries, Mrs Maguire surfaced to give him a smile she gave no one else – certainly not her own old fellow, who, as whispers in the bar had it, couldn't be coaxed out of his ball-sack restrictor if even Marilyn Monroe, or the buxom Widow Flynn in full flight, was to appear with nothing on but a filigreed negligee of September gossamer. She relieved him of that cardboard box, boy, as though taking charge of their firstborn in a carrycot.

'So there you are, my good woman,' says he.

Of course, he had looked up and down the way before

placing a hand fondly on her forearm to squeeze it firmly for a full sixty seconds – longer on sweltering days when her arms were bare – in a bare-faced exchange of some uh-huh-huh how's-your-father. He winked at her and kept flashing the killer smile – the one that the Doll said he had been renowned for in his carefree youth. From the passenger seat during that minute, I saw, as much as any small boy could, an entire kilowatt whack of plug spark, at least an electric-chair-full, pass between them as if they were Clark and Vivien standing at the top of the stairs in *Gone with the Wind*. It was just as well that Mrs Maguire had presented herself outside for the box, or who knows what would have ensued. Maybe he should have been called the Killer Rhett instead of what he went by, the Gunner Ryan.

Despite my old fellow's wiles with women, it's hard to know from which parent I got my talent: my ma, the Doll, was no drip either in the fine art of coquettish teasing.

Any time a certain Clark Gable lookalike about town, whom she referred to as 'the regular with the slight crumbling appearance', came in for a drink, the Doll fluffed up her down to splay out the eye-like markings of her peafowl feathers. And boy, did she flap wings at the sight of Joe Mac, the solicitor, when he stacked his briefs halfways to heaven on the counter of our snug and talked grandiloquence into his balls of malt before going up to the courthouse. The Gunner used to shout, with a shot of disdain, from his bedroom before I left for school: 'Today's the court. Go downstairs, son, and pull over the bench in front of the snug door to keep the place inside free for Joe Mac, the *solistor*, in case I forget.'

It was the one time in the week, apart from Sunday morning and the two doggy nights, when the Doll got herself done up to the nines, came down early, busied herself behind the counter and smiled so gently, almost beguilingly, at your man's low

orations between sups of barely baptised Powers' light gold –
given to him in shots from the bottle with the burned-gold crest
rather than the standard white one – that it knocked ten years off
her looks. She would place three or four mints beside his glass
and gaze askance at him as much as to say: I hope the old
District Justice won't get to smell your breath.

'He will be too busy nodding off on the bench to notice,'
says Joe, reading into her expression – and not for the first time.

'They say that the nose is one of the last organs to fail a
man,' says she.

'Should that not be his sense of hearing?' says he.

Smiling back at him, she of course had known this all along,
but it seemed to comfort her just to hear him verify it; and she
would get him to do so again in a month's time, when, as she had
already sussed about him, he would have forgotten about this
exchange. No fear, though, that the Doll would forget. She had
with the men she liked a way of boosting their egos, making
them feel good in her presence. She preferred to serve customers who held down salaried professions, letting the Gunner
take care of those who used their hands to make a wage – but
you'd need to have been living there to notice this division of
service, and taste.

There was, however, one customer, the AI man, who could-
n't be placed in either fold, but as she had clearly made it known,
his was a profession, though he mainly used his hands – 'And I'll
bet he's gentle with them too,' says she, having glanced sideways
to make sure the Gunner was within earshot. Those sorts of
remarks went over my head then.

It was obvious she had taken a liking to Dan, the artificial-
insemination man, frowning on people who referred to him as
'the bull man', and certainly regarded him as a cut above those
who called him 'Dan the Bull' or made vulgar jokes about wire

nails being driven into the backs of cow-house doors for him to hang his trousers on before inseminating receptive cows. Coarseness was not her style; most of all, she abhorred a certain brand of uncouth, country crudeness. The Doll looked down her nose, too, on slobs who lumbered in to strew their elbows across the rasher counter as if the place was theirs, whose fag ends, she was sure, clogged the urinal grating in the backyard privies and whose stink rose from the gully – or, most disgustingly of all, when they gobbed on the floorboards beside their bar stools. But catch her Dan spitting? Never. Dan had too much inclination for the good life: the old *Joey Viver*, as he called it.

While pulling his pint, her eyelashes flickered and her head cocked sideways to admire from the corner of her eye his tash-and-crockery set. Somewhere within the folds of her heart, Dan was *her* AI man. And then came the lingering moment when she turned to place the pint on the beer mat before him, and, jeepers, their peepers met – as the glasses on the shelves all but tinkled. It was hard to guess what went on behind his slitty bits of stone blue: maybe thoughts of how he would, if given half a chance, presently apply his trade, whereas her eyes clearly held affection, even if she had the measure of it – a concern in itself. I had to turn away in case she spotted my stirring of unease, over a possession of mine being somehow snaffled – a feeling I had never experienced when the Gunner got up to his tricks with Mrs Maguire. It was uncanny, the intuition that the woman had in these matters. But fear of losing the Doll, however irrational, would meddle with the insides of a lad's head.

Mind, it must be said: my assumptions about such matters, as I got older and started to sprout a winkle, were little more than simple deductions based on what might be inferred from all the saucy blather that flowed between the likes of Salty Burke, the sailor, and those other bar-stool godfathers whom no gossipy set of old ones could hold a candle to, ever. Then, refining the fuel of unease yet further, I added what might be surmised from the carryings-on of braggarts who had wangled fair-haired maiden-heads intact up Tanyard Lane as fair game, and had found married women with families to be the freest rides of all, as long as their husbands didn't find out. At times, though, as the rumour-mongers at our bar counter became despots of expediency dealing in sounds and signs, winks and nudges about people rather than by gossip direct, a fellow had to guess what these tasty morsels were – but when their exchanges intensified and became so teasingly set apart as to provide too much fodder with which to contend, an imaginative lad like me was apt to balloon his guesswork out of hand.

Then, of course, there were the doggy nights. Pleased with herself, probably, for having earlier spent a deal of time and hard effort before the dressing-table mirror, the radiogram relaying big-band swing to her from the shadows of the living room inside, the Doll instinctively pulled in the waistline and transfixed her smile to resemble the features of a cross-legged yogic-flying guru I had seen in a comic. 'I do love my décolletage,' she said. 'Do you approve?'

'Yeah sure,' I answered, ''tis lovely – as nice as the gap in the hills ten miles out the road, a sort of antiquated lovely, and from the same distance too, like.'

The character of Mrs Ryan faded, as Dolly the Barmaid in her black low-neck top and choker merged with the thick of the beer-brown, smoke-brown light, and time at either side of the bar counter, instead of there and then moving on with itself, stood stark still at first and then slipped backwards into the past till the ravages of being a mother on a woman's physique and insinuations of crow's feet were reversed – well, almost. Even the whirl-about of her one and only record of Carlos Gardel on the radiogram, pervading the living room above with tango – which she had once or twice tried to teach me – followed her downstairs, and something of its resonance came out in her strut along the passage behind the bar counter.

Content with inner visions, probably from the aura of mystique she was giving out, her head flicked to its maximum this way and that, causing her auburn-tinted hair to shake with the jauntiness of a young one, and nothing would do some noble bucks but to pick up on the demeanour and flirt with her in salute of this near-retrieval of a previous flowering. And the Doll's hand leapt instinctively to her mouth to cover an onset of giggling, as it probably had done when she had been jailbait. This whole circus of a thing – a bit too fecking decadent for my taste – had well and truly got under way, and before long buoyed up the entire bar to a roisterous mood. The racket could be heard outside on an otherwise still street, from where its palpable ghost drifted into the dark round Maguire's corner and up through Tanyard Lane to end its course, as any young lad would imagine, in the plucked twang of knicker elastic amid frustrated gropes and repressed grunts along back-gate alcoves – except from among those birds who were already near enough hitched, in the expectation of bringing forward their *big day*. Anyway, that's the picture I still have of those years, in which the bawdy-house indecency of it all was enough to rattle the lid of a young lad's haven – though no less enjoyable for all its edge.

Because the Gunner was absent, the place all the more readily became a breeding ground for desire, in which, I have no doubt, nature to further her own ends conspired. As the Doll at first circled her varnished nails in a sort of slow caress along the draught handles to lever them up and down, a hush fell outside the counter: eyes closely jigged after her, elbows were swapped, and lips puffed with desire twitched in and out to express what, though I couldn't quite reason it then, was meant to replicate the ultimate in thrusting, the Rolls-Royce of pleasure. I was, all the same, old enough to take in how those fellows lusted after the woman who served them drink, and the more they downed, the more obscenely they leched.

Although I gradually grew immune to the idea that the object of their gestures happened to be my mother, it was less easy to curb my objections to her willing collusion in such bouts of sordid, fucked-up debauchery. At the same time, to begrudge those geezers their bit of lechery would have been to deny my own nature, never mind the till – the germ and driving force of the show. As a young male with this thing pitter-patter pullulating around inside and a yen to do stuff to all the good-looking birds of my age, I had an interest in both camps, while my feelings were rightly fecking well bamboozled.

But comfort was at hand. The vodka left unfinished by fuddled customers, and which in all honesty I could not behind the Doll's back let go to waste, helped to make matters less mixed up. But that Russian hooch had to be well diluted and taken sparingly, at least till the end of each night's stint; that sort of stuff would put flutes on scarecrows.

But the business of flogging drink through till closing time was really all that mattered in our house; everything else was incidental; sensibilities certainly didn't count. As the evening went by, the browns of the bar, its wisps of smoke, the must of hops and babble thickened till the air got as dense as the bottom of a paint tin before its pigment globules are stirred to a state of suspension in solvent. And all the while, a barmaid's fingers went on pulling pints and dispensing liquor, as the till drawer heated up just the way the Gunner liked it to be. No wonder he took himself off, contented, to the dog track on Monday and Thursday nights, trusting his good wife to act as ringmaster. The man was truly all business.

He had got his doggedness from that excuse for a mother he had been landed with: a rapacious bag of bones who hawked phlegm, looked out in suspicion from under scalded eyebrows, and slurped tea from a saucer. Her inclination to be a hermit strengthened, the older and more senile she had grown. Then she came to live with us.

'There's nothing like a loyal friend,' says she once.

Her barb clearly meant for the Doll, Granny Ryan let on to be dotty as she addressed and petted an imaginary dog in her lap – long-gone pink poodles and old ghosts were the only gewgaws with enough patience and want of nose to venture near the bag. The badgering didn't end either when her daughter-in-law left the room: her voice rose in keeping with how far away she judged the Doll to have gone. But when she shouted, 'I'd sooner have my four-legged companion any day for a friend', my mother was ready for her.

'It takes one mangy bitch to know another,' says she.

But that didn't stop the granny rant. 'And as for that poor son of mine, may heaven save and guard him from the misfortunes that the spoilt brat of an offspring which she produced for him will bring upon the man's head. It won't matter to me when I'm dead and gone, but I hope for their sake they'll not live to rue the day when that scrawny thing will bring this entire establishment crashing wholesale down on top of them. She'll only have herself to blame. My own son is a soft wretch, ill-fated I tell you, not to have bairns other than an article like that under his feet. Anyways, I do have my doubts if it has one drop of my son's blood in it. Mark my words, it will never amount to more than an affliction on this household. Isn't that right, my little coochie-woochie friend? There now, don't you be worked up; settle down and go back to sleep. *Rock a bye baby on the tree top.*'

The Doll had been risen; she dropped her chores and went into the other room after Granny.

'Well, bad cess to your evil tongue, you old witch. You can be sure that the spoilt brat, as you call him, is none other than your own flesh and blood, but heaven help him if he turns out to be as rotten as you. *It* will be there to give you the last rites you'll sorely need, and to officiate at Solemn High Mass for the repose of your wicked old soul – as if that'll be enough to save you from damnation. And *it* will say the final prayers over your putre-fying remains going down into the dirt where you came from and rightly belong.'

Safe in her bubble, the Granny went on chatting to her invis-ible dog. 'Mark my words, but that yoke will say no Mass over me, ever. If it does, it'll be a black one, surely. There now, coochie-woochie . . . '

The old harpy didn't trust me and never took her eye off me once I appeared within striking reach of her crocodile-skin handbag, the leather of which her ferocious-looking talons indented and hatched even farther under her wing to ensure the safety of its crispy red ten-bob note, two half-crowns, two florins, a tanner, and the two threepenny bits that the dinosaurs had left for her to tend before removing themselves from the earth for good. Then came the afternoon when she lost control of both handbag and bladder, and was landed arse over head into the county home, to lie there, day in and day out, on an oil sheet and never again this side of kicking the bucket got to glimpse a china saucer; whereupon the Doll was once more free to wear whatever colour lipstick she wanted – as if doing so in daylight could any longer make a difference to her looks.

It was a glorious spring then that saw the demise of an incontinent Granny Ryan, an event that might have gone unnoticed at home if one old nurse on her way from work hadn't decided to venture in with the news, poking her nose through the main door, as hesitantly as a bishop stepping across the threshold of a knocking-shop shebeen for the first time.

Having picked her steps right up to the grocery counter, the woman's voice came across as shrill, sterile and cutting as the tools of her trade. 'I'm sure youse will be wanting to know,' says she to my mother. 'Missus Ryan has passed on to her eternal reward.'

Stacking bottles into crates farther down, I didn't at first quite catch her words. It sounded as though Granny Ryan had passed something and won a maternal award. At her age? Besides, I wouldn't have put it past the old dickens. If she had accomplished any feat, other than to leave something in her wake that required a big clean-up, I was certain she had managed it off her own bat, without the aid of man, woman or child, for she had never liked having to do with people; or rather, she had just never liked people, especially not her own flesh and blood.

When at last it registered with me that Granny was as dead as a frigging door nail, I was hardly woe-skewered and weary. Her passing was just an inconvenience for us – and the family business.

They found it awkward to close the premises for the funeral. 'What'll we do? How we will we manage?' says she, in that helpless manner that befell her over each and every family flurry. The Doll had this knack of turning a spot of bother into a breathtaking crisis; gone at the flick of a switch was our unflappable barmaid who mollified disruptive rowdies in situations where even the Gunner dared not stick his snout.

'Why don't we just pull the blinds and close the main doors?' says I. 'Hang out the black crepe but leave the side door ajar to let the regulars in, like we do on Christmas Day and Good Friday? And sure youse needn't worry: I can stay here to look after the place while youse go to the funeral.'

Apart from the chance to be on my own behind the bar for a day or two, I had dreaded the thoughts of that funeral, of being within an ass's roar of that old one's coffin.

'No, we can't do that, John son,' says the Doll.

The Gunner laughed at the idea, sounding like his own dead mother.

'Only offering to help,' I gulped.

Not to let them see how miffed I could get over their lack of trust in me, I turned on my heels, stomped upstairs, and carried my mother's wood-veneered radiogram from the sitting-room sideboard and plonked it in the middle of the bed in my room. I rummaged for something doleful but could only come across Sam Cooke in a 'Sad Mood' and his sullen state of mind in 'Chain Gang'. Anyways, I wound him up full belt.

At once, the Gunner's voice came roaring up from the bottom of the stairs: 'Have you no respect for the dead, boy?'

'Don't speak to the lad in that way,' says the Doll. She then called out: 'Please, John, turn down the music, like a good chap.'

Disdain, though, is a disease hard to cure – and infectious. 'Feck the dead,' says I, while doing my Sam Cooke thing. 'Let the dead take care of them-fucken-selves.'

The premises were closed for two whole dreary days: curtains pulled, doors shut, and no hope of hearing the least caper about the bar. I would have preferred to have been in Boxer Brennan's class below in the primary school, looking at dirty pictures in the yard at break-time with Wally Furlong and my old mates.

4

Unaware that its nestling days are at an end and the time has come for it to take off, a young bird can become so hesitant that it has to be whooshed off the nest — a gloomy occasion for any cockerel.

One night after the dogs, the Gunner let it slip that boarding school was firmly on the cards for me.

He must have had a few winners all right, for on his way home he'd gone into Tim Larkin's bar above at the corner for a couple of scoops and a hand or two of cards with the other doggy boys. He had come in late, unsteady on his feet up the stairs, into the kitchen, where my mother and I sat after cleaning and locking up the premises below. It was hard to say why the sound of the hall door closing and the unsteady thrum on each step had caused a quaver of trepidation, and my mother's face to stiffen: the Gunner, level-headed and beyond fault as usual, had never lifted a hand to either of us. But maybe the low glow of menace given off was because the man was overly self-contained for the saturated state he was in. Besides, something seemed to be warning my mother that if put upon, the Gunner just might burst through his clothes, sprout hair on his knuckles and turn pure pongid.

'Dolly, did you bring a drop of anything up with you when you were coming?' says he. 'Whatever sort of a dry old air there was on the track tonight, it would parch your throat.'

'A half-bottle of paraquat maybe,' I allowed.

Although not voicing outright disdain, she didn't let his excuse soften her expression or melt the sharp-edged, broadside-on iceberg of a woman on offer. Having already had the few bevvies, he had to wait till he landed home to get the ice: wife on the rocks. Dolly the Barmaid was long gone.

Either for fear that matters might worsen between them – which, as far as I can recall, they seldom did – or not to allow him get off scot-free over the way he had hectored his way into this private space of tiredness which I shared with the Doll, it seemed apt that I should let him have my tuppence-worth right between the eyes.

'You say the same blessed thing every Monday and Thursday night,' says I.

He turned round to get me in focus; his finger rose of its own volition, the way a jackass prepares for the arrival of another female in need of being serviced. It stopped, and kept pointing at my knees.

'Ah . . . who asked you for an opinion on anything?' says he. 'Let me tell you now, me bucko, come next September, and there'll be a . . . a halt put to your gallop.'

'How is that?' says I.

'How's that, he asks,' says the Gunner with contempt. And some seconds passed before a short snorted laugh was exhaled. By this time, he had got a proper fix on my whereabouts, but he could only look at my forehead and address the top of my head. 'Because,' says he. 'Because . . . that's how they knock the stuffing out of impudent pups that break college rules. You'll come home here next Christmas, my buck, with no head left on your shoulders. Isn't that right, Dolly, my love?'

But there was no Dolly: she had been replaced by that well-pickled stern-faced scalder whom I had earlier, and every other earlier, looked upon as my trustworthy pal – and what a boo-boo had been made on this score. Was there no one a lad could trust?

I stared at her for an explanation. She had known about this all along; it might very well have been her idea. But no doubt she would explain it all away by telling me they hadn't revealed the news to save me from the risk of being ridiculed by the others in sixth class, who, when they found out, would go: 'So the Brothers' Secondary isn't good enough for Mister Ryan. It has to be boarding school; college, if you don't mind. Will you look at what's going off to fecking college, then? Well, boys o' boys.'

It can't be said that I hadn't from time to time been suspicious of my mother's glorious designs for my education: firstly, boarding school, and then she would send her only son on to study for the priesthood. And neither the Gunner, whether he agreed with her or not, nor I, would have any say in the matter. Such an outcome would put the finishing touches to her dreams: a full-length fur coat, the son a priest, and maybe a new motor car – even a year-old test-drive model, anything to replace that van. Well at least she already had one out of the three, which was fair-going enough for the spring of 'sixty-two.

I had become even more suspicious after catching a snippet of gab across the counter one day. Since Dan the Bull had been at boarding school, the Gunner had wanted to know what he thought.

'If you've any sense,' says Dan, 'you'll not send him away. Let him remain under your own roof, where you can keep an eye on him. For five long years I was in that place, and learned how to drink, smoke, and chase women – and not necessarily in that order, either. Let him go down to the Brothers' like all the other shopkeepers' sons on this street, why can't you?'

Maybe boarding school had its hidden surprises after all, its good old *Joey Viver* side – though I doubted it. He was either fibbing, or else had been very lucky.

'It's her doing,' the Gunner mouths very quietly while point-ing at the partition.

The Doll, who was on the other side sweeping the floor, had been listening, but could no longer contain herself. 'We have to do the best we can for him,' she shouts. Then poses the pos-sibility: 'You'd never know, he might go on for the Church. We'll maybe make a priest of him yet.'

'Or a bishop, what?'

'Now, Dan, that'll do. He's not your son.'

It was the only time I had heard her get snotty with him. She came to the snug door to flash him a look, then turned back to storm the floor with a busyness that put those ears beyond hear-ing any more of what might impinge upon her grand scheme.

The Doll would see to it that her son should one day stand tall in his new soutane bespoke from T. J. Agar's in Dublin, the black of such holy attire matching those dark lovelocks buttered astern against his earlobes. He would immediately after ordina-tion administer his first blessing to a mother in furs kneeling awestruck on a freshly waxed timber prie-dieu especially rum-maged from the bowels of the ecclesiastical college's store-rooms: she'd had the master plan worked out for a long time. What a celebration of piety it would be, my heaven. And provi-dence galore for reaching this spiritual milestone: it would mean she was well on her way to an afterlife of the bar-and-grocery trade in the sky, where she might reasonably expect to be appointed as a blissful doyenne serving up cocktail shandies, or glasses of Blue Nun and Buckfast, to all seven serving choirs of angels, *in saecula saeculorum*. For days after the ordination, she would share our premises' well-earned social afterglow with whomsoever among her customers she thought fitting – those who were appreciative of the event. She would pick and choose.

Oh Mrs Ryan, but you only looked divine on Sunday. Your

new furs really set you off, and imagine your son's a priest: that young man would melt hearts of stone with one smile of his holy face. Will he be around here anytime soon to hear our confessions? I can't wait; would you believe that, now?

So by the time the Gunner had given the game away on the night, I had every reason to suspect that the Doll was behind the idea of boarding school for me, and how the fervour of her ambitions was too fierce to be let go off the boil. But I was disgusted to think she hadn't told me about it herself; felt cheated, somehow.

The world cranked round with pure vigour the summer long till at last the entry date stated on the college prospectus was upon us, and my being got possessed by a right glum demon, a maudlin fecker. Each thing, upstairs and down, showed itself in a new blue torpor, oozing an end-of-life preciousness of which I was already feeling the loss. As the final afternoon of my home life passed, familiar shapes became yet more salt-tasted, intimate; I both loved and hated them, all at once.

I marked every chore with a new awareness, as if they had never previously been carried out. The Doll was in the kitchen darning the last of my socks, having just finished stitching indelible-ink-marked name tags on each item of clothing, down to the last linen handkerchief and my new green tie, new this and new that, before folding them into a hard leather suitcase that sat waiting to become my companion through dodgy days ahead. Only a mother might foresee the importance of mementos to a boy in a fix within his strange new fastness. She, too, had become enveloped in a light blue haze, while he was outside washing and polishing the van. The blue glum was that compelling, so settled in purpose, it seemed like it might never in my lifetime lift.

He was just below my bedroom window. He glanced up once

to catch me staring at him. If looks had passed for talk in that exchange, we would have agreed that our existence as we had known it was there and then in its last throes. And as the day wore on towards my hour to leave, the value of that world, in all its tedious familiarity – *especially* its tedious familiarity – was getting bumped up greatly, as it had never been before.

Later that same sunshiny September evening, in keeping with one of the many instructions in the college prospectus – which had arrived in the post some six weeks earlier and which I had there and then instinctively known to be an omen of misfortune and wanted to see thrown in the fecking fire – the Gunner and the Doll made it there to the joint on time, just about, with their first and last, their sole shakings of the bag. They were set to abandon their one-and-only to the contrivance of a regime whose design was to mould and remove a fellow's inclination for the good life, the old *Joey Viver*, as Dan the Bull used to call it. So, when my old fellow turned the key in the ignition, more than just the engine under the bonnet got switched off. A thirteen-year-old's build-up of self-composure, which freedom had brought about, was being shunted into a siding for long-term docking in quitch grass and piss-a-beds; this was dry dock by 'The Well at the World's End'.

They were about to deliver up their dinky treasure: let someone else in future get the little fucker out of bed in the mornings to put rearing on him. Yet each of them leaned sideways with shoulders propped against their respective doors in front to regret, it seemed, having settled for such a second-rate choice. And had the stillness of occasion which attends a first parting of the ways not jam-packed my gullet with lumps, I would have fully savoured their unease, luxuriated in their predicament, with an acquired taste that had been fine-tuned for me over the years. The torpor begun in the early afternoon was by then thickening, as jelly sets in a bowl, with less blue and more dark grey, and came the sensation that we were being crowded out of our space in the same way as when the van had been full of cardboard boxes for the dump past the mill out the road at home. We sat there wiggling our thumbs, thinking – not lofty thoughts, mind, but backward mawkish ones. The blinding glisten off the bonnet further hemmed us in; it sharpened my memory.

In the bar earlier that day, Salty Burke, the sailor, had tried to cheer me up with his yarns of when he had pulled away from his home-port harbour pier. His mood, he'd said, was chap-fallen – it seemed more apt anyway than *crestfallen*, the word that Boxer Brennan, our teacher in sixth class, had dinned into us for use in essays: *When I woke to find that the snow had melted, I was crestfallen . . .* – and more cobblers besides.

From under the archway between the end of the chapel wall and a more modern block, the college's ecclesiastical wing for student priests, the last of the sun went on sparkling across the bonnet as if it, too, was in a mad bid to cremate my dominion. The sparkling light mesmerised our eyes in that funerary silence – before the removal of a boy's remains: *Let ye take him off our hands then and cremate him, the little fucker, anyway.*

But already, I was mortified, pure mortars. With all the cars parked in front of the college, the Gunner had had to drive the full length of the avenue, past the façade and its grisly tower reaching to the war clouds, the priests' house sticking out in an L-shape at the end, and into the farmyard beyond, in order to turn. And turn he did, dragging at the wheel to whirl the old charabanc about like it was a gravel truck he'd had under him, and then all the way back past the main entrance doors to find the last tight-arsed parking spot available, around the corner by the chapel's high wall. From the outside, at least, it seemed to be a place of lofty aspirations – but aspirations, perspirations: what the hell difference was there?

I wouldn't have minded so much if it was a Merc we owned, a big Zephyr or Mark 2 Consul, a Cambridge or Vauxhall Victor, a curate's solemn chrome-grilled Wolseley, a snazzy new-look 105E Anglia in black with hoods over the headlamps like the lids that sagged over Salty Burke's eyes coming up to closing time of a week-night in the bar; even a Morris Minor would have done. But in 1962, to have to emerge from a 1956 box-shaped 100E Ford Anglia, white, and a van, the only one in the fecking place . . . Well it was . . . a drawback to begin with. It smelled of tribal disadvantage, and there's a difference for you that *did* matter – if it's difference you're looking for.

The Gunner had bought that particular van two years before. The Doll had wanted a proper *kaar*, a sleek dark saloon of a thing, which in her finery she could step out of and onto the pavement to display from under her long fur coat a little silky ankle below the navy A-line costume. Although she had by then at least owned the coat, it was as usual her shortfalls that we had got to hear about, and every so often, when her fur-brown eyes had misted over, you just knew she was dreaming of the things she didn't have. Strangely enough, here inside the van at this time, amid the final confusion of an all-pervasive heightened mood-mix, it was on her expressions of disappointment that I most wanted to fix my thoughts, for I was at last ready to be in tune with the true meanings of loss and yearning.

'But Patrick dear,' the Doll had pleaded in her best Zsa Zsa Gabor – which, because of the fags (Goldflakes, to be exact), had come out more like Marlene Dietrich – 'we can afford to run a car as well as the van.'

Before she could make inroads to wrap him round her little finger, he was out the door and down the stairs to the bar and grocery, panting. He knew it was time to scoot when she put on the agony and called him 'Patrick dear'.

'Is it "Patrick dear" time again?' says one of the early-after-noon, regular roosting fuddlers, elbows on the counter like a pul-let trying to lay its first egg – or else he was keeping the weight off his haunches to allow an ongoing release of methane and avoid the build-up to an unspeakable detonation, a deflationary gust of dirigible spatter against our good ceiling.

'It's because of all the films she has been to see,' laughs the Gunner, passing off the observation. When what he would have really liked to say was: would you ever shag off home and leave a man have privacy with his wife under his own roof without drawing comments from a nosy tosser like you who hangs out of a pint for half the day and thinks he is making me up in the process? Not that he had minded her going to see *Gone with the Wind* – even if there was a dangersome whiff, or some prong of anxiety, in thinking about the Doll being seated alone above in the dark of the Scratching Post picture house. Afterwards, he had winked and said: 'Sure, amn't I all the better for it. Don't I get to feel the breeze when she comes home and shows me the Scarlett O'Hara side of herself, if you get my drift?'

'You're a shrewd man, right enough. Wish I could handle my woman like that. All I get is a lambasting for leaving my money here with you. Now, how about a quick one for the road to give me pluck to face this tartar of mine? Be a good man there, Gunner Ryan, and put it on my tab till I get paid my dole on Thursday. If you don't mind, *Patrick dear?*'

But the dreams-don't-boil-the-pot approach that went with owning premises such as ours had been the only one the Gunner knew how to take. He had recognised little difference between the premises and its attendant, live-in chattels of a wife and son. So then, let her have her aspirations; he needed a van for his deliveries. And that had been that.

The run-in to parting was at hand. Wistful, and unable to word our thoughts, we were there together inside the van for the last time as the sun's glisten on the bonnet died and the great shapes of pied-faced cut stone prevailed more in the lesser light.

The moment was here. Somebody would have to make the first move. The Gunner must have been reading my thoughts.

'We had better get going,' says he. 'Or they won't take him in.'

Dare I hope? No. Then the final snatch at silence – by way of our goodbyes.

When the Doll bumped open the door to produce a left ankle for all the world to see and stoically clacked her high heel hard on the tarmac, she did so publicly with the eminence of an official who, at the end of a court's business, stamps documents to make irreversible the decision handed down and give the executioner the beck to set in motion his preparations – those final few checks and balances: nothing left but the formalities to be seen through. I knew by her act of avowal that there was no way out for me. The empty walk up the tarmac to the tower doors leading to the inner dark would have to be made; to where, as the Gunner had said, a fellow would have his head lopped off before Christmas. The imagined masked Titan was resting on his axe all ready by his block; in another minute, the doors would clunk behind me to shut out the very light, the last delights of a September-evening sky, the end of the world as known to mankind. The end of independence: nothing would ever come freely and openly again. Goodbye to a boy's sovereignty.

But not quite; for this would have to be one hell of a joint if it was to succeed in beheading a fellow of his tendencies, or con-vert yours truly from his fondness for the bit of old *Joey Viver* and make a priest of him. Not on your granny's nanny; *yab-a-dab-a-fucken-do*, boy.

5

Birds of a feather flock together, it is said, but so do those that as yet have only a few barbed quills sprouting. Don't they, Johnny Boy? Go on, don't stop the story now.

To sit the entrance exam and get streamed into first year's three classes, we had been brought there a day ahead of the main-stream mass of boarders. Our first morning was spent cooped up in the big study hall. Come Halloween, we would have a whole blessed week of house tests, and the same again at Christmas, Easter and June, before, at last, we would experience the high jinks of another sensual summer. If the place was to be taken seriously, the prospects of living under the shadow of exams for the foreseeable future, hands being chafed between the knees while awaiting the results, was enough to send a wide-eyed lad to bed with such biliousness as might never allow him in all sensibility to get up again. From then on, every test would be treated with the same regard as I was showing for these first ones. But that was only one of our tribulations there.

An almighty ongoing effort would be needed to resist the sway of that monstrous place. Right from the beginning of the day, I had been aware of a certain whirlpool-like pull, the draw of a magnet, and with it the sensation that time had either been suspended or altogether skewed. A month, it seemed, had passed since the Gunner and Doll had zoomed off for themselves the evening before, away from this all-pervading smell of paint and lacquer freshly slapped on over old surfaces. Down the avenue they had gone, to swing north towards home.

Out of bed at ten to seven to face a low-lying pall of dimness across our dormitory quarters, through the dark-brown morning cloisters, the chapel, the refectory, with its scalding, weak, tan-coloured tea like hot piss, and finally into the big study hall, where even the light coming through was being borrowed, if not outright stolen. We stood in a flock, waiting.

'Sit, one to a desk, and remain silent,' says this man. Not really a man, he was a long hank of misery in a cassock, or soutane – as yet, I couldn't tell the difference.

Though it was only September, still bright and balmy in the outer world, in here the cold was everywhere: a solemn fucken chill, no matter how you tried to shake it off, seeped into your shoulders and downwards, till you shuddered and got frustrated enough to attempt to lash out and leave a winkle-picker stuck up the arse of some weaker little cherub in a desk nearby. At one stage, I was on the point of taking off out the gate to hitch home before lunchtime, and be able to climb into my own old crib again that night. But I feared that the white van would come tipping up the avenue for a second day running – and the ignominy of that then.

Though the urge to run away was easing as the morning passed, that blood-curdling chill, together with the strange pull which distorted time, were hatching me into a morose fecking egg, a state in which there was every prospect of a fellow being stiffened for good. We were in a place that was hard to put a fix on, other than to say it was not unlike 'The Well at the World's End', a story from primary school – though not from Boxer Brennan's class, where the only stories that counted were ones about characters with four legs, and which ran in the three-thirty at Fairyhouse, Newmarket or Down Royal. Not only had I arrived at the well in the story, but I was standing on the side of a perilous cliff at the World's End, where the only choice was to follow the herd of boys being shepherded onto this leviathan-like viaduct that lay veiled from view by a pall of dim murk, from which the only means of escape was to jump off the edge. But one thing was for certain: there was no going back, no shagging going back – time distorted would see to that.

Question papers were then landed in front of us. Without the least smidgen of diversion the morning long – and since we'd been barred from standing up or going out to the jacks till after the exam – I sat twirling curlicues in answer to questions I couldn't make head or tail of, till the hank of misery in a black soutane, or cassock, at last told us to put down our pens. 'The time's up,' says he. Then all at once as we traipsed from the big study hall, a chink of light broke through the high south-facing windows to signal our right royal release from the hassle of arithmetic. And a pale-faced little pilgrim with dark curly hair bumped into me. The offer of a lark with this hick was hardly a chance to be snubbed.

'Come here till I ask you,' says he. 'What's this your name is now? Where do you come from, anyways? How did you get on with number six on the paper? And where in heaven's name did you get them shoes from – they're queer pointy, aren't they?'

Was this 'Twenty Questions' or some other quiz? No, Inspector Hammond of Scotland fucken Yard had landed.

The pilgrim, molly frog, put a fix on me with the eyes, as I flicked my head back and held out my hand the way a bishop in imperial shimmering regalia descending from his high altar after some fancy Gregorian-calendar rite and plainchant would offer his ring to be kissed by menial Christians, the church's main mass of underlings – though all that old Latin grand fuss was already on the wane. The Doll had loved nothing more of a Sunday morning than to drop to her knees at the sound of *Oremus*, the organ hissing up a head of steam before it let rip, or at the sight of the golden-robed Aztec god turning round to address his flock. (And hell, but wouldn't Johnny Leary, the circus promoter, the size of him, have made a mighty bishop? At least he was one of our own, a fellow townie.)

'Well, my good man,' says I, 'if you care to wait an hour till I get through your list? You want to know how number six went, and I will tell you. But can I let you in on a secret? First you must promise not to give away as much as one word to a living, breathing soul of what I'm about to tell you. Have we a deal here then, old son? Do we have a deal, or not?'

Spit-gobbing dottle-sucking old fellows slurping black pints at the rasher counter had warned me. The best way, says they, to handle *funny fellows* I was bound to come across in boarding school was to treat them with the same ceremonial disdain that a bishop uses to keep his flock in rein: some of our regulars were not only well up in the ways of the world, they also had a profound grasp of religious affairs. Salty Burke, the sailor, proclaimed that he'd regularly been exposed to experiences of a spiritual nature during voyages on the seven seas he had crossed at least seven times over – which makes it at least forty-nine seas in all. He also used to go on about the Vienna Boys' Choir and what had been done to its best singers to keep their voices from breaking. Castrati, he had called them. And like the Widow Flynn, he too had been to Rome. Was I not privileged, so, that a man of such familiarity with both the sea and the Holy See had consented to give me a few tips?

'Son, whatever you do, don't let on you can sing, ho-ho-ho.

Stay away from pretty boys with dainty wrist movements and girlish expressions, ho-ho-ho. Beware of shirt-lifters. Keep your back to the wall at all times, especially in bed at night, ho-ho, and you'll be safe enough. Don't forget, either, that when – and not *if* – you sprout a little *nuragh*, keep it to yourself and you'll be as right as rain. Now that's a fact, ho-ho-ho.'

And a *ho-ho-ho* again, like it was Christmas. Every day at home had been a Christmas Day, or so it seemed from this place.

'Listen here to me, lad,' another old fellow had butted in. 'What you need with you going to that college is a strong corset, one with wire stays like what your mother wears.'

Salty Burke didn't take kindly to being upstaged. 'Aside altogether from being familiar with the type,' says he, 'how do you know the good lady even has a corset on, or for that matter wears any article of underclothing? Have you been in the yard again pimping round the clothesline? There must be an organisation where people afflicted by that complaint can meet: Frillies Anonymous, maybe. I'll make enquiries for you.'

But the second fellow forged on regardless. 'I have,' says he, 'the very thing at home for you, son. It's an old pair of long johns I didn't need since I got married – not like some people – and I'll lend them to you . . . at a small fee. But, first, I'll get the missus to stitch up the gusset for safety's sake. They may be a bit long but—'

'They may need to be sterilised,' says Salty. 'Ho-ho-ho.'

To keep the yarn going, I said: 'Did either of you ever have your shirt lifted?'

They looked at each other and changed the subject. As canny as those old codgers were, they hadn't noticed how, against my will, I played along with their guff: the Gunner, with his eyebrows bristling up and down, had regularly got on to me not to be smart with people, or back-answer them.

'You may open your ears,' says he, 'but keep your mouth shut, *dúnta*. I don't want to lose custom, mind, over you. Now heed what I'm saying.' And he had for emphasis pounded the cash register with his index finger, pumping the drawer in and out. It had been one of those times when he'd come across in that heavy way of his.

Here at the World's End, where time, it seemed, was not the only thing misshapen, I would have to hide my singing voice and be on my guard against any *funny fellows*.

And since his approach was sudden and his face leaned a mite too close to mine for comfort, this curly-haired pilgrim appeared to be odd . . . strange . . . funny, and I flicked my rump cheeks in and out to check for the whereabouts of the hem on my shirt-tail. Or maybe it was just that the fellow had no idea of propriety – another tweedy thumb here from the woods at the back of beyond, the likes of whom the place so far seemed to be full of. Either way, he ought to have allowed me more room to breathe: it's not nice when anyone other than a female in a hip-hugging skirt, or a newly married woman with lust on her mind, encroaches upon your personal zone.

'You have my word,' says the curly-haired one, 'honest.' When he shook my hand, I thought he was going to put it in his pocket and run off.

'Honest?' says I. 'Well in that case I will stake my integrity on your veracity' – a spake borrowed from a speech that Joe Mac had practised in our snug. 'Would you take an oath on that in open court?' says I. 'Have I got your solemn bond?'

The little apprentice castrato before me was stumped. It was time to render him the final, bishop's blow – or what Joe Mac had called the *coup de grâce*, as he stabbed the air with an invisible sword while holding his other hand over his head. So I bent over and whispered: 'Milord, not only did I finish question six, I did the whole paper twice over to make sure I'd got all the answers right the first time round. And I assure you of this with my utmost unimpeachable integrity.'

He believed it too, and stared at me with a lost-for-words look that was not unlike my mother's veneration of Joe Mac, or how she went in church of a Sunday morning to the sound of *Oremus*. 'Well glory be,' says he, 'but you must be a pure whizz. Did you get every last one of them right twice over?'

'What did I tell you? Are you questioning my sincerity, or just plain deaf?'

'No, no; I'm very pleased to meet you. My name is Shamie Doyle junior – my friends all call me Shay. I come from near a village that sits on the shoulder of the Blackstairs mountain like a loose slate about to slide down a sloped roof and drop onto someone's head. I'm here on a county council scholarship. You may call me Shay, if you so wish.'

'May I, indeed?'

After what passed as an excuse for lunch, Shamie the pilgrim and I followed the others out of the refectory, along the cloisters, through a narrow passageway, across a yard, and beyond, to where the college grounds opened out into a sports field, the lay-boys' field, where at last the air was free.

Here was an area of open space that sat away from the frenzied cloisters and the regime's immediate clutch. A fellow had a chance to be at one with himself, if that's what he was into, or brag to his new cohorts about the glorious summer he'd had; the next one was far too many sunsets into the future to bother mulling over.

The lay-boys' field at the side of the college was bound to have been an honest-to-heaven sloping piece of natural farmland once, tilled to produce food crops on the upper edge of town, before some mastermind of a school president got the notion to bring in a 'dozer to shelve it into two playing pitches, leaving it about as fertile as a bald eunuch in charge of a honky-tonk of curved-flesh fresh concubines: a big double flat-backed eunuch of a thing.

The field held something else though: a prize nugget of precious facility, one pure gem of freedom – or at least the access to freedom. Thank heaven for the back gate, and its location down in one corner, where the field dipped away.

At the sight of its neat little wicket door, which beguilingly sat ajar, I felt at once a soft glimmer of possibility douse away my hollow chamber's torpid dim. A ray beamed in through my skull's pair of cross-lying loopholes, which were surely far too narrow to admit any future inklings of calculus and coordinate geometry, or such clutter as the elder lemons of fifth and sixth years would seem to be obsessed with when they would arrive that evening – and who would from the following day onwards pass us on the tarred path as if we, first-years, didn't exist. The gate's allure – along with my luck for coming upon hidden places – would, I decided, become the main antidote against the endless confinement ahead. If it was to be my last task on this planet, I would find out what was in the lane beyond the gate, where it led to, and its reason for being there.

Though neglected, with the paintwork as sun-bleached as that on any other out-of-view side door, the back gate still held far more appeal than did the college's main entrance, which, with all its coy full-frontal stateliness ahead of a cutesy avenue winding from the road right up to the front door under a castellated tower, was just part of the previous century's fad for putting up grand plasters in neo-Gothic as mock-ups of older establishments that had rested on medieval foundations – classier buildings by far. But modest and without pretence, this entrance had its own style, an unborrowed honest look that offered real prospects, a touch of hope. But, of course, it also gave off its own right-royal old-town aroma, and the fecking stench of that.

The reek of rotting vegetation came in from a lane that was rife with empty beer bottles and their serrated caps, strewn across the path and by the hedge. And in the days yet to come, the smell of student tobacco smoke would add to the blend, so that this corner eventually became infused with a distinct whiff of home where the Gunner's black bushy eyebrows were, as ever, like the feelers on an insect, still steering him up and down the long narrow space behind the counters – and had he at last begun to miss me? But there was something else that slyly mingled with what my nose had already identified: a waft of mystique I preferred to think of as the after-smack of raw, messy lust – at a time in a lad's life when such a commodity was still scarce enough to be mysterious. The entire giddy jumble hung in the air thereabouts as if to tempt my senses with the likelihood of hidden magical discovery: for as long as the least enticing tinge of possibility anywhere in this place should remain, a fellow's heart would hold on in hope and his spirits continue to defy the regime's clenched grip. Even if this hope should prove to be deceitful, no more than fruitless wishful thinking – the bald eunuch's kind – what the hell matter? False prospects too can betimes drag a fellow from the mire.

The inside of my head during the early days of first year was so doused with this expectation that any normal yen for home got lulled a fair smidgen, and I eased past the things that tugged at the coat-tails of my cohorts, forcing them to huddle in clusters and wear long dolorous gobs as they walked the path round the lay-boys' field.

But on the afternoon of our first day there, so many bedraggled newly weaned lambs had gathered in a spot by the lower wall that I felt obliged to help lift their unease and cheer them up. Though tempted to run a mile from them, I set about the task of lightening their five-year jail sentences with a little lark about a few flashy dames I had met over the summer.

The girls I described for their benefit were those big-rump candy-mountain creatures, in ready-to-rip skirts above their knees, who had clip-clopped into our snug, puffed Woodbines, climbed on the bench and craned their necks to peer over the partition at hunks in the bar who were in the process of tanking themselves up ahead of the Sunday-night dance in the Athenaeum.

One used to wiggle a profound arse at me and snap: 'Do you mind?'

Did I what?

'No, Mae, he doesn't mind,' another insisted. 'If he was over in Soho, he'd pay the peep shows to see the likes of what you're giving him for free. Tell me, Mae, is my Jack inside, is he? And what's he drinking? Guinness? Oh no, not that stuff? I told him I'd never let him kiss me again with the smell of it off him. Wait till I lay hands on him, and he'll get what for. Murder him, I will.'

'Bring the Spearmint with you,' says Mae. 'And feed it to him before you let him near you. Murdering him, though, I think will be last thing you'll do to him tonight. Won't it, Babs?'

'You're right there, Mae, so you are,' says a third, adding her ha'penny-worth.

'Quick, Babs, get up here till I show you. Look at your man there, isn't he only gorgeous? I hope he asks me up to dance tonight. Wouldn't I just love to lay my fingers across his potato-crisp bum that's as tight as a drum. Will you just take a good look, oh Babs, ooh. Crack my whip off it, I would.'

'You're awful, Mae, you know that?'

'Well, why not say it as think it? Isn't that right, young fellow, young son of a Gun-ner? You'd never go inside and cut us an ice cream, would you, good boy? I'll pay you tomorrow, honest I will. There's a longing on me all of a sudden for something cool to calm down me nerves, something stuck between two wafers to get my tongue round. Are you sure you haven't an older brother hidden away in a room upstairs?'

'Leave him alone, Mae; he's little more than out of nappies.'

'Nappies, Babs? Who are you kidding? Just stop and take a look at the cut of his jib. I'd be willing to change that fellow's nappy for him any day. And to slap those round wafers of his with talcum like you'd knead dough for a loaf. But sure you don't soil your loincloth any more, my little dishy horse's door? Come here, tootsie-wootsie, till I gives yez a wee kiss. How about a big smacker for your Auntie Mae here? Has Auntie Mae's babbie never kissed a pretty miss before? I'll bet you have them all dying about you.'

'Leave him be, Mae, or he'll blow his trumpet at you.'

'Oh lovely,' says Mae.

It had meant little to them to climb on a bench and put the heart of a callow lad crosswise to see skirt seams balloon beyond bursting point, sheer nylon vie with suspenders in testing the limits of tensile strength. My hands leapt to my eyes for fear of an explosion, a splatter of flesh to the four corners of the snug. But as long as the peep shows had lasted, neither material nor leg ever gave out, thank heaven.

The minute they heard the Gunner's step along the boards, out the door they trotted, as pertly as they'd come in, and without offering to buy as much as a box of matches between them.

'Get down out of that!' roared the Gunner, one time he caught them stomping crisps with their heels into the grain-stained seat – though not before he, too, had for a moment been struck by the view.

'Ah, don't be so scaldy, Mr Ryan. Weren't you young once yourself?'

'Show your fine legs to Mr Ryan,' says Babs, 'and make him feel young again.'

'He won't feel none of my young, Babs, for all the tea in Timbuktu.'

'"Tea in China," Mae. You're meant to say "tea in China."'

'He can have his tea in bone china,' says Mae, 'for all I care, or in jam jars if he likes, but it won't be on my account. I'll tell you that now for nothing.'

'Be off with you,' says the Gunner.

'Piss in his tea I would, if I ever got the chance,' declared Mae on her way out.

He saw them off with the face of a monsignor whose last claim on the bishopric had just been passed over. He then turned on me: 'Why didn't you tell me those scent bombs were here? The next time they land on the floor, I want to be called right away. Surely it's not too much to ask you to look after the snug till your mother gets down. Open the window wide and let out the fumes.'

No sooner had the street window been fully opened than a dissonant *Yoo-hoo* was proclaimed: colourful birds out of tune with the dawn chorus. Then a flurry of reaching hands waved in at us as they fluttered past the top, clear pane, which the Gunner had once referred to as the clerestory window in a snide at the Doll over her attachment to all things pious. But that had really been about something else, to which I wasn't privy – not that I had wanted to be either, mind. The wild elegant hand-movements passed by too quickly, leaving me with a swanlike wraith of after-image not unlike how some crows had swooped past the clerestory windows during confirmation the previous year, when I had been half-expecting to descend from the church roof a marvel of those curved tongues as shown on the cover of the catechism book our class had learned off by heart for the occasion. At last, when least expected on a Sunday night, ahead of a dance in the Athenaeum, my confirmation-day-mystery delight had come about, the occurrence of which had not only been well worth the wait – it was to become a prized nugget for recall, or as a sweetener in my fellow first-years' ears.

If the defiant flock's resilience had been fascinating, their high-spiritedness had been outright contagious. So taken was I by the mix of calling-bird freedom and ceremonial sense of occasion, with its eerie hint of devotion even, that at once I had to go and peep after them from behind the door jamb. On one of their visits, I got an inkling of how a zest for life was indeed a hallowed thing, not to be violated – a star to follow. But if this latest truth about human beings was to be sought out, it would amount to a feat that a fellow could not pull off while he served porter behind a counter, or as a black-soutaned gouty priest in some mid-diocesan parish among tight-arsed farmers not one of whom would have to take to the boat or learn its name. This inkling soon became a certainty.

Their latex legs were restive, and wobbled down the street. With an impetuous, frantic flurry, the girls then flapped cardigans and shoulder bags at each other in an absurd mockery of some free-for-all cockfight. When Boxer Brennan one time had seen a stir in the schoolyard and muttered something about anarchy and freedom being linked, this surely was what he had meant. As quickly as it had begun, the fracas ended, and with their feet homed in on the next port of call, an impetus of loose shoes again clattered on in search of other *fine things* whose potato-crisp rumps were about to face the same scrutiny as livestock in pens where cattle jobbers pinched round for prime meat.

All too soon, the latex legs would leave our streets for the gangplank of the *St Andrew*, bound for Fishguard. But not before the girls had dared to make free with the revered of our town, leaving behind them an allure of charm as elusive and dappled as the leaf shadow up Tanyard Lane in sunlight, lasting long after they had gone. For one whole summer, their defiant spirit soared and slighted the old-town panjandrums who had squeezed the lard from their grey-faced elders.

There was no point, though, in going on about these things to my first-year cohorts. All they wanted to hear about were tits, arse and legs. Not that in the foreseeable future we might get to see such bodily bits and bobs – unless, maybe, as a view from the back gate. Hope on, boy; hope on.

6

It's not easy for any prima donna-ish coxcomb to survive crash landings and having its feathers plucked.

By late morning of our second full day in that joint, the weather had changed: the dark sky dropped so much it was being propped up by the field boundary, and anyways, those walls that ran right the way round were tall enough to contain the most wilful inmate. Behind the goalposts, rusty mesh on sky-scraping iron uprights abutting the walls stretched the full width of each pitch, supposedly to keep in high balls – high or low, what matter, it was all a balls: we were entirely hemmed in.

Here and there, where it had broken loose, the mesh clinked in helpless rhythm against its stays, while the sough of a strong breeze through wire above our heads gave backing accompaniment to the ringing of metal against metal. The sound was as forlorn as the strum of a tuning fork in hell – where, or so it's said, bagpipes, organs and things pronged are the rage – if that's what you're big into.

If a lad who had scarcely been weaned off his mother's teat listened to the anguish being prompted by that rigging device, he was sure to ache for home and heave glottal-stop sighs in his dormitory cubicle at night. The soughing rush still in his ears sharpened his recall of a liquid, *dolce* Nat King Cole jiggling round on his mother's wood-veneered radiogram – enough to bring gloop under eyelids and soak the foam of a pillow which was strange to the touch. 'That wire contraption is there on purpose,' he'd mewl. 'It has something to do with being herded onto the institution's solitary viaduct, leading to where I'll become, five years on, another dour, arched-overpass young man – Gloom Glum, there's Master Glum, the college boy with a poker up his ass.'

Watch out for trapdoors, son.

Well, as they say in only the best circles, we shall see about that. All we had to do on that particular day was to await the results posted on the noticeboard, telling us what classes we had been assigned to – 1A, 1B or 1C – to sort out and collect our books, and be given our places at table in the refectory. Apart from that, we were left to rummage about for ourselves and get used to the place. No harm either: I needed the time to accustom myself to the smell of paint and varnish, regain my whereabouts after the exams of the previous day, and learn to handle the quare hawk who had fussed me over question six and since attached himself to me like Lester Piggott down a home straight, with the marks of his knees on my flanks.

'You're down in 1C,' says he.

'Is that a fact?' says I.

'I thought you said you'd got all your sums right.'

'They *were* right, and twice over, but you know how different the system is for this year. They asked me if I minded going in to lend some brainpower to 1C, just to raise the standard. "Not at all," I told them, "always happy to oblige." The way it works this year is: the bright boys are being divided between all three classes.'

'Oh, well of course they are,' says he, in a drawl that I hadn't thought was in him.

Such indignation as showed up on this new flipside of his at once alarmed me. Even then, I knew tolerance was a spirit which lads of our age gave each other only in half-measures from the optic. So his fervent esteem had gone the way of all devotions lavished on those who'd ever become his wide-eyed centre of interest, till he'd found some paltry glitch in their makeup. And a fine-tuned look of vitriol practised on previous fallen icons flared across his gob, denoting the extent of his pangs at being let down – and, like hell, you'd feel for him. Then, in case the message hadn't got through to me, he gave a further cocksure tilt of the head and inflected his voice skyward so much that had he been in Austria, he'd surely have managed to squeeze himself into a pew, where the Vienna Boys' Choir so prettily chirped their strumpy butts off all the way up to the rafters.

And while his change of manner had jolted me, the sudden grasp of how far off the mark had been my first impression of him as a total nitwit really rocked the old dignity back on its heels. Maybe I ought to have supposed that, squirrelled away under his belt, he had some scrap of savvy in dealing with people, but it was hardly possible to guess how sharply he'd honed the skill. And though I had rubbed shoulders with the wiliest of wide boys amid the snappy vagaries of town life, he was the expert here at putting on petulant faces and adapting poses: ruses that belonged in my stash of tricks rather than to some buttonholer who had probably never seen inside the front door of a pub, not to mind dealt with patrons the likes of Salty Burke.

Could the molly frog separate mad topers from their last-glass *dríodars* at closing time of a Saturday night, or pick out codgers who talked shite at a mile a minute to get away without paying for their drinks? Hardly; for if such a thing as a round-robin junior tournament of streetwise one-upmanship was called for, and yours truly was a contender, there could only be one odds-on favourite. To end up, then, in a situation where the likes of this pilgrim had the drop on you: was it any wonder that the old sense of aplomb might slacken? Of course, such a frame of mind could be tolerated only for a jiffy – during which, though, I waited for him to cut and run from our day-old friend-ship the way he'd abandoned fallen idols in the past, probably. But a fellow just had to recoup his pose quickly: pick up the poise, boy; pick up the poise.

'Where did you say you were from?' I asked. The question was designed to amuse: a fresh attempt at talking down to him. And on realising how he had already answered it, he might instinctively lapse back into his menial-minded mealy-mouthed hayseed self and hesitate over why he was again being asked that. But it was I who got confused when he replied.

'At evening-tide,' says he with resonance, 'my home is situa-ted 'neath the shade of the Blackstairs mountain.'

Holy shit, is it a poet we have? Be done with friendship then; take the pilgrim from under my feet or I won't be responsible for where a winkle-picker will end up.

To shore up their spirits under the comforting umbrella of camaraderie formed on the previous day, the same bunch of first-years, to a man, again gathered on the wedge-shaped sliver of grass by the lower wall. After a little awkwardness, the caper picked up till it seemed as if no break had occurred. At once, each wanted to be an entertainer, yet the shape of a tightly hud-dled audience was emerging. This set-up changed, too, as fellows drifted to talk behind their hands, while the yawp and yammer grew as discordant as a morning hen house on the Blackstairs – the one owned by the pilgrim's mother, maybe. The molly frog had taken up with my old classmate from primary school, Wally Furlong, to become ensconced in a new-found conspiracy of sniggering. Martin Doran, the great bumpkin with the shoulders of an ox, who had slouched across his desk the previous day to allow me cog his arithmetic and grammar, had joined our core group of six, and laughed heartily at my saucy jokes. He, too, was there on a county council scholarship: the place was littered with brainboxes.

Although select offshoots of new-moon affinity showed, they were as yet too strange with each other to break from the main coterie, as every now and then they went still to tune into the mother-teat hub of fun. Feeling too awkward, coy little auld men preferred to fingerpick their lips with plops and take every-thing in from their bunker-safe say-nothings than to risk even the sound of their own farts in company. But when the yarns dried up and the buzz fizzled out, the entire group drowning in a mix of expectation and speculation, it fell to the master of cer-emonies here to keep the pot stirred.

'Has nobody here ever rummaged in a booby hatch?' says I. 'Or paid the devil to let a lass dress him down at the scuttlebutt? Or spliced the main brace after garbling the grog?' To take the wind from the sails of upstarts who tried to best him in banter, Salty Burke had resorted to these remarks – not a word of which either my new comrades or I understood. But we laughed, because big Martin Doran was beside himself with hysterics. The chortling spread quicker than a wave of toppling dominoes, till there was another pause of expectation: *More sir, please, Mr Coco the Clown. Don't you dare stop now.*

'Lads, it's all my eye and Betty Martin,' says I. And we went on laughing at nothing. 'What do you think girls are: pretty boys with tresses in dresses, wearing lipstick? Did Mammy never take down the book to show youse about the birds and the bees and all the slack arses under hazelnut trees, and did you never stop to check what was in the crow's-nest at the top of a tartan-sail two-master schooner plying her trade between here and the coast of Malabar?'

'Where?'

'Malabar. It's up there near Castlebar.'

And the chorus troupe replied: 'Nope, not at all, at all, at all.' For fuck sake.

The more they were fed, the more ravenous they got, till the caper took on a grotesque life of its own, with no way out for me but to go on slaking its breathtaking excess. It didn't matter that this was gibberish compared to Salty Burke's commentary: the genuine article of lewdness and hints hidden in ship-jargon. His well-timed sea dog's nuggets of suggestion, which had to be unravelled, were more comical in their insinuations of misbehaviour than any crude story I had overheard in the bar.

My comrades were delighted to be fed scraps, and to be in the presence of one who had associated with downright villains: the least taste of pickled naughtiness or decay would do to fortify them against the bell-tolling isolation ahead. They needed to have it affirmed that the world outside was exotic and awaiting their arrival.

'Well me hearties, where the hell have youse fly-by-nights been? Too long below the poop deck, I reckon, or gone by the board down Davy Jones' locker, ho-ho-ho.'

'You mean Joan Davis's locker?'

'No, he means Joan Davis's *drawers*, ho-ho-ho.'

'What a catch, by heavens, when a trawler-man hauls in such an article? And hangs it on the line to dry with the rest of the things? So heave-ho, my boys, now heave-ho; then heave to – for five shagging years, after which we'll bring on all the weird astonishments.'

A fellow could get tipsy on their reaction, the tremor of power at being able to sway laughter a little bit this way or that.

Yet the temptation to try it out further, even take it to the limit, was hard to resist – till the entire rigging came apart on me.

At the next pause, Mr One-upmanship, Shamie Doyle, put his oar in. 'Don't mind him,' says he, 'that fellow's always telling lies.'

And to add a heckling chorus of opposition, Wally Furlong brought up an unsavoury moment from the past. 'Lads, did you ever hear the one about a stowaway who swigged on a bottle of piss, thinking it was soda water . . . '

It's no worse than reading filthy magazines from under your old lad's bed, beside his chamber pot, I was about to say. But what was the point in further denting the audience's goodwill towards their show's top-of-the-bill entertainer by going all crabby? It was best to save face and laugh it off, as if the slight was on someone else; to ride out the storm while gathering my wits to transfer the spotlight from Wally to his new-found pal. Animosity was a mount that needed a jockey as good as Lester Piggott.

'Well, me hearties,' says I at last. 'Let me introduce you to Shamie, the boy from the mountain, where it's so cold in winter he has to put on his grandfather's long johns to keep his little sack from disappearing up his big end, and so hot in summer he wears his sister's light frilly knickers to— '

'I don't have a sister. Why don't you go get knotted, Johnny Boy?' says he.

But as good as it was, the pilgrim's timing would not be let scupper me that easily; no petty side whiffles would thwart the course of a craft in full sail – Bosun Burke keep a firm hand on the tiller. And at once, I burst into Elvis's song 'Wooden Heart', which we all sang together. Forgotten, of course, were those warnings of not letting on to be able to sing. Not to be outdone, and in a voice that would crack the Gunner's best sherry schooners, Shamie Doyle sang 'Edelweiss'. And could he sing.

To cock a snook at him, I pulled up the legs of my trousers, shuffled round on my toes doing a ballerina's pirouette; then jumped, and tapped my feet together in a batterie action. The laughter rose; even fat Wally's belly shook as he chuckled grossly. But, with his face demure and eyes shut tight, the pilgrim didn't baulk or quiver till he reached the end. The group was finding new sources of pep. Next up, and sporting a crew-cut, came Neady Beird, a laid-back stocky geezer. He sang of his sporting hero, to the air of 'Davy Crockett' – at least, he too was making an attempt to contribute. And his credentials seemed good: no room in the Vienna Boys' Choir for a voice the likes of Neady Beird's.

Then up stepped this mighty fellow, with the same unruly glint in his eye as I had last seen on the faces of Mae and Barbara. He wore his shirt collar over his coat, as if he was about to cut up rough against the system – any system – and took over the show. He sang a ballad, 'The Leaving of Lily Poole', or of some such bird. The geezer should have been out on the football pitch kicking all kinds of shite out of the stuck-up knock-kneed brigade that had arrived the evening before. Using his fingers for a comb, he swept the mane from his eyes and sang 'The Irish Rover' at a rate of knots. But who would dare to object?

A pal of his, called Tod Mayle, who looked more like the comedian Ken Dodd than did Ken himself, and with the same curly hair and buck teeth, whispered sidelong from the corner of his mouth: 'That fellow is pure animal when he plays football.'

Spewing spits of admiration, Ken D. turned about full-face to see if I was awestruck – and petrified, I was, but of being bitten by horse's fecking teeth. With a faint tic at each side of scanning eyes, and the nose of an anteater, here was surely another member of the scholarship brigade; my chances of shaking up the joint academically were being reduced by the minute. But I might yet leave my mark in those hungry halls, if only by raising my leg like a dog against the front door of the tower on my way out.

Nick Loan kept leathering into songs. He had all the signs of an individual who thirsted for life, and whom the regime might find hard to catch, hold down and get their pincers on, if they should decide that his soprano voice ought to be preserved.

Eventually, as the entire group took to circling the field, the harbour came into view. We talked of old sailing ships criss-crossing navigable channels to pass through the sandbar beyond – against which waves ceaselessly rolled to white. If only we'd had a conch with which to listen to their sonorous breaking; if only a fellow could make a break for it – for home, or freedom, anywhere. Had Salty Burke really sailed from those quays below and crossed the sandbar on route to the coast of Malabar, where, like he'd said, bronzed bindi-faced females in saris loped to meet him and ran their hands across his receding hairline? Had he called into the premises at home yet on that very day to hold forth from the crow's-nest with his usual garble, which appealed more from a distance? Any sailor who swapped venturing to far-off lands for the routine confinement of a high stool in Ryans' must have at some stage left his pate exposed for too long under a tropical noonday sun. Still, memories of home came easily.

I pictured the Gunner routinely bent over wooden crates checking for empties, and the Doll inside the other counter tut-tutting that a cockroach had managed to zigzag by her ever-flattening feet as she turned to grab an iron bar from beside a keg to poke out corks, peas and coins from under the bottom shelf – everything bar the devil's coach-horse.

'Where in heaven's name has the dickens got to?' she'd mutter. I could almost hear the whoosh of the bacon slicer, and

whiff the slivers off the flitch that the Gunner held out as a sample of pink flesh to a customer. His voice rang in my head:
'Here, missus, smell this for freshness.' I wanted to be there to
swish round the red knob and serve meat to some gawping gorgeous bird, married or single, who would flick a leg to see if the
young clerk was watching her new sheer-stockings or if little
Johnny Conch might poke his head, uncalled-for, through a too-
tight white Terylene shop-coat. No wonder the Gunner always
had a smile for the ladies he served. 'Are your hands spotless?'
he asked anytime I went near the slicer. 'They do look at your
nails. You keep the hands clean, and we'll hold on to our customers.' To this day, the least feel of grit under fingernails sends
a dry metallic taste to my mouth.

At once, the tarmac path on which we tramped, framing the
field as if it was a sum diagram from the entrance exam,
imposed itself upon us. The laughter of earlier had faded. The
institution had begun in earnest to insinuate itself. Great efforts
would be called for to resist it.

7

But that's just the start, a tousling of the feathers; the plucking and crash landings have yet to come.

In the afternoon of our second day, the background sun tried to break through the intense grey over the lay-boys' field. Because the mainstream mass of boarders had arrived the evening before, the poor prone beast of a field was sopping with creatures crawling every which way across its spine. Then, in a remarkable show, the swarm divided in two, as those on the field retreated to the ranks sauntering along the paths. The pitches themselves were beset by a race of ogres, great grisly geezers togged out for games. Some of them supported enough Desperate Dan chin stubble and hanging-basket tufts of black chest-hair over the V-neck collars of sports jerseys to pass for duffers with wives and batches of squawking children from whom they had escaped for respite, rather than the fifth- and sixth-year boarders whose credentials Nick Loan could sorely have tested with his big feet, had he taken a mind to.

The teams who played hurling took over the upper ground, and two smaller groups veered onto the lower area to thump a clump of heavy leather as best they could across soggy earth with only clompy boots and white knobkerrie knees as weapons with which to prod the air and goose each other. They shouted 'Eh-heh, will you look at that for a root?' every time the sodden thing levitated above seven feet: not really ogres, just simple big gawks, easily amused.

Such uncouth pastimes, though, didn't grip me. Ping-pong, where players had a roof over their heads and girls too competed, was more my game. If those fellows had come from my street, their pursuits would no doubt have been the same as mine.

The paths were by then colonised by puncture-proof groups of blisters whose elite occasionally stopped to mingle with the select members of other squads and swap tales of summer in a knocked-up ribaldry – an exclusive thing, an irreverence in which I would have given anything to take part. But since the existence of first-years had so far gone unrecognised, their joviality only magnified the gulf separating us in the student pecking order. It intrigued me to see them reassemble so easily in tightly knit groups, and pick up on camaraderie as if their three months apart had been less than, say, a day.

Still lapping the paths, first-years shoaled yet more tightly together till we stood out from the main mass like Teddy boys at a hunt ball. All we could do was chant amongst ourselves some mad-monk mantra from the Himalayas as an acceptance of fate. The isolation from mainstream goings-on only increased when someone remarked how hard by the institution lay to the edge of town, as near as dammit to my kind of habitat, where the call of shopfront verve merged with a brackish tang off the harbour beyond and rolled in unseen frills over the bottom wall to taunt our senses. To this day, at the first whiff of salt air, I do feel an itch to be on the move, to escape – ah, yes.

All very well but, as far as threads went, those hard-tack boarders looked a sorry bunch: scarcely one natty dresser among the lot. But had flannels, groin-rash-inducing tweeds and twills been in vogue, this hub of haute couture could vie with the salons of Paris.

The gales are howling, sweetie, it's minus five on the catwalk, and here comes, oh là là, Mr Great Outdoors, How's-it-hanging Joe. His top button is undone, trouser-leg garments delightfully flap at the jay-nay-say-kwa angle of a fare-thee-well two-master at half-sail out of harbour, and such a generous amount of cotton collar over the coat; some tough man, boy, and look at that strut. Whoosh, there goes a real American GI. Shall I open the door for you, mister, or would you prefer to kick it in? Oh, you sweet thing.

With manes greased back like the dictionary picture of a great crested grebe, some of the older fellows did sport decent tight pipes and 'pickers, but they either wore them a touch slovenly or didn't have the upper-body matching accessories: narrow shirt collars, slimline ties, or the essential unrumpled clean-cut college blazers. Unquestionably stylish when new, the green blazer was of a flimsy, lesser fabric, one with too much fine wool in the mix or whose fibres were a tad short and too loosely woven: an item to be set aside on a hanger and taken down only occasionally, for it to hold its shape. Why anyone would drub this article about till it got tatty, and his general appearance showed he had nothing else left to wear but tawdry hand-me-downs, was beyond me. One fellow's even gave off the violent smack of having been worn to muck out his mother's hen house – on the Blackstairs.

Would you believe it, a second-year cad was actually kicking football with the classiest pair of brand new silver-buckled black 'picker boots, which I would have given my right leg to slip my tootsies into, featuring sloped heels and slender uppers, probably procured by mail order from London, or Paris itself. Almost cried, I did, watching scored hard leather brutalise gentle matt-black calfskin. The Doll's words came to me: 'You can douche the little bum, wash its face and dress him up, but you can take him no place.'

At best, fellows wore nifty items of dress as a nod towards

the latest style, rather than from taste, never mind a sense of elegance. The exquisite tingle of pure fashion, with its added freedom of expression when mixing and matching, seemed to have gone undiscovered inside this corral. Most fellows' articles of attire were, however shabbily, displayed as badges of compliant belonging to the overall fellowship of the joint – and by funks, too, who wished to avoid being baited for appearing to differ from the norm. Of course, the scholarship eggheads, whom you'd spot at half-mast a mile off, dismissed all taste and trendy garb as fads with which only glib goofs occupied their pea-brains.

It goes without saying, then, that no other first-year had evolved enough from the wooden-clog era to have acquired a pair of pointed toes for himself. And, heaven help us, farmers' sons were, don't you know, still at the dawning of the age of latex – lost Aquarians who pined for one last good squelch inside a gumboot before being forced onto that monstrous ghostly five-year viaduct ahead. Such was the nature of wellingtons that they left scotch marks on both legs and brains, as well as on scrotums.

But, style or no style, we were all lags under detention. Or, as someone else commented, 'the clowns of Duffy's Circus': harmless, if not entirely gormless.

Although it was the better of the two playing pitches, the upper one did have a soggy-wet patch of heavy going towards the middle, where the made-up area adjoined the lower ground, and, running all the way across, a ridge bank separated them. It was there, on the afternoon of our second day, that I came across the fiend, Billy Curry. Or rather, he came across me. Of course, I hadn't heeded the warning: 'Watch out, lads, here's that anthropoid from third year, and he'll hit you a dig you won't forget in a hurry. Lads, did you ever see the likes of them fists? And there's nothing that they relish more than beating people up. Come on, let's get out of here.'

But Billy Curry didn't seem like a threat. He was togged out, and too busy inflicting himself on fellow Neanderthals to be bothered with anyone else.

The sky had begun to blacken again, and it weighted down the white-grey puffballs that sputtered non-stop from a two-inch pipe in the wall beside the college farmyard. Or the opposite may have been the case: the dark goings-on beyond the stonework were being vaporised and sent out to bump up the murky kite that hung over the whole institution.

'In there, they kill the bullocks for the refectory,' says Jimmy Codlotin. 'And make savoury sausages of pigs' blood and doodles.' He ought to have known: he'd been here the year before. 'The stringy white bread we get,' says he, 'is made of lamb's wool and gut.'

A howl of a character was our Jimmy. He had just joined us, having been told he wasn't allowed to go into second year. And no wonder he was being kept back.

'Lamb's wool and gut? Is that right?' says I. 'Like Shamie Doyle there, you must be here on a county council scholarship, so.' And I chanted: 'Jimmy Codlotin knows nothing only guts. Next year, still in first year, he'll know all about sheep's caecums – tee-hee.'

He was irked no end. Blood gushed across the big pustular-red forehead under a swirling sandy haycock; it was scary to look at. Boiling into a right dither, his sharp-featured face could take it no longer. He chased me off the path, along the ridge between the two pitches, till the hair collapsed onto his great lugs, like lustrous taffeta down the loins of a concubine raddled to the hilt with rouge inside the fug of a sheikh's tent. I daintily winkle-picked my way from sod to sod, aware that I wasn't doing my shiny blacks any favours. Tsk, mud had already crept up the seams of my drainpipes. With any pace at all in those legs, his hand must soon land on my shoulder.

'Damn you to hell, Codlotin, you great cack-handed bride of Frankenstein.'

I ought to have had more savvy that morning than to don my good clobber – as if there was any chance in this kip of catching a girl's eye. But the temptation to indulge in style had got the better of my brain, as had my fellow inmates' need of an introduction to some modicum of pizzazz. An off-white speckled polo neck inside a tight-fitting Fair Isle V-neck jumper would set the outfit off and exude an air of casual ease that befitted the return of a well-heeled old boy sashaying down the cloisters, and offhandedly displaying a graciousness that I had no need some day to aspire to: I had already acquired it.

Far from taste or style, that afternoon, two hurling teams belted to and fro, for all their worth, a leaden chunk of round leather on the upper pitch. Spattering muck and hopping off each other, they roared and cursed to hell their rivals' luck, as if any of it could ever matter. And between Codlotin's bawls and players' shrieks, I never heeded Billy Curry shout: 'Out of my way, you stupid-looking fart!'

Besides, he must've arched his back and dipped his shoulder quite a bit to get such leverage on impact. The crunch flashed down my right side and centred on a point somewhere below my waistline. Whilst airborne, I got the sensation of viewing a large screen where hundreds of meteors flew past. My cheeks felt the chill air of travelling apace: Yuri Gagarin, the shagging astronaut, had at least got a pressurised suit on during his itinerary off the planet. The back wall of the farmyard, with its puffing pipe and the set of goalposts, was all turned on its side, and blurred under an increased hail of stars and meteors before disappearing beneath my feet . . .

It doesn't seem like the usual dream, where a trillion grey dots and flecks assemble in a haze before vague shapes emerge. With all the haze at once flitting away, this one is lucid and quickly comes into focus. Faces, too, are familiar; they will be easy to recall afterwards. It's as bright as if the sun was bursting through Mrs Flynn's kitchen window after a good cleaning. But here is Nance Flynn herself. I recognise the foothills of her enormous silky-pink bosom, as she bends to store away the items I've just brought in – the good woman likes to have her groceries delivered. She fondles the root vegetables. This is a fine realm, indeed, for any lad to find himself in.

Maybe it isn't a dream, but an old black-and-white movie in the Scratching Post picture house, opposite the chip shop – the nicest, crispiest chips in town, which Nance insists on calling *frites* ever since she made that pilgrimage to Lourdes in search of a husband.

The film, however, is not set in her house, but far off in an Eastern harem, where the turbaned Sultan of Turkey, with scimitar, pouts his lusty chops at sultry-eyed, half-dressed odalisques – all in severe need of a good pilgrimage themselves. 'And where do I start tonight?' says he. The juicy-fleshed belly-buttoned beauties with spinning-top-shaped hips wiggle-waggle their enticements to make the light fleck, the way a flock of knots pulsates after dropping onto a pebble beach. The off-white enclosure is on a hill above a town of well-ordered bazaars, and muezzin-echoing minarets that outreach bronze domes. As lucky as a cut cat on a night's tearation, he is. The women all wear silk – see-through silk, by heaven.

The outlines of bodies underneath appeal like Little Chip Marmalade on Earle's oven-fresh slices – only one side toasted, mind – beside a blue-rimmed mug of scaldy tea, with a fried egg, rasher and two sausages on a plate first thing of a frosty morning. And, for a moment, the picture is adjusted to bring me my home comforts: the Doll, tray in hand, knocks on my door – lest I go to school with nothing in my stomach. She just as quickly disappears.

But I have seen this film before: it was a week-night showing. A zonked, Let-me-at-'em Larkin walked in off the street, swayed in the doorway at the back of the cinema, and lashed into a bag of *frites* before he thought fit to check his whereabouts: 'Where am I?' says he. 'What's this, and who have we here now? Why's everything gone dark? Someone turn on the kitchen lamp.'

On spotting the half-dressed women, he flung the chips across seats nearby, dropped his pants and lurched towards the screen. He bawled out the same words that had given him his nickname: 'Let me at 'em. Stand back till I show 'em. Here I am, my little brown-eyed beauties. Don't you go running off till I have my supper . . . where's it gone?'

He got halfway down the aisle before his trousers fettered and tripped him. By the time the lights came on and the film projector was stopped, three men with *frites* in their hair had rolled him over onto a fold-up chair taken from the ticket kiosk to stretcher him, snoring, and legs dangling, as his drenched trousers sprinkled a trail along the foyer tiles. They left him outside on the pavement. Within weeks, Let-me-at-'em got landed in the County Home – beside Granny Ryan, probably – and wasn't heard tell of again till his remains were brought to the church, where less than two dozen souls turned up to see him off. Yet people sing about him in the pubs nearing closing time. Bloody hell, the things a fellow has to go through to be remembered amongst his own.

But here comes the shagger now, party-pooping across the screen of my movie. Feck off, will you? He is chasing a lithe belly dancer round an enormous bed; the circling makes me dizzy. At the very thought of one bed, a second comes into view, then another, and another, till the place is covered with beds: enormous satin-sheeted divans with lace pillows rise from a low cloud. Am I in heaven? The ladies giggle, roll across the satin, and kick their slender legs in the air; they laugh all the more when they spot me in the doorway of the auditorium. As the drunk chases a female off over the hill, the entire scene mellows into one of exclusive luxury; I've become as tipsy as Larkin was on that night; my body teeters along the passageway, reaches the screen, and arrives in the film – now, I'm a big star.

The dancers are like those on the magazine pages which Wally Furlong had tried to soft-soap me with when I had vomited from taking a slug of the urine sample he'd sworn was a new brand of soda water. I'd told him, too, that my mother would call and have a word with his father, who was said to be a dirty old man on account of the magazines, pork-pie hats and other things he got in the post from his brother in London and which he sometimes showed to customers. 'Don't let the Boxer catch you with them or you're finished', a voice calls from the desk behind. 'So what?' says Wally. 'We'll say they're pictures from the *Racing Post*: Ladies' Day at Ascot, or Leopardstown.'

A force draws me to the nearest bed, where a beauty on her back stretches one leg in the air and arches the other at the knee. Awaiting a visit from her overdue sultan, she for the moment replaces him with yours truly – 'any old port in a storm,' she says. When she wiggles a finger and whispers 'Come here, my little sultan man, and sate yourself down', my mouth slobbers so much saliva, it trails out along the floor tiles of the foyer. Although her face is hidden behind damask, the foothills of one mighty breast look familiar – so that's who she is, but how can it be? What matter, it's all exclusively for one pair of eyes. Who wouldn't want to be an apprentice sultan?

Dream movies are strange things. Having tied my single-humped dromedary to the gate outside, I draw closer to my humid beauty, with her messages in my sultan's gold and silver bags: enough rashers and sausages, onions off Shroughmore Hill and root vegetables to sate any full-bodied concubine. She swings her legs off the bed and sits bolt upright. When her arms reach out to embrace me, I totter onwards with my pants round my ankles, and feel my head collapse into the hollow of her great springy chest. My river of slaver flows down the gorge between her peaky pair.

I look up to see the sultana-in-chief, Mrs Flynn, smile her motherly smile, and the world fills with liquid pleasure, which would go to your head like the bubbles in the bottle the Gunner kept on the top shelf for show – till I popped its cork and swapped the champagne for ale-shandy one time a pair of barflies bribed me to share it with them as a bit of seasonal was-sail when the Gunner had gone to the bookies in Irish Street.

I feel her hand round the small of my back pulling me into her so hard, my head begins to throb in agony . . .

8

And there's yet more. For it must be said, the regime knew good and proper how to pluck unruly fledglings and swipe them from their high perches. It was part of our training.

The pain was shooting the roof off my head, and I could hear myself moan. The soft mud felt warm on my cheeks, when I woke in a puddle on the bottom ground, a few yards from the ridge between the playing pitches. A foot was resting on the small of my back, and amid the laughter Jimmy Codlotin's voice was the loudest. I tried to slip back into the dream, but Nance Flynn's face and chest had already gone from me. Then the ungelded voice of Nick Loan guffawed: 'Is he dead, or just having an afternoon nap?'

The next thing, the bell went for five o'clock study. Within minutes, a mass of boys, no longer uproarious, was being sucked towards the field entrance.

Jimmy Codlotin and I were sauntering through together when we were singled out by a bald, raptor-eyed priest. This must have been Baldy Klops, the one all the talk was about, who appeared in doorways to glower and bring to heel boys who jostled or ran, and whose speciality was stealth in nabbing smokers in toilet cubicles.

'Lads, has anyone got a match?'

'Come out here and I'll give you one: the palms of your hands with a few strokes of my cane.'

The dean of discipline's reputation had gone before him over the previous two days. Conversation had baulked at the mention of his name; it was said he had the heart of Pierpoint, the hangman, adding trepidation to woe with stories of inflictions.

Without looking up from his breviary, Dr Quigley's presence by the pillar was enough to quell disorder and quieten the clatter of gangly legs on the tarmac. His head suddenly came out of the black calfskin-covered book, like a heron's reaching over a current to pick out a fish. Although sessile-eyed under ledges of thatch, he was scanning the tailback; we all knew it. And I somehow guessed that his focus would rest on us – me and Codlotin.

'Stand aside,' he said in a deep clear ring – no trace of alto left there.

Codlotin shivered while we waited for the last fat straggler to huff past, throwing us looks of pity. Baldy read till long after the last student had turned the corner beyond the toilet block. I wondered if there was anything in that book about compassion. We were there so long, we didn't know whether we should go or stay. Eventually he spoke.

'Well, Master Codlotin, are we to be graced by your presence for another year?'

'Yes, Father.'

'Well, in that case we had better have your hair seen to, hadn't we?'

'Yes, Father.'

'Why didn't we do so before we returned, huh?'

'I don't know, Father.'

'*We don't know, Father, do we?*' Baldy mimicked him. His hand rose slowly, and caught a tuft behind Jimmy's ear; as the hair was being wrung, his victim's face squirmed and his hands convulsed.

'And your name is?' says he then to me. When I told him, he

looked me up and fecking well down, cold as a trout. 'Why are you covered in mud?'

'It was a bit of an accident, sir.'

'Huuh?' he harrumphed. 'I didn't hear you. Speak up, boy.'

'An accident, sir.'

His first blow was the slap of an open fist across my ear, followed by the reprimand that I was not to call him *sir*, but *Father*. *I will like fuck*, I thought. *The Gunner at home is my only father. Why can't these hoors be called something else, or Reverend, like the Protestants do?* His second blow, by way of confirmation, was a close-fisted bang to the northeast corner of my skull which knocked everything about inside.

'Go clean yourself up. I will call round to your study hall and see you later.'

'I will in my arse,' I said under my breath.

'What did you say?'

'Nothing, sir . . . Father.' But it was too late: wham-bang again on the other ear, and again.

My mouth was no longer connected to my brain, and both ears chimed as if the offertory bell in every half-parish church in the diocese was going tinkly-boo all at once. It was said that he was a Doctor of Divinity – well, fuck me pink, now I knew what that meant.

I went to the first-year study hall without cleaning myself, and sat in my desk while 'Jingle Bells' played on through till suppertime, and during recreation afterwards. I had only begun to pick out other sounds clearly when the bell went for the eight o'clock study period. By nine, Dr Divinity Baldy swished through the door and spoke to the prefect at the top of the hall before he spun round to glare. His eye landed on me.

'Master Ryan,' he called, with a shrill strain on *Ryan*. 'Come hither, please.'

My long walk from the back was a one-man-band Patrick's

Day Parade – or Corpus Christi procession, more like. All eyes were watching and mouths open – and anyway, I had begun to look like one of them: a lad in from doing a day's ploughing. But what the great doctor didn't realise was that I enjoyed performance, and, rather than be made an example of, I would turn the receipt of further punishment into a spectacle from which our year's first rebel hero might emerge. Each step up the aisle between desks was a jaunty one, and I didn't look at the enemy in case I might catch his glare, laugh, and lose poise; for I had sensed the burn of his eye.

'You didn't clean yourself up, Master Ryan, I see.'

'No, sir.' This time the *sir* was deliberate, and well he knew it.

'And why not?'

'I forgot, sir.'

'You forgot, sir. And you also see me dressed in a layperson's attire?'

'No, sir . . . Father.'

And deliberately, he placed his breviary on the prefect's desk, reached inside his black serge, and pulled out what looked like a miniature shepherd's crozier – or was it a fairy fop's walking stick? No, this was Wyatt fecking Earp at the OK Corral drawing his long-barrelled weapon. Would I be shot or pistol-whipped?

'I see we are going to have to rid you of the manners of a corner boy before beginning to inculcate some decorum befitting a student of this institution. So shall we begin right away? Your hand, Mister Ryan.' The dean of discipline brought down his buff bamboo on my palm, again and again.

To keep from blubbing out – either do or die, but never cry – I focused on the sliver of white crescent about his neck and the hoop of collar – which for a moment seemed hell-bent on absconding through the cutaway notch of soutane under his

Adam's apple – and thought about the Scratching Post picture house at home. I could not afford to see my fingers tremble and twitch inwards like robin's claws as they switched between registers of numbness and pain. A loathing of the dean and his intemperate sadism kept me from going mental, and an instinct for self-preservation didn't allow the least compunction to take hold of me. From then on, right and wrong were standards that would not apply in that joint. All that mattered was survival.

'Your other hand.'

This time I counted them: six whooshes through the air – twelve in all. The aching and numbing went on switching, and this hand too became another throbbing appendage.

'In future, Master Ryan, when I tell you to do something, you will kindly see that it is done right off. And, by the way, don't forget to address me as Father, not as sir. Isn't that so, Ryan, harrumph huh?'

'Yes . . . Father.'

'Now go to your place.'

The first time I had come across anyone in the business of ritual violence who savoured the effects of his own hand as much was the day I had gone up to Furlong's on a message and waited while Wally's old fellow hoisted a hogget from a beam, slit its throat and opened its stomach. Blood had, as the useless thing it was, run past me down the yard, out onto the street and slurp-slurped into a cast-iron council gulley-guzzler, while my own ran cold. From the gratification across his gob, it was obvious he had enjoyed seeing my ashen face, but differing sharply from his porky-pie-hat cheeriness, the primal vileness of taking the animal's life, not to mind how it was done, had left a haze of ghastliness across the yard.

Here in the study hall, however, the harsh difference between the holder of a doctorate of Divinity and his actions was more difficult to pin down. But if a fellow was to survive, he would have to get used to his personal domain being intruded upon and violated, ignore how degraded he might feel, and take for granted the onset and spread of brutality under its various guises.

For, in a few weeks, our class would see how force was used to help us understand maths, when Alfie Bra, our teacher for the subject, would wham-bam Jimmy Codlotin's noggin against the blackboard for not knowing, second time round, his fecking pons asinorum in geometry. But Jimmy, too, was a resilient scut, and nobody's toady. And whether the class was maths or any other subject, the lesson was ever the same: how to get through unscathed. Sur-fucken-vival.

On my way back, I pulled an insolent grin to meet the eyes of my cohorts, and when the acclaim due to me began to unveil across their faces, I was tempted to bow, as an actor would at curtain call. My fellow inmates' silent commendation, except for Shamie Doyle, whose face showed scorn and whose eyes were turned away, kept me from cracking up in my desk when Baldy had taken himself and his leprechaun's stick off. It wasn't till afterwards, on the dorm, that I could afford to let go, check the fingers, or pity myself. As at last the shock caught up with me, I craved my home: to see the old faces of the pair and sleep in my own bed. Anyway, these flipping foam pillows were useless for soaking up wet.

It's easy now, from this distance in time, to see that behind his casual display of unconcern Dr Quigley really was a tyke among loons who hadn't a clue how to reckon with fellows. The real problem was the clapped-out apparatus of a system, the leviathan-like viaduct that lay veiled from view by a pall of dim murk, which they ran there at the World's End. It crippled its operators, turning them into a frustrated shower of old gits.

Otherwise, somebody would have said *to hell with this for a lark* and given your man a peal of offertory bells in the ear, or sent him and his black breviary packing down the avenue.

But in another way, fair dos to Baldy for his even-handed approach, in that he had the one contempt for all of us. He had the same lack of bias as a butcher in an abattoir – one who runs his eye over the animals, while lining up the best – only the very best, mind – to slaughter first.

9

What happens to one or two fledglings affects the flock. In springtime, farm-ers string up braces of slain birds to put the frighteners on any 'murder' of crows or 'unkindness' of ravens with a fondness for the corn of newly seed-ed fields.

By the time *Lá le Bríde* – the Brigid's crosses and all that jazz, there since the days of the coracles – had slow-chauffeured in the spring, first-year boarders were well used to institutional noise. Frenzied skitting across wet quarries re-echoed along half-lit cloisters, to which a rain-lashed evening restricted the boys. Then an impromptu overture to begin study period was performed by our offbeat ensemble, led by Nick Loan, experi-menter-in-chief of wacky music, to find the force and sequence of banging desk lids, which offered the same percussive possibilities as the battering of a Lambeg drum in a ceilidh band, or the thwacking of a bodhrán at an Orangemen's parade. And there was no escaping that ceaseless cussed fizzle of fluorescent lights overhead in the study hall, till the sounds of the day had finally run out, almost.

'You can put away your books now,' says he – the jackdaw-black prefect – from his drawer-less bureau facing us.

We banged again to end another day's drill marathon, stretched and stood to attention, and droned out a collective dose of night prayers into the humongous fecking pitch dark

beyond big windows – a duty that carried as much spiritual fer-
vour as did the hum in our public house near closing time of a
normal Saturday night. The final sounds before lights-out were
those of slippers flapping at linoleum up the centre aisle of the
dormitory, past narrow cubicles, on a venture to the jacks at the
far end, and their slosh-slap on return – as evidence that some
sods couldn't piss in a pot if they were paid. They were country
lads at heart, who were used to the wide open spaces: say what
you like about townies, but they could when sober discharge
themselves through the eye of a needle, and if not there, then in
your eye or anywhere besides.

But a condition we could never accustom ourselves to was
the cold, even during recreation. Only on rare occasions after we
had gone out for a slash did Shamie Doyle, Jimmy Codlotin,
Wally Furlong, Kenny D. and I venture beyond the toilet block
opposite the locker rooms for a brisk walk across the top of the
lay-boys' field. Then back with us, like rabbits in heat, through
the cloisters, to hunch down on the warm pipes by the skirting,
to quake and jibe one another till the bell went for five o'clock
study.

'Youse'll get piles from sitting on them pipes,' Nick Loan
called out.

'You'll get blisters on your tongue from telling us,' says I.

'Don't let him hear you, or he'll give you a clout you won't
forget,' says Kenny D.

'Big Loan? No, he won't. That fellow's all right.'

Even the brand new pair of Hush Puppies I had persuaded
the Doll to get from Cullen's window during the holidays amid
the after-Christmas bargain rush to help make me look older getting past the doormen of the Athenaeum at new year's for my
first dance were failing to keep my feet warm. I half-envied the
comfort Shamie Doyle's must have had inside his tightly laced

clodhoppers: great tugboats polished up to the last, which had surely carried a long-gone ancestor of his to the pig fairs in town the century before. Fecking hell, Scott of the Antarctic would have been envious.

Because the chain from the crank to the pull rope had just given a jingle-click-ding, the bell for first-study period was about to go. We had come to regard this advance notice as a bell-wether of loss. It tinkled a million miles off before the peal to wake us at ten to seven, and preceded every other ring that regulated our lives: the one for Mass, those at the beginning and end of each class, and this full-blooded summons to our study halls. Ready, altogether now: one, two, three . . . clunk-bang, clunk-bang.

Three of my cohorts jumped up to jostle for space in the window embrasure to see which theologian was today's bell-ringer, and who would come up with the funniest things to say about him.

'He has the face of Korky the Kat from *The Dandy*.'

'No, he's more like Podge, with the pointed nose and all.'

'Methinks he's unquestionably got the chin of Corporal Clott,' says Shamie Doyle.

What was the point of standing up? All theologians were the same: great gawk-eyed ecclesiastical students who, after secondary school, should have stayed a while on the outside to debauch, before their six-year stint across in the seminary. As if yanking the frillies off a dressmaker's dummy, Holy Joe's fists would stick out from his black-cassock sleeves to reach up, and he'd crook his trunk to tug downwards on the rope outside the porch at a slant across the square from our window, the fifth one down.

Codlotin wasn't pushed about gawping at your man either, and stayed stuck to the pipes. As the bell drowned out our voices, Jimmy and I grimaced at being in a gang with nincompoops

whose idea of putting on the agony was to hold forth in a confab on the difference between Dennis the Menace's shirt and
Smasher's. By the following year, maybe, they'd have left their
infancy behind, and we could all move to the benches in the next
corridor to play push-penny – or trade on the property market,
since Shamie Doyle had agreed to bring back the Monopoly set
his mother had promised him for next Christmas. Till then, we
might make do with what we had: watching Wally Furlong get
fired up over the pilgrim's latest fad as he stared sheepishly into
the little lad's face. This was Wally the rebel, who the year before
had flaunted dirty pictures in primary school.

I dared not show them my latest copy of *New Musical
Express*, with its list of the official UK charts, which even the
senior year had probably only ever heard about. And any lark
about girls entirely stumped them, not to mind when I got in the
groove to 'Love Me Do' by the Beatles with a full-belt paradid-
dle on the lid of an empty, resonant desk. But of course, they
liked 'Edelweiss', and Bridie Gallagher, and big Burl Ives, who
crooned on about grey geese and plump white ducks. Could
there be a code to 'come-all-ye's that I wasn't getting? At least
Codlotin liked Elvis.

The bell had gone when I jumped up, out of dismay, and did
the stamping-out-of-a-fag routine on one leg to show Jimmy
how to dance the Twist. But the spasm I added for effect
became lost in the pandemonium of last-hurrah hysteria that
was building round our ears. Our dim corridor had crowded with
fellows winkling the last ounce out of recreation – how they had
savoured the supreme of sweet-and-sour during the final hours
of their holidays. Such an unrivalled sauce – the hindmost titbit
of any good thing, as ever, being its most luscious.

Suddenly the scary bonce of Baldy appeared at the top of
the steps and put an end to excess. The sound level dipped to a

murmur; the same as had happened one year at the Corpus
Christi procession, when some gobshite had tripped over a wire
and set the loudspeakers along the street on the blink.

Tantum er-go Sacramentum ve-ne-re-mur ce-rnu— *Isn't that a lovely
priest, that new man? Novo cedat ri-tu-i*— *And how's your husband keeping now, Missus Maguire: any sign of a pick-up? Ne'er a sign; that man's
dying since I married him, especially in bed; other than that he's fine, Nancy.
No sign of anything permanent in your life at the moment? The hell of a
sign. A-men*—

As boys fused into lines outside their study halls, a corridor-
full of columns jiggling again reminded me of how that summer's day procession had swayed along concrete while the tarred
road ahead shimmered. The company of FCA men leading the
string had gone a tad out of step, as their sly eyes searched out
girls along pavements. And in turn, great-thighed, long-suffering
married girls who were free for the day on grounds of pretence
to devotion had made no bones about accommodating, with
more longing than their single sisters-in-arms, glances from
moustached grunts whose fetching hams almost breached the
seams of their uniform trousers. Hup, one, two, three – down,
boy, down. Meanwhile, spouses forsaken for the time being were
in retreat behind Ryan's doors, and other premises, to recuperate
a little lost essence.

Our prefect, another Holy Joe from the *far side*, the ecclesiastical side, arrived to turn the key and clack up the hefty latch for
first-years to mooch glumly over the raised granite threshold and
knotty boards towards their places. By five on the dot, all corridor queues had shuffled inside to bang desks; each lad could
either withdraw into his work for the next day, or pretend to, as
he lapsed into a two-hour reverie – a choice no regime could
enforce. Then hark, as they say in all the best circles: the lopes
of those who were late for study resounded in the cloisters

outside. Our communal ear pricked up when Baldy spoke.

'Masters Loan and Beird,' says he. The tone got sharper with: 'Master Doran, I do believe. You boys are late, huh. Can you explain?' The dean was more matter of fact than usual, cutting off in advance the offer of genuine excuses. So, no caustic touch of cat-and-mouse play about him this evening, then: probably no time for it.

'We were delayed, Father, togging in after games,' says Loan.

'Were we now indeed? And is that explanation sufficient?'

'No, Father.'

'*No Father*, indeed. You won't be late again, will you?'

'Yes, Father.'

'Harrumph huh?'

'*No*, Father.'

We awaited the sound that would resonate both outside and down the inner corridors of our skulls. The first swish cut into sparsely covered phalanges and metacarpals; its flight righted by a flap against soutane serge before it arced into the next stroke. There was no pair of shoulder blades in our room that each thwack, as precise as an executioner's axe, didn't send a shudder across; no heart that didn't feel the cut. Even Shamie Doyle's unsympathetic fingers must by proxy have sensed some tingle.

Outside, the flogging echoed on.

Still, hardship forged ties between unlikely comrades. And every boy contributed to the room's rising wave of sympathy for three of the college's most promising young athletes, whose mitts after games were already on fire – not to mind this. But a bond of fellowship was about all we could muster as a serum against the toxin of cock-eyed correction that got meted out for the least misdemeanour.

You could sense, too, the brand of rancour that was the seed for revolt germinate in those who were so inclined. They were there all right: the quiet ones who, with enough experiences like this under their belts, would become dyed-in-the-wool rebels. I watched as heads pivoted in the supporting cups of their palms to find others who, in like revulsion, dared to pull faces at the lack of compassion being shown. You didn't need to be there on a scholarship to pick out those who'd turn out to be men-to-matter, rocks of the world to come, and their momentary reactions registered more weightily with me than did any fear of that baldy bollix or his fairy cane.

For a moment, I shivered to think of what the future might hold for humankind. As though from the edge of an abyss over a cataclysm beyond our unseen viaduct, I was getting a glimpse of events yet to come; of a humongous upheaval in which activists would, with a force of nature, ring in untold changes upon the globe, while institutions such as this one would get wiped out, and those who ran them ossified into fossils. Yet strangely, I didn't want to take part in such a revolt; the thought of it left me cold. I only wanted to observe and bide my time.

Despite being at my desk beside the radiator near the back, these old carpals and armpits shook, and the voice of Sam Cooke singing 'Chain Gang' on the radiogram at home came into my head. I took my hands down from my face and began to drum like fuck on the pipes. The prefect roared at me to be quiet.

'Or else you won't have far to walk to report to the dean,' says he.

This joint would need some cataclysm to clean it out and remove the infestation of tendrils creeping and twisting in a dry-rot-like network beneath the paintwork along the walls towards every room. The blight crept up through the legs of chairs to plant its nerve ends in prefects' brains. It could be found in the fusty dust that swirled in dank cloisters: an oppressive thing. Its eradication would have to include Baldy, at the heart of the fungus, and the likes of big Billy Curry and his mates.

A hard slogging over little or nothing would not affect the unflappable Neady Beird or Nick Loan; they would get by unscathed. But for a finely tuned big goof with a soft centre, like the unwary Martin Doran, whose size and strength bizarrely made him even more vulnerable, the outcome was bound to become more than an evening of nursing sore fingers under oxters. Violence both stifled a fellow's aspirations to be inventive, if he had any to begin with, and turned him into a surly bucko with a glum-awful gauge of himself. Martin Doran was that sort. So I reckoned he needed a little support.

Later that night, on my way to the jacks down the dorm, I spotted your man in his pyjamas sitting on his bed, hands wrapped about himself, feeling down. So I went back for a little drop of something in a bottle from my medicine cabinet.

'This'll do the trick,' says I. 'Since Baldy gave me the works the first time, I like to keep a ball, or two, of malt handy. It will tide you over the night. Take it neat, mind.'

This wasn't the last time, either, that I would share my supply with the big fellow; certainly not.

10

May a fledgling amid heavy weather avail of each opportunity and make the most of every delicate chance to savour such goose-summer days as come its way.

The dishevelled procession plodded from side to side down the corridor, as if it might never get to where it was meant to be. Every last man-jack of 1C was loitering towards the woodwork-and-drawing room for forty-five minutes with Mickey Mortise, a half-deaf semi-retired lay-teacher, to avail of a chance in our schedule to cut up rough, knife-throw compasses at desks, bang heads with T-squares, and louse up each other's diagrams – the sumptuous treat of a little hands-on anarchy. We would hatch and cross-hatch more lewd shapes for the old duffer to decipher; budding geometers jockeying for status, we had reputations to enhance. Also, we had reactions against the regime to air.

Armed with an instrument box, two sharpened pencils, a pencil parer and rubber in a vicelike grip under one arm, and in the other an A3-size copy that held between its pages pictures torn from a *Playboy* magazine which Wally Furlong had brought back after Christmas, I ambled behind Jimmy Codlotin at the tail-end of the group. I was daydreaming of gong home for Easter. Then, all of a sudden, I got plugged into a two-hundred-and-twenty-volt generator, with the shock of seeing her.

Straight from *Playboy* but for a tight strip of blue Terylene work-coat to cover her shape, the apparition came towards us. Her arms, too, were loaded with the appliances of toil, each loosely but stably held: a bucket and bundle of cloths in one hand, another bucket and a long-handled mop in the other. We might all have joined forces as members of the Irish Transport and General Workers' Union and marched outside to go on strike: let's place a picket at the front gate and take the Easter break early this year. The sudden rush of current jolted to life every idle circuit; my limbs and brain at last warmed up. A move had to be made; something had to done. It was an impulsive thing. And I felt hope at the possibility of a smidgen of enchantment amid the chaos.

This very urge had driven tom-cats to wail in a nearby alley at home and to rip their groins getting over broken-glass-capped walls for scarcely a mouser in hell's chance of the all-important first tilt at some receptive honey in anguish atop an asphalt roof down the neighbourhood. Never again when one would wake me would I fling a bottle at it – the noise of which had caused the Gunner to ask: *Was that the sound of breaking glass I heard last night. I wonder, hmm . . .*

For we were, the soft-furred species and I, kindred beings, gentle at heart – except that the scent which it chased was fecking odious, while I preferred to tail the whiff of lavender given off by a gorgeous honeybun whose rear end independently held sway from the waist down. As lick-alike as we were in the *amour* department, with each of us falling into a seizure of craving when lovestruck, I would, whatever else, keep my groin store intact from spiky objects. Once more the conditions were just right for nature to take its course; this had to be love, yeah love – instantaneous love, boy.

Catgut got wrung from sheep's intestines rather than felines' probably because our sort's entrails became too frazzled from fervent ardour before they could be removed and twisted into fiddle strings. I ought to have consulted Jimmy Codlotin, the one for sheep's caecums. What's more, if my innards didn't there and then receive a good dousing, nothing would be left of the entire lot but a tin-can lid of burning ash on the floor outside the refectory, the whiff of which would have been a delicacy compared to the tang off Sister Spud's leather-soled roast *boeuf* and cat's-pee-tasting potatoes. Was the old tuber that hard to wash?

Indeed, if the flash of a girl's leg movement kindled the least internal organ stirring in lads who were normal, the arrival of a female who wobbled a tight tush as delightfully as this one was doing, while she motored on by, had to be enough to put an urge on the most flaccid josser confined in that joint. To add a touch of Eastern mystique, her eyes were turned aside the way pre-Vatican-II convent postulants shunned the sight of males approaching. I could feel my ears, and whatever else, grow outwards like a lolloping kangaroo's. Cats and kangaroos: what difference? We were all of a kind anyway.

My rash craving was even more sudden than what I had experienced during the Christmas holidays at my first dance while tight-smooching a scent-doused coal-blackhead in the middle of the floor where the bouncers wouldn't notice, and after I had accompanied her home, she pushed against me in the open porch with a force that had made it an ordeal to keep my arms round the hydraulic ram of her waist and to breathe. Then her old fellow bellowed from upstairs: 'What's going on out there?'

'Nothing, Dad. I'm saying goodnight to a boy.'

If that was her word of goodnight, heaven save us from the effects of her long-haul conversations. Indeed, had the girl been able to pull as hard as she could push, no doubt she would have been a sure-fire candidate for the famous international tug-of-war team from Boley.

'Are you from Boley?'

'I am.'

'Can you pull?'

'Both pull and push.'

'It's going to be a torturous night, so. But Boley will do well in the world championship this year. Ready, steady, and lie on the rope. Pull. Hisss . . .'

For their own good, pretty women ought to have been barred from working near where virile students were so tightly crammed; fellows already had enough impulses to contain without the added taunt of seeing maids in tight polyester strut across their terrain. The odd glimpse of puppy fat carcassing in warm folds over white elastic-top stockings while catwalking through cloisters was one thing, but the arrival of a real smasher amongst us, or of any vaguely tumbling beauty, was entirely another matter. Even Jimmy Codlotin's mother, on visits to her bright bundle every Sunday and Wednesday afternoon, was an imposition of torment on repressed would-be geometers, as through our windows we waited for the clip of high heels along the avenue beyond.

As the weeks passed, she became ever more like Zsa Zsa Gabor, till by the end of term her fur coat and heels alone had begun to look not half-bad. Get 'em off you, Mrs Codlotin, girl.

Girls in bobby socks who worked in the kitchen were at risk when they walked through cloisters with meals on trays for codgers and malingerers who lay in bed letting on to be sick. But how was a creature of such delicacy, plucked straight from the upper reaches of pure imagination, surviving here? Certainly, over the months, as the legs had got longer and my pride-and-joy 'pickers cut more into my toes, I had thrown an eye on her, but on this day her appearance in blue Terylene became over-whelming. Was this a vision floating under neo-Gothic arches, or had big Billy Curry again come up from behind to send me head over heels into dreamland? But this was no dream; it was an opportunity. If quarried rightly, life in here might yet throw up a golden moment.

This vision wiped out all the powers I'd had of recalling my regular old fetish, the tug-of-war black pearl, an obsession so well guarded since the holidays that I had never once mentioned her name to my by then best pal Martin Doran, lest its element of bedtime comfort be diluted. For I had found that, from other titbits hard-garnered during the Christmas holidays, as soon as they got disclosed to my cohorts, their appeal had become so watered down, I might just as easily have put myself asleep at night by fixing on the sabotage of Baldy Klops' black and white Sunbeam at the front of the college, the one car Mrs Codlotin, oddly enough, had so often leaned against to fix her high heels.

It was just as well I was at the tail-end of 1C in the corridor, or else the others would have noticed my face change colour and got on to me for fancying kitchen girls. You could brag about any big-jawed convent bird you wished, with tubes under her for legs, from downtown, and be applauded – because you were such a bleeding ladykiller. But you became rightly jinxed if word got out that you'd jutted a whelk in the flannels over some curvy-arsed kitchen girl. It was only a lubber like Wally Furlong who got the horn from watching skivvies – and we usually gave him the razz.

'Hey, lads, will youse look at the red face on fat Wally? He's after the kitchen staff again. Oh, lads, Wally is in love with a skivvy.'

It was easy to cover up my predicament by lowering the copy – the unwieldy thing had a use other than to carry naughty pictures to draw for Mickey Mortise's perusal; not that it mattered, for the dotard had probably never in his life seen a bowly botty in the raw, apart from his own.

'What's that you're drawing there, son?'

'Sir, it's just the tail-end of a horse, sir. I always begin there and work backwards.'

''Tis a very peculiar-looking horse.'

'It is that so, sir? But it'll shape up when I shade it in, sir.'

'I take it then that you intend to draw a mare?'

'Oh, yes, sir, yes.'

'Sir, you'll be able to saddle it by the time he's finished,' Nick Loan said.

I wasn't the only one in the corridor suffering from a bulging whelk. Immediately ahead, Jimmy Codlotin lowered his copy, and as though a line of old clippers were stuck in the doldrums, the copies of many other lads also slipped to half-mast – except Wally's, oddly enough. For the hell of it, I whistled 'Red Sails in the Sunset', and all but heard the Doll humming Jimmy Kennedy's song as she ran the spatula across a pint glass.

Instead of following my class into the next cloister, I swung back in the direction we had come from, where the apparition twenty yards on was headed. I popped into our empty classroom to shove my accoutrements into the desk before continuing after her.

The line of flesh on display beneath her work-coat as she disappeared at the top of the stairs was such that, come what may, Mickey Mortise would not be seeing me, nor would Alfie Bra in the maths class to follow – for whom a good excuse of absence would be needed. I glanced in each direction along the cloister before swinging sharply right to take two steps at a time upwards.

The dormitory door was still open, so I poked my nose round the corner, where the sight of her strutting action up the aisle at once made me drool. Sharp-edged shafts of sunlight that narrowed and waned in the distance burst across her path from a line of slim cubicle entrances on her right-hand side and caught the flesh-tint of long, contoured calves. She was enhanced in a shimmer of brightness each time she emerged from the contrasting dust-brown shade of a cubicle bulkhead, and as she went in and out of light, the flecking of her movement, the effect again of knots pulsating, sort of confused my eyes, just short of dazzling them.

Yet the scene held a touch of sadness that went with all things lovely. Its presence was maybe brought about by a struggle she'd undergone that had tested her to the pith, or perhaps such a melancholy was the forerunner of some experience she might yet have to endure – if so, I hoped that the steel-blue radiance of her beauty would not be spoiled, ever. Then, as if to back up my misgiving, her demeanour in the distance appeared to flag, and the one stitch of gloom came over me, as it did whenever I thought about the Doll behind the counter, sullen and removed from the world, even though she had the moment before been sharing a laugh with 'Dan the Bull', in for a pint. What a queer thing: to gaze on magnificence, only to feel downcast by its oomph. For though her ongoing sway still marked out new contours, her step lacked the side-to-side flounce of the catwalk she'd shown in the cloister, and her shoulders drooped ever so slightly, as if her grip on erect poise had been prised loose. It concerned me in case she was suddenly filled with the same miserable angst as overtook boarders during their return after the Christmas break. Her shape had changed, definitely.

Then I remembered what our science teacher – the sleek-haired one whose eyes, beneath dodgy, twitching brows and shutter-speed lids, appeared to close from above and below, akin to those of a bird infested with stickfast fleas and who, from the way he might look at you, would give you the shivers – had taught us that *amplitude* was the technical term for the height of a wave, and that this height, when it changed, was said to *modulate*. The bit of old science had its moments after all, and it was helping me to spot how dolls changed their swagger when they got downcast. *The dame has modulated her amplitude, the dame has . . .* Yeah, but wasn't that the nature of girls?

I waited till the subject of my experiment had gone three-quarter ways up the aisle and turned left out of sight into the recess, where the jacks were, before I went through the doorway. I'd never felt so inclined to be furtive.

But furtive was exciting. A fellow could use it to probe things; stealth ought to have been an item between the beaker and the Bunsen burner up on the science-room shelf. *Pass me the loan of your stealth, Wally, till I test this out.*

Jimmy Codlotin's was the nearest cubicle on my right. The untidy wretch had left a monster-sized jar of Brylcreem open in the basin opposite his bed: a wire trellis, rather than hair oil, was what he needed to tie up that peruke of a thing, where all sorts of insects and wildlife were procreating. So I popped inside, and at once felt the relief of a little time out from the chase.

I dug out a daub of cream to spruce up my hair in Jimmy's smeared looking-glass. Shame on you, Squire Codlotin: you ought to be reported for not having the mirror clean when a friend in need calls. I lobbed another daub against the underside of his washbasin, from which to dab the scuffs on my aging win-kle-pickers, and used a corner of his bedspread to buff them off. Not at all; Jimmy wouldn't mind. And for good measure, a blob to the underside of his bed as a preen gland in which to dip his bill, should he wake in the night with an inclination to primp himself up. Better still, a dash onto his cotton sheet to help him sleep, and one for his pillow to get him back for the time he chased me across the field. This felt good.

For a moment, a moment only, I had forgotten why I was up there on the dormitory.

11

It takes gumption for a moocher to drop everything else and follow his nose in pursuit of an opportunity that comes along. Chase that dream, my friend.

Slip-sliding along the lino towards the shadowy end of the dorm, I abruptly picked up on a matter of importance that had been overlooked, and my legs all but skewed off course into the nearest cubicle. Things had been happening too fast for a fellow to plan his crucial approach, and what excuse he might offer for his presence there when he should have been in class. Even outside of class hours, the dormitory was off limits till bedtime, unless a student had gone to the surgery to be certified sick by Sister Polyps – provided that the cad was prepared to take on the spot her all-purpose dosage of two horse tablets and a glass of water. Glug, glug, and thanks very much, Sister.

However, with the triumph under my belt of having seen home the black pearl of Boley at Christmas and the likelihood of doing so again over Easter, there was no reason in the wide-earthly world why this venture wouldn't succeed. If I walked up to her and blurted out that I had followed her because the sight of her body had sent me into orbit round the earth, would she react with surprise, a smile and a pair of big eyes expressing: *Mamma Mia, how luck favours me today?* And why not? Wasn't this guy here the most charming, suave bloke in 1C, and the best dresser in the entire school? I'd hold my glass at the proper bartender's angle for her to froth out like a tap on the end of a freshly connected keg – well, if ever there was the black stuff in heaven.

Baby.
Yes, honey?
Drop the bucket, and get off of your broom.
Oh, wow!
Show me what you can; let your body swoon.
Oh, bow-wow!
For here I am, baby, your winkle-picker man.
Oh, heaven, good heavens!
Yes, baby.

But from an inkling that a female's nature was un-straightforward and things might not work so simply, I decided to add caution to daring, and prod onward with discretion. A good glug of hooch from the remaining bottle, the last man standing, hidden in the middle of a neat pile of Y-fronts on the middle shelf of my locker, or a handful of Sister Polyps' horse tablets, would calm the nerves. Without them, a fellow had to make do with his own vim in working up a head of steam; besides, time was down to a phial-full. So on I went, till the splash and plop-drip of water in a container could be heard from around the corner. My prey was close by.

That she had wasted no time in getting on with her chores was enough to make me want to funk the situation and leave her there undisturbed. But this other urge wouldn't let me be; the corner ahead had to be turned. So I stepped into the alcove.

And there she was, framed in the soft light through a frosted-glass window on the off side from the sun, stooped and turned away. Her back arched yet more each time her wrists twisted to wring from a cloth last drops that became jewels glittering downwards into one of the buckets, and so delectable was the snap, the sound of work so divine, that even the scouring agent smelled like cedar wood. If only it had been possible to winkle out from the institution's dreary hours this one sparkling instant to hold for keeps.

But the yearning for lip-smacking a fellow had to contend with began to cut up rough inside, burning like hell from groin to fingertips, as time pressed on: at any minute, the bell would jangle in the jungle downstairs. The thought of facing into Alfie Bra's class would put a black knot on a first-year's intestines and douse this pleasant saline tang on his tongue. Both yearning and loathing at once focused themselves in my fingertips, and touch was the one sense that needed redress.

In here out of view of the main aisle, a fellow could fix himself and afford his mane another stroke of the plastic brush that was such a leading thing of its kind, with a ringed handle to house his crooked sweaty finger inside the pocket of that Donegal-tweed jacket. Cupped in the palm of the hand, it made grooming in class an act so reflex as to be discreet, except of course – shiver my hairy fecking timbers – during Alfie Bra's. One country clod had dared to dub me *Johnny Hairbrush*: it ought to have been *Johnny Pizzazz*, for goodness sake. But one self-caress doesn't ease an itch.

I perked up my gall in readiness for whatever the girl's response might be. And in an effort to appear as unconcerned as James Dean when drawing a bead on some voluptuous chick, I leaned with one 'picker crossed over the other against the partition wall of the cubicle nearby, sucked in a deep breath, and opened my beak.

'Excuse me, Miss, but didn't I see you at a dance in the Athenaeum after Christmas?'

No, I hadn't seen her there. She might have been in Timbuktu, or Dublin, where Billy Curry was from – heaven forfend she had as much in common with him, or else I was faced with a harpy instead of the maiden-like replica I had imagined. It was too late for me to funk it and run. The ball's in, the game's on, and there was no turning back till the final whistle. Martin Doran's words, not mine: he was the one for the more robust sports. But let feral mousers in alleyways tear out each other's eyes; this cat preferred the more genteel quality of fixtures indoors, ideally a good purr on a boudoir chaise longue. Meow, Ginger; shove over on the pillow.

Believing herself to be alone but for the sound of her work, this girl was out of the blue faced with having to deal with someone who was sassily quizzing her. Maybe the twitter of his voice, no matter how handsome the bounder might look, was only an imaginary one. And did she fall headlong into the bucket with the start? Well, if she had been in any way stumped, it didn't take her long to recover, turn round, and face her intruder.

Without any hint of a red cheek or eyes dropping to the ground, she managed to tap into that reserve of composure she'd so breathtakingly shown downstairs, stood straight to size me up, and checked my freshly oiled bouffant for recognition. It was clear that the girl had not seen me before – not even vaguely from the corner of her eye in the cloisters – and I felt the smart of a slight. And, so, she instinctively had the advantage of setting the pace of our exchange; even of deciding if there should be one. She gripped and twisted the cloth before giving me an answer – which, when it eventually came, was by way of a casual question that overlapped another splash-dribble of diamonds into her bucket.

'What dance was that, then?'

'The one in the Athenaeum,' says I.

'And where might that place be, then?'

Her voice, which was not as sweet as I had expected it to be, had on the second question softened to a warble of indifference compared to her hollering of the first one. She had to be concealing a mechanism for sizing me up. The straightforward leg of this chase was over. Her change of tone meant she was content to play me along, the way females, in what is little more than second nature to them, are able to string males along.

I recalled how the Doll had passed off gougers full of guff when they were sodden beyond inhibition, and whose ebbing manners had no place in the presence of a lady. How with her patience stretched, she had squinted her eyes in a pose of disdain for the benefit of others who'd not yet lost the run of themselves, and pitched the glass she was cleaning against the light in downright refusal to let the least smear go undetected. She then pinged the tumblers with her painted nails before placing them upside down on the back shelf, and each ring echoed the point inside sopping brains, where words failed, that customers were obliged to remain staid and low-key as guests on her premises. And anyone who persisted in testing the tether of her feline tolerance got his clock cleaned with the sphinx-like distaste she held for cockroaches.

She had also schooled me in the art of female reverse-side action. Letting on to be intently listening to some dolt across the counter who jabbered on non-stop and who, the more he talked, the more money he spent, she subtly continued with her own tasks, but the sly nods and asides she threw in my direction were enough to let me know what the woman was up to. Otherwise, I might not have realised that such a lady's aid of intrigue had even existed, never mind suspected it to be as lethal as a derringer up the sleeve of a bar-room belle in a Wild West saloon. A glare of contempt spun out before spurning their demands for service was a device she used on arrogant jacks who imposed themselves or irked their hostess by not tendering proper niceties, maybe even a little flattery, as a down payment of appreciation for such customer care as only the Doll, with eyelashes flicking, could give.

At the same time, lest she commit treason by giving away womankind's secrets, the Doll had never gone into explanations of what was behind her bouts of furtive signalling, even though she must have realised it would someday stand her precious only son in good stead for him to be well versed in these matters. But I had seen enough to know that behind the fluttering lashes of the smiling chatelaine lay a complicated lady who revelled in her own ability to outwit most male specimens of the species.

So here I was on the dorm, sure and certain that the girl standing before me knew very well where the fecking Athenaeum was.

'It's to be found in my old home town,' says I. 'Where life is lived to the full, where nobody has too much, and everyone has a roof over their head and enough to eat.'

A little corny cant was what the situation called for to put the girl at ease; it might serve as a first instalment of appreciation in exchange for whatever hospitality was on offer, or a means of dinting a good first impression.

'Your old home town must be a great place to live so,' says she.

Although getting on with their business, the girl's hands had grown more hesitant: her attention had been distracted. Was she having ideas? Were those fingers itchy for want of touch? Of course they were: this was me, Johnny Valentine Ryan, here. For good measure, my mane got another brush-through when she wasn't minding. Yeah, this was the man.

The opportunity for success looked good. Rather than dismiss my approach out of hand, she had engaged in conversation: a hint that she was prepared to give this caper a whirl. By continuing to work as she spoke, though, and glance in my direction only while standing upright to move the bucket with her foot and wring out the cloth, she was dictating the game at which women were the renowned masters, and I might hold my horses. In this chase, the hunter had become the prey. The reverse-side action had kicked in: I hoped the dame fancied her quarry.

Come and work for it, boy, if you want my notice. You have so far not earned the right to replace this chore as the object of my attention. A girl likes to see a certain grovelling about her suitor. Males and rove beetles should fawn before a lady.

Splat a cockroach round the college close, the college close . . .

Sure who would mind currying favour here, if in the end favours were to be had? But I needed to winkle out more than just notice from a bird who was upping the swell of her appeal as the game went on. The lure of touching her body surged in me as she once more bent over, and more lovely leg than ever I had seen lovely leg on a girl extended from beneath her workcoat: fecking tantalising. This is the way a racing driver must feel as he gawps at a new model being reversed from his neighbour's garage: too overcome with craving to rush over and caress the streamline curves of its off-red arse; too mesmerised to stir a limb.

'What will Dr Quigley say if he catches you here talking to me?'

'Oh, old Baldy Klops, is it? It's not so much what he'll say, but what he'll do.' To make her laugh, I again put on the corny droll manner; how much a fellow gets a girl to laugh is a sign, surely, of how well he's doing at enticing her towards seduction – the sound of that one word alone, boy. But no laughter came; not yet.

'Would he slap you?' says she.

'Would he what?' says I. 'He'd slap me out the front door and up the road home, for good and all. Why, do you think he'd do otherwise? Maybe compliment me for being a credit to the school uniform and shake my hand, saying, "Well done indeed, John Ryan, boy, for your taste in pretty girls"?'

I was glad of the chance to flatter her – an offer of more down payment. When at last she found this funny, I asked her what she was laughing at – which I had planned to do anyway at the first sign of a chortle. She stood up and faced me full-on. She looked fucking lovely.

This was the moment to be seized. I sidled over right next to her, again cocked one 'picker over the other, and leaned against the toilet wall at the risk of getting distemper on my coat. Once more she chuckled, nervously this time, and seemed to hesitate over what to say next. She'd gone all shy. I put my arm on her shoulder and, in a way that was almost too playful, chanced her with another question.

'Do you think he'd compliment me for giving you a wee peck on the cheek?'

She neither looked at me nor pulled away. What could a fellow think but assume he was doing well for himself. The rate of progress, and not much time left for dithering, made my little heart *pink* a beat. My arm slipped naturally, of its own accord like, down the back of her Terylene work-coat and about her waist, where it remained, momentarily.

Well shiver my timbers, below these fingers was the arch of her lovely tush, this protruding thing of splendour that had jelly-wobbled along the corridor and which I had longed to squeeze hard on like it was a sponge ball. Here it was. But steady on there, fingers, my friends, don't rush it: just think of how the wondrous doings compacted into the last few minutes have outshone all that has happened since Christmas.

Yet her waist and hip bone felt no different from the ribcage of the whippet with which the Gunner, half-locked, had landed home one night after trials at the dog track. As everyone else turned on their stools to check him for signs of psychosis before eyeballing each other, he'd dragged the reluctant beast, yelping helplessly as it pulled backwards, across the bar-room floor towards the back door. The pair of bulging brown eyes on a startled hound is the saddest thing on earth. Thank heaven no start showed in this girl's eyes.

But when she stopped wringing the cloth and dropped it on the floor, I couldn't be sure whether she would slap me across the face or respond in kind to my latest move.

'You're some chancer,' she said.

'Now tell me, why's that?'

'*Why is that?* says he,' she called out in pretend amazement.

'You're right. But you know what: I'd whirl an arm round Sister Spud in the kitchen below if she was in any way good-looking.'

That got her laughing so loud I would have asked her to shush but for the delicacy of the moment.

'I'll tell her not to live in hope so,' says she. 'My, my, is that the name youse fellows have for that old rip? Mother Iodine is what we call her. She always carries a bottle in her bib pocket, ready to whip out and sterilise you for the least scratch. You know, she once dabbed it on a girl's mouth, mistaking lipstick for blood. I think she likes to see pain on our faces when the stuff stings.'

'She's not an old rip,' I said, sparring with her for another reaction.

Her bluff scorn of the wimpled prune, however justified, took me aback. Whatever right to contempt there was for the regime, it belonged to me, a direct victim. And if we both were to have the same opinions, we'd only end up outdoing each other with smart remarks. Besides, I couldn't help but feel sorry for the gaunt Sister Spud, whom I'd seen feebly slip along by the cloister walls, scared stiff of getting keeled over by some ploughman gouger, oblivious of the white habit passing behind him and of the outcome his flapping about might have on a hock-spavined old vestal virgin, should they collide. It seemed that this girl, whose high-pitched voice marred her good looks, and whose name I still didn't know, might be more headstrong than I had hoped for.

The most important matter, though, was whether or not she was game for a spate of canoodling, a touch of fingertips along the fringes for a while. And then . . . come what may – any activity towards which our law-of-the-lever animal instincts might lead us.

I tickled her ribs. Despite rabid cackles, she had as many tickles as a beer keg left out overnight. Was it my approach? Did her quarry not know the correct formula? Again, I felt a little taken aback. No matter what, though, he would not funk it. Lester Piggott had never jibbed, however scrawny a jade he'd saddled.

When she stopped laughing, I deepened my voice in the style of Marlon Brando – James Dean had served his purpose and was stood down. Marlon, the man, whispered in her ear in case the millions of cinema-goers the world over might hear him without having to crane their necks – and why shouldn't they make the effort, all those women who loved the great taurine neck of Brando? Moo, Marlon boy, move over; this here is John Valentine Ryan, taking on the lead male role in this scene.

I stood on my toes to reach down – which, since she was tall, meant stretching straight across, fornenst my nose. I gave her a kiss on the cheek. One good slow-sucking peck you'd lay along the flank of an ice lolly of a summer's day. And did she mind? Did she what? First impressions are the ones that last, I told myself again.

Not only did she not mind, she turned her face more towards me, till our maws sort of drifted together. But our lips didn't glue as if stuck from the juice of gumdrops, like what had happened with the black pearl: no shortage of know-how there. It was more how, of all things, the sides of raw meat that the Gunner used to keep for the hound had melded to the side of the ice-cream fridge out the back. My mouth stayed firmly on duty, awaiting the go-ahead to delve farther into the rictus opposite. For some reason, it reminded me of a last-supper cup of warm tea I'd held against my breath at Christmas, before being shagged back into confinement here.

My hands drifted down the curves of her backside and pulled her in to me. When the crockery of one open mouth clacked against that of the other, she pulled away, stood erect and stared at me. Words were rising in her throat.

'I don't think we should stand here talking, where Father Quigley or anyone else can come up on us.' Was that what she called this: *talking*?

'Do you always refer to him as Father Quigley?' says I. 'We have another name for that lad. And where will we take ourselves to so we can continue with this little chat?'

An enlarged Brando sweltered beneath uncomfortable woollen undergarments that had seen him through the winter. As we moved away from the lavatory recess, I tried to coax her into a cubicle nearby, one in shadow – the light along the aisle was a nuisance.

'No, not that one anyway,' says she. 'It's too near the hatch door to the priests' stairs at the main entrance. Any of them might appear here on top of us.' *On top*: some way she had of putting things, and with these damned wool shorts getting itchier at her every word. 'Do you not know that Dr Quigley's rooms are on the other side of that door?' says she. 'He often cuts through here as a shortcut to the middle of the school. Whatever about you, I don't want to lose my job and end up with references that wouldn't let me work in this country ever again. When I take the boat to England, it'll be out of choice, and not because I have to, for any reason – if you get me?'

''Tis tricky right enough,' says I, agreeable to anything so as not to mar proceedings. 'And I don't want to see you getting caught either. I didn't know about this door being here; is it a secret entrance, a magic hatch to fairyland? I have only ever been to the other end of this dorm.'

She didn't answer.

'Tell me your name,' says Brando. 'Wait, let me guess: it's Marguerite.

'Marguerite?' she laughed. 'It's surely not Marguerite. My name is . . . Jane. Where did you get that from? Marguerite, how are you? We're not in Paris, France, you know.'

Oh, but Paris, France, as we sidled down the dorm and into a cubicle more to her taste, was coming up: Paris and Cork; New York and London; Tokyo and the Taj Mahal; Tashkent and Tomnalossett – wherever you're going yourself – we ought soon to find out and experience them all. Each and every one of them was a star place. If only a fellow might first of all return to earth from this orbit, he was in above the atmosphere.

12

*And on he goes, with his charm and sweet-toothed smile; my cockerel friend
is not one to turn away in the middle of his hiatus and leave unfinished such
a morsel of delectation.*

Having bounced up through the hollow, concrete stairwell and
come at us in toned-down waves along the dorm, the racket
below of classes changing seemed so distant it might as well
have been happening downtown. Yet, it was possible amid the
clamour to make out Kenny D.'s huskiness, Wally Furlong calling Shamie Doyle to wait, and Nick Loan off ballad-singing
again as he kicked a beat on the heating pipes. Bless him, but
nobody else could mither the system with the same defiance, as
he went: *It's not the lave-in of Liverpool that graves me, but me darlin'
when I think of dhee.*

Their noise gradually went tinny, and then lonesome.

The outbreak and waning of sound didn't register much with
Jane. She had stopped short of supplying me with her surname;
as if for the sake of intrigue in making the most of our escapade,
she was prepared to dole out only what I should know, or else seeing the giveaway of information as leaving herself open, she
wouldn't chance the risk. But this was only a thing or nothing, as
we sat on a cubicle bunk well away from the mysterious hatch.

As her hemline rose, an array of sheer-stockinged leg
unveiled a bit of this is to that as that is to the other: a tasty

morsel of proportion for a budding geometer to feast his eyes
on. What other lesson, besides, did a lad need to dig ratio? And
from being on the inside of famished lips, I felt akin to a pouch-
mouth camel bound to pout and belch a niffy breath as it waited by a windswept tent for the turbaned Sultan of Turkey, the
randy git, to emerge. I again slipped a ravenous arm about her
slim Terylene waist, and would have swapped fingernails for cat's
claws to get a grip. Out of propriety, though, I let an ocean of
exasperating quiet pass before giving her a gentle tug towards
me – ooh, the bliss of that then.

With one and a half eyes shut, I stretched my head closer to
hers, as if we were in the back row of the Scratching Post
picture house waiting for the lights to dim, the Sunday night
feature to roll, and off-screen fiddles to quiver like crazy, turning
girls to mush. After long-drawn-out feel-up sessions, all self-
respecting beatniks in speckled polo necks would flash their
thumbs-up or, with whichever fists were free, piston-pump the
air for the benefit of gawpers who'd hang around by the wall
down the aisle for signs of conquest from their agents. Having
often longed to take my place in the back row, here I was at last
getting initiated, and not just as any old associate member. Bring
on the string section, boy, quick. Straining the thumb against the
forefinger, fillip another *Wrigley's Spearmint* gum wrapper in the
air to land on some up-do hairstyle three rows down.

Half-expecting to be beset by a Mark II version of the black
pearl of Boley, I braced my torso against the onset that would
knock me skew-ways off the bed; for Jane had the athletic look
of an Amazon. When the big push didn't come, I relaxed and
moved my noggin forward till our temples touched and our eyes
met off-focus with a concentrate of simple doting fondness – an
action I recall to this day with such ease as only the staying
power of first impressions can enable.

As I adjusted position slightly, a shank of light broke through the shade to bronze the front of her hair, warming an already lovely flesh-tinted face. So that of all the others above, below and fornenst us in the universe, the planet to which we were claiming squatters' rights had to be the one that was most in accord with Creation, while all we lacked was a note of plain-song to tune into from some infinite-world basilica beyond.

But the pull of gravity was fecking fierce, boy.

That racket downstairs had tailed off to a rustle. Jane's eye-lids flicked open for an instant, as if to find her bearings, and then closed. Our lips touched, this time with a tingle of salt-cured ham, and when it shouldn't have, home crossed the bead-line in my head. A flitch from the bacon factory lay along the counter, as Babs and Mae, bloodhound-like, stretched over the partition with their wan shanks exposed over stocking tops, ready to explode. I missed the cheer of our front snug – as if a fellow had a divine right to old familiarities and their delights. But it seemed that once begun, needs had no end to them.

Gradually warming and inflaming, her salt lips grew moist, though her body stayed taut. The hard dint of her gums and teeth pressed, till I had to move back to breathe and recoup myself; it was clear that her kissing skills were at a level that needed more coaching than I, with my experience, could supply.

Bloody hell, girl, lips: pretend you're a puffer fish from the National Geographic. *Those squidgy bits of sponge are pleasure pads. Look it here, let me show you.*

I thought it best, though, not to spell out what I was trying to get her to do. Big Brando just pouted his mouth and made squelching noises. She eventually followed suit. We again closed eyes, poised buffered faces in each other's direction, and once more moved in. This time there was no rictal impact; just a hit-and-miss, peck-and-recoil ritual in what must have aped the mating rite of a pair of orange tropical fish. Sure, that was how love stories got off the sand, or at least how this one might.

Jane revelled in a slurping that sounded not unlike how Granny Ryan used to sip tea from a china saucer held level with her stark-black cavernous mouth. Sweet feck, was she going to turn into another Granny Ryan? And for a moment – only for a moment, mind – I felt the mockers being put on my inclinations. I had to wipe away grandma's *phizog* and fix my brain on the business in hand, and my eyes on those glorious features.

A funny thing, though, how the noggin works: the weight of one thing drives you to do the opposite. The voice of our spiritual director, Father Jerry Rev, bellowed that I would burn in hell. His sermons were fixated on us keeping our hands over the bedclothes at night so as not to be interfering with ourselves … down below, or we might go palsied. He probably meant a bad dose of the clap – which we couldn't possibly pick up during term, since all girls, loose or otherwise, were barred. What Jane and I were up to seemed to be harmless enough; it certainly didn't warrant your man terrifying us about an eternity of flesh-roasting. Besides, his advice sounded more like rules he'd made up – ones to be broken – than sacred laws from on high. So, not an iota of guilt or fear of damnation pressed on my principles; I had no scruples about pushing on with things. What did press, though, and chafe, was this tight ball-sack restrictor – damned Y-fronts. If only that priest could see me there, he might have said to himself: *Well fuck this sermonising business for a lark.*

In any case, when gravity tugs and mischief enters a fellow's brain, he gets taken to task. My arm coursed in farther over her shoulder, and fingertips slid down onto her right breast, like Humphrey Bogart crossing the Sierras with his mules on an expedition to a goldfield, when she whacked my hand, lickety-split – *Schlap.*

'Keep them roaming spiders under rein,' says she.

The rebuke sounded so well-rehearsed she must have either picked it up from the hand-me-down wisdom of female friends or forged it after some other geezer had tried her out – which, going by her lip-smacking experience, was the less likely grounds for her stance.

'But, Jane dear,' came the deep voice of Brando again. 'Don't you know that if you don't use them, you will lose them? Even the doctors will tell you that the parts of the body which are left go idle tend to grow stale.'

'They can go stale,' says she, without an ounce of sympathy for the ever-tightening state of a fellow's jocks. And on she fecking well went: 'Do you think Doctor Quigley would like you having that sort of approach to a girl's virtue?'

'Not that virtue has much to do with it,' says I. 'But I don't think he would like me having any approach to a girl right now. And, besides, I don't intend to ask him.'

Using nautical manoeuvres to tack a southern course, I sent frigate *HMS Second Finger* forward in line with *HMS Forefinger*, already in an advanced position off the coast. But again not a bit of her would let me sail beyond the hemline of a work-coat, which was so tightly moored above the knee, anyway, it put me off further attempts to run that blockade. Kneecaps to fiddle with was all she would allow, and I had to content my sensuous inner being with biting her lips, as a dunnock would in season peck at a hen's cloaca. Pleasing though the sight of corncob knees were, one clamped against the other, all I could do was to glance downwards and grope on in vain, every attempt to inch upwards bringing a scold. A fellow would need to be as well endowed as Hercules, with his must-bag hanging, before this girl might yield. The problem in dating kitchen girls was one of scruples: they had too damned many of them. I was picturing a rove beetle in a zigzag towards the bottom shelf as Jane's hand gestured a splat.

'Pry-vaat,' she insisted. 'Sto-op. Keep your paws off what's to be held in safekeeping for the one who'll lead me down the aisle.'

'Aisle?' says I. 'What aisle might that be?' I was trying to shake off the rebuff. A fellow had to make light of the situation, or else wind up proceedings and go off in a huff – an inclination which, if followed through with, would provide a fairly feeble alternative.

'Why a church aisle of course,' says she. 'A church flooded with organ music and confetti flittering mad outside it. It will be a white bride on her daddy's elbow who'll march up to say "I do" and glide back down alongside her tall handsome husband, with honest eyes on him as big as granny's china saucers.'

'Leave grannies out of this please,' says I. 'Come here and take one look at these peepers of mine. What do you make of them for specimens of porcelain?'

Jane held her head back and fixed me in the beam of a stare – a scanning laser determined to maintain intact a lechery-free zone to her domain, or at least to the part that stretched down along the central plains. This forbidden area went from the Sierra foothills in the good old North Country to the hem of a light blue work-coat in the luscious south – the only margin that in the meantime might vary, should the aisle-stomping Hercules of her dreams come along and hit the right sequence of buttons to unlock her defences. It had been made clear that no nifty frigate-finger of mine would plunder what she saw as the greatest treasure to be given to her dreamboat as a dowry on their wedding night – or a night in the immediate advent of nuptials, if he was lucky enough, but doubtless not sooner, for even Hercules wouldn't get to steer his mule pack far among those there darned hills before he and his party got slapped down.

Maybe my shortcoming of approach was a failure to give her a good tickling, to indulge her in footsie or thumb-twiddling, and to fondle those ear lobes, which appeared yet tastier since I'd found out that she was storing herself up. She ought to have held the same disdain for me as a householder holds when he finds impaled on his garden fence a cat burglar who has fallen from a drainpipe while attempting an upstairs break-in and whose skewered nuisance of remains must still be dealt with before decay sets in. This intruder failed not only to lay a hand on the booty, but even to see what it looked like. My self-composure dipped yet more when I thought about the probity of kitchen girls.

But Jane was hard to fathom. The honest-to-goodness expression on her face held no aftermath of dislike or offence.

She bore no mark of hostility, either, towards those who looked down their noses and shouted *Skiv-vy* when a member of the kitchen staff passed them in the cloisters. She'd had to suffer the jibes from snooty little shits of the well-to-do – horrors of boys who weren't supposed to as much as speak to kitchen staff, let alone taunt them before an audience of gawpers, who either tittered behind open palms or flaunted their chortles. I'd seen the shudders of trepidation in girls' pink calves brushing off each other as they picked up speed to pass pent-up gangs of students fit to explode from too much hanging around cloisters. Yet Jane showed no tinge of resentment or desire for retaliation – as if she understood that students had nothing else to do on wet days. My little heart *pink*ed a humble beat at the thought of her tolerance and good decency.

What mattered there and then, though, was where I stood with her. However much of a sucker she was for good-looking, well-dressed geezers, she still may have seen me as a heckler, one of the bunch in which she'd lumped all oafs. For fellows from the brotherhood, on whom Baldy Klops and Billy Curry liked to prey, at times formed into lynch mobs of corridor cowboys and doled out the same grief as they'd experienced. First-years, too, would in time get fouled up in their own conceit, from all that traipsing up and down fucken cloisters. *Mammy, come and get me out of here.*

In a craven effort to avoid a final admonition before she blustered off, I felt compelled to placate Jane. With as much screwball enthusiasm as could be mustered, I grabbed her hands, and pulled her from the bed, and out of the cubicle. Crooking her hand round my left arm, I marched her down the passage, humming *Here Comes the Bride* – and if he must, let the Baldy bastard appear from his hatch. I swung her round into another cubicle, and on one knee pleaded with her: 'Was that not a good enough walk up the aisle? Look at this lovely little vestibule of a chapel here' – its resident was tidier than Jimmy Codlotin. 'Why do we have to wait? Will I go down for Doctor Quigley right away, and get him to perform the nuptials?'

She laughed and said, 'You'll do no such thing. That doctor will have no say in my nuptials; nobody like him will. He's not like a real doctor that can heal.' Her voice had changed down a gear to the eager whisper of gossipy siblings. 'It's a fancy tag he wears for status. If I was on my own sick, he'd be the last person in the world I'd let near me. I won't settle for the garblings of an old bald-headed half-priest. I want to be blessed by a holy man and wear twenty-four carats on my finger. I won't throw my love away and give myself over on the cheap like I was the Vincent de Paul man going round coming up to Christmas. I'll hold fast, as my mother before me did, and keep my principles and privates . . . Do you get what I'm saying now?

'You know what you should do?' Her voice had returned to

its previous pitch. 'Join a youth club, you should, where young people learn the ins and outs of how to conduct themselves while keeping company with members of the opposite sex. What's this the nickname youse have for Father Quigley?'

'Baldy Klops,' says I.

'Baldy Klops?' says she. And she laughed wholeheartedly. 'Old Baldy Klops. That's a queer one for you now.'

''Tis right enough,' says I.

And somehow the Granny Ryan's *phizog* was back jiggling about inside my head. Her bockety rictus gave out stink, and her mighty black cavernous mouth got ready to swallow me up.

Fuck off and find another haunt for yourself, you.

13

Along with each delectable morsel comes a risk too great for the nerves of ordinary fledgling cockerels. But my friend is, let it be said, no common cock; he never was.

If the girl had thought our tryst had been a fully fledged fiasco, she would not have agreed to meet me there again after Easter. We took better precautions this time and moved to the end cubicle, Jimmy Codlotin's – though whose it was meant nothing to her. From there we could hear steps on the stairs as well as the access hatch squeak at the other end and have enough time to react. But the willies still went hair-raising down my back as the unknown of that hatch loomed. Jane had brought along her bucket and mop, just in case. And I turned on the tap, filling Jimmy's basin to the brim, ready to splash over onto the floor should anyone come: so that supposedly having noticed it while passing, she would appear to have stopped to turn off the water and wipe the mess. How careless of the boarder who resided here to leave the stopper in the sink and the tap running: typical!

We were a few minutes into our opening parley on the edge of the bed, as I thought of ways to overcome an adherence to her youth club's motto that romance be conducted at arm's length, when we heard the warning squeak.

There it was again: the door at the far end. It closed with a creak and a thud. Hell. Steps began striking a tempo along the floor towards us. I recognised that slow, even squish-plod he used while reading his breviary – damn him! Jane looked at me in horror.

The approaching steps were heavier than the slip-slap of fellows passing my cubicle last thing at night while I was ready to nod off, and I tried to let their primal plod distract me in that same benumbing way. The trick was to forge regular humdrum sounds into a comfort soother of absent-mindedness. All that surround noise in a classroom, even the silent static, was at hand for a fellow to use as a device to offset the jittery jumps ahead of being caned over missing the pluperfect of some dead-language load-of-cobblers, like Latin. But to learn stuff excessively doesn't mean it is learned right, or understood. On the other hand, boarding school, it must be admitted, was the place to pick up a few useful, basic tips on survival.

Like chain lightning, I again turned on the tap, pulled out Codlotin's two suitcases from under the bunk base, stacked one over the other on the bed, and splashed the floor.

Having whispered a few sweet reassurances and instructions into her suddenly irresistible succulent lobe before giving it one final salty suck and naughty nibble – 'Ouch,' says she – I hopped up on the cases to sail horizontally over the partition and onto the bed in the next cubicle.

Come the college sports day and I might enter for the high jump – like hell. I felt the blood warm in my veins. Boy, was this caper vibrational, my performance that of a star, and was I not already a natural in the winner's enclosure? It would have to be kept up. Where's my hairbrush?

Shifting the pillow slightly sideways, I tucked myself virginally tight into the corner behind the locker bulkhead. But did my shiny-black coiffure maybe stick up a jot too much over the top rail of the cubicle?

First thing for definite come the summer holidays, I would flatten it to a mop-top and buy the full new rig to give myself a spanking fresh George Harrison look – yeah, yeah, yeah. My head brimmed with this dapper image, ready for the warm summer nights around the streets at home – oh boy. As my loincloth elastic stretched tight on the groin, I could all but hear girls squeal in the June gloam of Tanyard Lane. The new look would have to match these peepers, the enticing black pools which one downy maid at a dance over Easter had remarked upon to her friends as *lurey* eyes she could allow herself to be ogled by all night long. Word of what she'd said had got back to me within the hour – no girl could chance a *spake* like that about a fellow without him hearing of it, not when he was as well-got in his home town as yours truly. Moreover and besides, as they say in all the best circles, it was time to move on from Elvis and his huh-huh-huh shaky-crotch, just-gone-to-the-jacks look, or else I'd get left behind the times. Pickers, too, had seen their day; I would paint mine gold or silver and frame them as keepsakes up beside the Gunner's giant bottles on the top shelf of the back bar for generations to come to gaze upon and utter: 'Did they actually wear things like them in days gone by, oo-fah, bloody hell?'

A grandchild of Mae might crane her neck over the partition and say: 'How could a girl kiss a guy in shoes like them?'

And her friend, a descendant of Babs, would in fine family tradition reply: 'Maisie, you don't think that in times gone by they used to reach down quite so far for something to kiss?'

'Oh, Barbara, you're awful, you are. You realise that?'

'Indeed, Mae, but you don't know the half of it, oo-fah, bloody hell.'

Darker and more leaden the steps struck as they neared. But on this occasion, fear was something that stimulated.

At last, the sludge-pump thuds and swish-swash of soutane serge were upon us. But were they actually passing by? They were indeed – ah, blessed luck be with us. They went by the other cubicle, too, and out onto the landing, to echo gravel-like through the stairwell. They pulled up, though, and scuffed round. By fits and starts, they carried their owner's black-art carcass back towards us. Your man, something was telling me, had at once decided to defer the reading of his Divine Office.

Most of a minute lapsed, during which I could hear only the drum-wallop of my chest and the hurried slush-about of a cloth describing circles on a wet floor inside. The girl's sham task dragged on till she in all honesty could no longer sustain it under his glare. And then came the spill-drip of liquid in a bucket: its soft, pristine tinkle for some reason soothed for a jiffy in the same way as a stream under trembling poplars, or the wash of water against the arches of the bridge at home. His voice broke in on the woodland-like quiet – well, bad cess to Baldy Klops, and all belonging to him.

'Leave it,' the dean growled at her. 'I shall locate the boy whose berth this is and bring him up later: he shall see for himself the product of negligence.'

His sharp, clipped 'product of negligence' sounded like the snarl we were used to in Alfie Bra's class of horror-induced maths: both men must have had the same short-fuse training, maybe even from the one how-to-get-irked-quick tutor in that badass seminary they'd both attended. Hidden from his glare, I was for the first time able to be detached at close-up and see how he dealt with females – a species with which deans might not be familiar. But it made no difference: he behaved badly towards her too. Both he and his function were revolting, and by extension so were all jumped-up johnnies in authority.

Was it possible to winkle that creature from the dean, and to replace it with a human, anyone? Even I would have made a better fist of the job, with one of Salty Burke's old-style shirt collars on back to front as a badge of clout with which to issue unholy shagging orders. For an instruction from the mouth of a cassocked caballero was as good as a bull from Rome itself, or a diktat from that other bald-headed one, Nikita Sergeyevich Khrushchev, in the USSR – or from wherever a person's loyalties to hairlessness lay. But for the time being, it seemed like we were stuck with Baldy as the captain's dog, the bosun of this ship, to psych us all out.

With his papal-like infallibility on boys' behaviour, especially when they'd left flotsam behind, Klops quickly got a clear picture of what had occurred; to be so well armed with the power of insight, and evidence as plain to see as albatross droppings on a porthole, there was no need for questions. Any time he had asked, it was just for the satisfaction of seeing a boy trip himself up, and for him to have his assessment confirmed, with the Mona Lisa-like smirk restored. All the dean wanted was to hear the miscreant deny ever having had hand, act or part in the offence – not that the occupant of the next berth to me there would remember if he had left the tap running or not.

My fingers grew numb from clinging to the top of the locker.

When he again shuffled his feet, my body froze. I recognised the squish-squash of leather on vinyl as shoes once more swivelled round. Had the moment come for him to check the adjoining cubicles? I was for it, surely.

Three steps this way, and another long electric pause. And *pause* sounded the same as *paws*.

He was all touchy-feely: Reggie Run-the-Paw, who was Baldy's cohort – the geezer whom nobody, as the unwritten rule went, was supposed to remark on, or even to think about. But there and then I needed another distraction. The Reggie man was sometimes alluded to by older fellows, though only in whispers, lest his spectre demonically appear before them with his dirty tool lolling out. If he came after me with that thing jangling, my right 'picker would skewer it from his torso and I'd send it, garnished with a fig leaf, on a platter to the kitchen for Sister Spud to do up as a prawn cocktail for Baldy's Friday lunch. But at the thought of lunch, this distraction also got to be too much.

Had Baldy spotted that the bedspread was creased from my downward dint? Surely it wasn't so easily seen from the dormitory aisle. The weight gained since I'd become a boarder would scarcely allow a fellow to wrinkle a piece of taffeta, never mind furrow a mattress.

Baldy's ability to see around corners was well known, but could he look through solid objects as well? Maybe part of my nether end was protruding. Pleased with himself over his own ghoulish flair for ferreting fellows out, he just had to be waiting for me to yield and climb down. Fuck it; he could go step into the cubicle and catch me out, barefaced.

But as my knees weakened, it seemed I would have to end the strain and show myself, or collapse in a heap on the bed. What would I tell him? This meant expulsion. As the seconds dragged, it got to be too much, nearly.

Once more, leather squelched on vinyl, with an about-face in direction. Again, three strides were taken. Was this a changing-of-the-guard rite before the presidential palace of a South Seas banana republic on an island where Salty Burke had been?

The voice issued another diktat: 'Wipe your shoes when you're finished, and don't trail streaks along the corridor.'

So he dictated to the kitchen staff too, without as much as a *please*, a *thank you*, or a *kiss my fat holy ass*. But with the personage and makings of a bishop, the non-medical doctor had fish to fry other than quizzing some kitchen girl whose sole concern most likely was the local hall's billing of showbands for upcoming Sunday night dances – even if she had shown enough wit to spot and make good the mishap on the dorm.

Sure, to him, she was no different from any other wench with simple tastes – of whom he'd seen so many come and go through the college kitchen. With those looks, though, she might be fortunate enough to land an honest manual worker, instead of falling for the first hideous-looking beatnik in drainpipes waiting to wangle her with a Presleyan wiggle of his crotch into the back seat of his jalopy for a five-minute despoliation-of-chastity-and-impregnation job. One way or another, she would marry all too soon; simply and quietly, because of a showing bulge, on a week-day morning; then produce a litter which in turn would add to the pool of servants available for the college's future needs – to which his life, too, had been so dedicated. In all high propriety, and as a man of his personage might expect, this was part of how control and order in the world would be upheld. But did the man himself ever during his life get a tinkling feeling down in the Willie Winkle department? How did those old lads manage non-stop without putting their hands up a piece of skirt, ever? Well fuck me, the pain of it. What a way to live.

The dean humped off with himself down the hollow-sounding stairs, leaving behind a state of affairs beyond his ken, or control.

It was over; and not a moment too soon, either. Allowing a few minutes for this little heart to settle, I let go of my nether muscles, climbed down and went in next door. With blood gushing hot in my veins, I hugged Jane in a mixture of passion and great relief.

'That was a quare close shave,' says I. 'Jane, are you all right?'
Spent-looking, she was leaning against the wall.

'I have to be honest with you,' says she – and how could she
be anything else? 'My name is not Jane.'

There it was again: that sense of the girl not being quite the
person I'd expected her to be – but it was hardly dishonesty.

'So you're Marguerite, after all, or maybe . . . Petronella?'
says I.

'Petronella, how are you,' says she. 'My name is Rose, Rose
Brien.' I knew she couldn't be anything else but honest, eventually.

'Rosie O'Brien?' says I. 'That's a lovely honest name.'

'No,' says she, 'just Rose Brien.'

'Same difference,' says I.

Adversity, they say, cements a friendship – or something like
that. Ah, but isn't it the quare old life all the same? And she still
looked good in the April sunlight, there inside Codlotin's cubicle. Would she let me feel her tits now, I wondered?

14

Part of the nature of young male birds is to crow, fluff their plumage, and throw shapes at each other.

The six-of-the-best on each hand that followed weren't lost on Codlotin's personal habits. And by the next Sunday, when we again hit up the stairs to hide in his cubicle, I could see myself in his mirror, and the sink was free of grease. Jimmy and I regularly went there to dodge the senior of the house and his classmates, getting our arses kicked off by the more hideous louts among them, for the once-a-week ritual in which first-years were rounded up and made to pick up papers on the college grounds.

Jimmy had also got his trademark coiffure hacked off – without which he looked bare and bony. And despite a show of blustering strut, he was bound to feel out of sorts after the slogging he'd got.

'I don't remember leaving the water turned on,' he kept saying. 'My brother in fourth year always grills me not to leave the stopper in or the taps running. Just can't remember leaving the water on. I'd nearly swear I didn't.'

'Of course you can't remember,' I said, while sliding my finger down my pocket and through the ring of the blue brush to give my own quiff another slick-up. 'If you could, you wouldn't have forgotten to turn the tap off in the first place, would you?'

Codlotin went quiet to digest this.

Wally Furlong sat alongside us and non-stop thumped the cases underneath with his heels, as though on a mission to follow and pester me through life. It was obvious from a spate of short coughs to clear the throat that he was cranking himself up for something. A certain crackle showed in the voice, which only recently had begun to pupate into that of a full-blown master butcher's. Not that he had ever been applicant material for the Vienna Boys' Choir: a Vienna sausage, maybe, but not the choir. Dying to butt in, he jerked his body forward, and at once the hum of mutton grease he'd given off in primary school again rose and merged with an out-of-the-blue sunburst against the dormitory wall to produce the effect of being in two places at once, or watching two films overlap on the same screen.

Or maybe the impression was of something entirely different. That as soon as conditions were right – the floor got washed, the smears were wiped off the mirror, a reek of mutton hung in the air, and the seventh son of a butcher went on kicking the shite out of two suitcases under the bed – Jimmy Codlotin's cubicle underwent a sea change. It became a contraption for coinciding times and places so that at the push of a button every clock-tick of the past, present and future got compressed into a single ongoing instant that was apt to fit in a vial – one that also held an alchemic concentrate of all places and events, ever. And when the machine's switch was pushed, life as we knew it in the joint got transformed so that our day-in and day-out tedium of timetables – which passed at the rate of strand after strand of horsehair-for-ticking being teased out – finally ceased. And as everything got exciting, enthusiasm and pleasure became the order of the day. But for all this to happen in the first place, our machine needed another lever to be pulled, a last condition met, one which only a certain boy and girl, if given the right amount of time and quiet there alone together, could achieve. Yep, she and I were the ones to set this old lab frame in motion. Seduction, boy, was the secret lever. I'd have to have a good chat with Rosie Brien about the matter the next time I'd see her.

'Do you want to know what really happened?' says Wally at last.

'What?' says Jimmy.

'I know exactly what happened all right,' says he, trying to sound compelling and to make the most of the interest Codlotin was paying him.

'Well then tell us for shite's sake,' says Jimmy.

Again, Wally was up to his old tricks of trying to shock and enthral by making out he alone had the answers to secrets nobody else knew about – which was true when it came to the mysterious hiding place of his old lad's dirty magazines. Yeah, under the bed: some mighty secret that.

But in recent times, Wally Furlong was changing. For one thing, his trundling walk had lessened. As his face raddled more and the upper lip jutted out further, he gave off a new aplomb when foisting himself on fellows from second year, and without fuss got accepted into the clique-claque gangs of third year. Not content to remain for long in any group, though, it seemed at times as if he was fraught with the same maverick itch as I had: the urge to mingle with every cat and cad of interest in the joint. But while I liked to flit about the fringes of a gang and just hang round for no more than one period of recreation at a time, to see what its capers were, Wally inveigled his way in to get caught up with the jostling for hen-status and palsy-walsy goings-on of the members. As ever when the lad made a nuisance of himself, carried tales or put fellows in a pickle with each other, the group kicked him out. As Furlong changed, so too did the amount of vexation, doubts and qualms that he managed to leave in his wake.

Although a monkey-business addict, pure and simple, who had been mistrusted over singling lads out to stab in the back, he every so often got accepted back by a mob, provided that this time the laugh he was usually good for came at his own expense – hardly a condition to make him baulk. In exchange for which he didn't mind doing the oafish hulk, or playing the simpleton-from-first-year act he was so good at. Yeah, anything to get accepted: that was our Wally for you.

'Give over with the shagging suspense, Wally, will you, and tell us,' says Codlotin.

'I'd say,' goes Wally, 'that Johnny stole up here on that day to wash his scaldy taws in the sink and then left the tap running after him.'

I just knew he had been brewing up mischief. 'Hey, Wally,' says I, playing on his fear of spiders, 'look out behind you, quick.'

'What?' says he, turning the head.

'The tap is running after you.'

Jimmy laughed, and Wally's taunt drifted. Well, not quite: he didn't let go of things that easily, and the point at which his prank lost its froth while he persisted was usually the one where his real menace showed.

'Go on, Johnny boy,' says he doggedly. 'Own up to it, why don't you? My father says your old one used to come in to our shop to tell us she had never seen the likes of the nappy rash you had; couldn't be got rid of. Go on, admit it, you still have scaldy balls that need to be watered all the time.'

Even Codlotin sensed the intimidation, as he looked at me under foxy eyebrows that would turn to light sand over the months of sunshine ahead, and changed the subject.

'Didn't Baldy Klops, the bastard, tell me to get my hair cut immediately?' says he.

'I like the convict's hairdo all right,' says I. 'You'll shift a right deal of bimbos down on the beach this summer with a head on you like that.'

'Not like yours, anyway,' says he, and got up to pose before the mirror. 'I don't need to become a scrub-brush beatnik to do the business. At least I've got the looks and charm to shift birds one way or another.' He was by then pouting faces of admiration at himself in the mirror.

'You do to be sure,' says I. 'It's a pity all the same.'

'What's a pity?' says he wistfully, feeling his face for the least sign of bristle. Some hope. But it was best not to slight him over what had become a sore point of late: the lack of chin-sprout, while his brother had the hair of a yeti.

I couldn't help myself, though: I had to hit him with something. 'It's a pity to lose your own personal wildlife sanctuary,' says I. 'The laws of nature were surely broken the day you got rid of the flora and fauna off the top of your head.'

This was the last straw: to really rile Jimmy you only had to scoff at his haircut. It took a good minute for his blood to rise and colour the barren gradient of chin-gob silhouetted in the glass before he turned to chase me from the cubicle. Wally's quacking mocked me all the way down the stairs. At least between us, Jimmy and I had kept the lid on Wally's heaviness.

Anyway, ever since Furlong had copped on to our Sunday-morning ruse and imposed himself on us, I had thought of finding another hidey-hole. To be cramped up with those two hoors for an hour wasn't such a great alternative to picking up papers these times when the seniors had final exams ahead and had lost their zeal for bullying. Besides, I disliked seeing Wally's carcass sully another spot in the college that had come to mean so much to me.

Jimmy Codlotin didn't need to know that his berth had got its little secrets; speculating on such matters would only keep him awake at night. And after our spiritual director, Jerry Rev, had bawled us out over scandalising others, I didn't fancy the punishment – of being pegged overboard into the big swim with a slab of granite for a necklace – that went with this offence. So a fellow just had to be wary of feeding fellows sweet-scaldy morsels to do with girls: the act of defiling their virtue by telling them a few old yarns seemed to be a grave business. When Jerry Rev, in his weekly homily from the steps of the chapel altar, got going on the subject of morality, you could all but feel the flame-tips of damnation rise through the pew to toast your buttocks. With fire and water as eternal tortures, you sure as hell hesitated before blathering on about dolls' diddies and velvet crannies. But was it that the sin was more in the talk than the doing?

And what tittle-tattle of scandal, I wondered, did all those other brown-stained cubicles and distempered walls, with their year-in year-out silent vigil, conceal? Did any boarder ever before have a fling with a kitchen girl, or smuggle in a ravenous moth from outside – one who liked to have a boarder's hands sail her sloop close to the wind? Oh boy and oh damnation, at such sweet thoughts. It would make your teeth chatter, though, to pic-ture the unfortunate, under full sail with trousers down round his ankles, being scuttled by Baldy Klops ruminating over how soon he might expel the lad while waiting for him to put away that reluctant-to-be-rehoused little prawn. Expulsion was such a shock-inducing word, like *execution*, *guillotine*, *hanging* – especially for scholarship boys, such as Kenny D., Shamie Doyle and Martin Doran.

But there must have been other, more outlandish, things too: secrets so bizarre and damnable that even the tower ghost would rather fade to a lesser shade, or even dissolve, than reveal them. Were there, indeed, acts so vile that nobody could bring himself to whisper about, and for which names suitable enough had yet to be coined? During the summer, I would quiz Salty Burke about this matter; no other person in the world knew more than he did about the strange ways of humankind. He was bound to come up with something good.

I would tell him about the fling a certain fellow in my class was having with a kitchen girl, and no doubt he would spiel out the same advice as I had heard from him before: 'News is never so startling as to last beyond the tat on next week's local rag.' 'Nothing's so strange that there isn't something more remarkable to be heard round the corner.' 'I tell you this for nothing, son: quarer and stranger things than what you speak of have happened in college rooms. So, impress on your friend the next time you see him to set his mind on his books and to keep his hands off fair maid's booty – he'll have time enough for that later.'

I would probe him again: 'And what, may I ask, Mr Burke, are the quare and strange things that have happened in college rooms?' But his reply would probably not change much from what he'd already given: 'Why does every long peeping Tom in these parts want to prise up stones in search of titbits of dirt on people and then drool over what they find?'

He would issue the same line as he'd given me before I went to boarding school: 'Beware now, son, of old sea dogs and bawmen who want to dance with the cabin boy: they'll scuttle a lad's entire voyage ahead. Be wary of Mr Bawman who wants to tango. So what will you do, son, if one of them pirates corners you?'

'Kick him up the goolies, Mr Burke.'

'That's right, son, kick him up the . . . You do that, but first make sure your aim is good and true.'

15

It would appear that not all birds of prey have sharp talons and hooked bills. Some come equipped with measuring tapes and graph paper.

Since the beginning of first year, with its September already gone into a world apart, the matter of whom to trust and whom to shun, because of a long-set gulf between staff and students, seldom had arisen, especially for our class. Among the small number of teachers who did try to span that divide, one or two quare hawks were much too given to reserving aside their chats for cute-looking little mollies backed into window embrasures along the cloisters to be in any way fecking wholesome about their intentions. Luckily these oily wads were few and far between, and most of us instinctively recognised them for the dodgy geezers they were.

It was easy to pick out the genuine ones who did have concern for their students' welfare and made some effort (though not enough) to draw off the swirling bilge-water of forbidding drabness there.

Take the old Latin teacher, Oculus Lippus, who, guffawing in great bawdy chugs, showed an essence of homespun openness that everyone took to, even when doing so went against discerning taste – mine. The bulbous peepers on his face were scarcely portholes to such an unbounded store of generosity as seemed ready to bubble up and tide the globe over with glee simple. It didn't matter that he was too brainy for that corpulent blob, the soutane front only a little less grimy than, say, a baby's bib after a mighty spate of burping, or that he had a camel's lip which quivered with the same droopy drool as the Gunner's after a bazzy in bed with the Doll during the holy-hour closing time of a Sunday. A caper from which they had, thank heaven, long and ever before desisted: picture your old lad and old one at it in bed, hammer and tongs: yuk.

When the old goof bobbed through the cloisters, a good many, wanting to be in his sights, dared to joke with him; for others, the mention of his name often was enough for a sending-up lark. We, in 1C, bunch-huddled in desks like cattle under hedgerows ahead of a storm, got rowdy and instinctively took him for granted. Only as a last resort did he ever whack us with a soft split-leather strap that was too slapstick to cause anything other than a flurry of sniggers; his face under duress perplexedly flushed red. Doing his nut didn't suit him, whereas in the hands of Alfie Bra, aggrieved vexation was as fecking lethal, boy, as a Beretta strapped to James Bond's ribcage.

But to offset such nourishing kindliness, let me tell you, first-years had another creature to contend with: a quare hawk who, despite the velvety smile, looked out upon the world through the strangest eyes you ever did see.

'Reggie Run-the-Paw, is it?' older students had laughed when they heard who we were having for history and geography. His name painted a picture of lice-infected maulers crabbing up boys' thighs towards their buttocks good enough to put the mockers on any suck who for approval wished to catch teacher's eye – and the lad got a dig in the ribs as a reminder from the boy beside him, going *suck, suck, suck*. Most of us sensed that Reggie, unlike Oculus Lippus, was not a character to be alligating with, for safety's sake. Yet what exactly it was necessary to be kept safe from, nobody knew – or if they did, they weren't saying. In so far as none of us had been murdered or gone missing, what was the big deal? What truth lay in the warnings? Besides, the more you attained the knack of keeping your head unfazed by things, the easier it was to get through the day. It probably was the same for the staff. No place of benevolence, this here was the school for survival, despite all the efforts of the likes of Oculus Lippus.

'Old Reggie man, himself, the last of the great private investigators,' big Billy Curry had laughed in a Dublin roll that did its best to belie its owner's innate spite. '*You're* safe enough though,' he says, pointing to me. 'He's not partial to greaser goolies; shites in drainpipes are not his dish. He only favours pretty boys,' says he, and lands me with a kick up the hole. 'But be careful; be very careful, indeed, when he asks you to collect the copies and bring them to his room. If he produces a sheet of graph paper, a measuring tape, and asks you to slap your little snail on a table so he can see how it's developing, tell him you don't want to because you're forever pissing your trousers and there's such an old one's whang of ammonia off you it would knock a horse in a knacker's yard. I reckon that should do the trick, don't you? Hey, greasy Johnny, I'm speaking to you: he'd need a micrometer screw to find out what you've got. Ye-aw, haw-haw.' Thump again.

'Get lost, you manky wanker.'

'What did you say?'

'I said the frost makes my hankie danker.'

Then one more thump from him for good measure.

When I had told Kenny D. about the copies, his crockery started to chatter as if the air round about had suddenly dropped to minus five – but he needed to have no worries either, I allowed, going by what Curry had said about looks.

'Let's make a break through the back gate now and away from this place quick,' he rattles out to me.

'You can't,' says I. 'You're here on a fecking scholarship. Anyway, Shamie Doyle told me you liked to suck up to Reggie. Imagine how low you'd drop in teacher's estimation if you ran away.'

'Go feck off,' he spluttered. 'I'll kill that other little coon when I see him. If any teacher asks me to bring up copies to their room, I'll put on slippers, drop the bundle outside his door and run like fecking Ronnie Delany.'

The day after Codlotin had chased me from his cubicle, he and I were leaning back in our usual window niche, hoping that a pair of muscle-legged kitchen girls with big tits would pass for us to ogle and dig one another's ribs over. But who comes along the cloisters only Kenny D., with a bundle of copies under the arm and a worried look across his gob.

'Here comes Doctor Fang-Tootles,' says Codlotin.

'Where are you going to with the bundle?' I asked.

'Reggie gave us a map of America to draw; he told me to bring the copies to his room.'

'We are only on long-legged Italy with him yet in our class,' says I. 'That's why I opted for 1C instead of 1A at the start of the year. I do like to take my time and explore these things in depth. We are feeling our way up Leghorn while dreaming of Genoa.'

'Italy is where the pope lives,' Codlotin cuts in.

'Well holy fuck, so it is,' says I. 'This nugget of information means you are sure-fire certain to get into second year. Now all you need to do is learn off your *mensa*s to become priesthood material. Where are your slippers, Kenny?'

'Why?'

'Why! Have we forgotten? You told me, months ago, you

wouldn't venture near priests' rooms without slippers. When Reggie hears noise at the door, he'll drag you inside to *scrawb* the marbles off you. Go get your slippers, quick.'

'I can't,' says he, his teeth chattering so much they might crack. 'Our dorm is locked during the day.'

'Jimmy's dorm is not locked; he'll lend you his. Jimmy, go and get your slippers for Kenny there, or else he's in the soup.'

'It's all right,' says Kenny. 'Old Reggie is nice, really, I think. The last time I brought up copies, he showed me his collection of James Bond books, then put on a record, and went off with himself, leaving me on my own. I got a quarter-ways through *Moonraker.*'

'Moon-fucken-raker!' says I.

'Did you really?' says Jimmy, not in the least bit perturbed by the revelation. 'Oh, lads, Reggie showed Kenny his collection. *Suck, suck, suck.*'

'Shut up, Jimmy,' I said. 'I know the moon-raking, Kenny, you're in for with Reggie. You actually went into his room and sat down? Hell, Kenny, you're really up the Swanee now: that's the tactic he uses to wheedle fellows. The next time you're up there reading, he'll suddenly walk back in, tear the trousers off you, grab you by the knob and get you to do things.'

'Oh yes,' says Jimmy. 'Get you to clip the clinkers off his hole, the way farmers dag sheep in summer.'

'Shut up, Jimmy, that's crude. How do you know he didn't go inside the other room to watch you through a spyhole in the wall, or something? He may have a camera yoked up capturing your every movement to make you into a film star: Kenny double-O seven-and-three-quarters Bond, what?'

'Oh hell, Johnny, what'll I do?' says he.

'Suck the marrow from your bones, he will,' Jimmy comes out with.

Kenny's face was in two minds about turning either all-out crimson, or whitewash; tics at the sides of his eyes pulsated down an anteater's nose, making the nostrils twitch – what Reggie saw in him and his black brushwood head was bewildering. Then again, that's what made this place into a circus: any split-faced clown was liable to cartwheel into the ring before us to do capers that had neither rhyme nor reason.

'Kenny, boy,' says I, 'we do hope you haven't already been scuffing about in the poop deck. There's a terrible guilty look on your face.'

'Don't mind the Boy,' says Jimmy. 'He's only exaggerating; it's not that bad, is it? I mean, Reggie's old pooper isn't that hairy at all at all: he shaves it every morning. Doesn't he, Kenny?'

'How the hell do you know?' says I.

Kenny D. bent over to retch.

'Mind, don't puke on those copies or Reggie mightn't like it,' says Codlotin.

'Oh lads, will youse come with me?' says Kenny. 'I'm scared.'

We stepped out of bounds without approval and went up with him, then waited on a level of the stairs below that of the main landing. He crept along the wide passageway above, and placed the bundle down outside a door.

The door opened. We ducked. Although Reggie twice looked up and down the way, he didn't spot us, or else his hairy tentacle of long arm would not have reached out to wind around Kenny's shoulder. Never before had I seen a priest out of his soutane: the black silk waistcoat over a white collarless shirt was like a picture at home of the Gunner's old fellow taken by a seaside hut years before; except Reggie had no batwing moustache or hat on, and looked much less rugged than the guy in the snap.

The Reggie man, using his piper's fingers as pincers, slowly tightened on Kenny's shoulder to draw him inside.

Next thing, we heard steps underneath; I knew that footfall. We looked over the banister, to spot the top of a shiny bonce approaching the stairs. Codlotin, the twerp, hawked up spit and gestured a gob at the target.

'Don't,' I warned. Having forgotten that Baldy's rooms also were up near Reggie's, we were as much out of bounds here as if we'd been downtown.

I followed Codlotin as he dived across the half-landing and through a door – allowing us to escape in time. We climbed three or four high steps through the dark to a small door that opened out onto a dormitory. So this was the secret entrance I had been wary of when meeting the wild Rose. Although relieved to be free, we were no less mortified over abandoning Kenny to his fate at the hands of the ghastly one.

We pelted along the length of the dormitory, down the main stairs, and through the cloisters to our classroom, where, without a word, we opened desks to arm ourselves with compasses and a tin-opener I had brought back after Easter – for the two dozen cans of beans in my locker that were helping to stave off this term's fierce, quickened hunger.

Out by our window niche again, the exact spot where this circuit had begun, we bumped into Nick Loan and Martin Doran. On hearing our story, they changed their minds about togging out for football and instead chose to go to war beside us. Kenny D. – or what might be left of him by then – had to be wrested from Reggie's hairy tentacles. We asked Wally Furlong to come, but he declined. 'I'll follow youse on up later,' says he.

The group marched with fire in its demeanour. We strode out of bounds beyond the stained-glass door at the head of the cloisters, marched through the hallway curving past Sister Polyps' surgery, and up the priests' stairs. Nothing short of sheer brute force this time would stop us from rescuing Kenny.

Without knocking, Loan turned the handle. The door was locked; all was quiet.

It took a good two minutes for a key to rattle and the door to open. We sidled in past Reggie. There was Kenny, standing by a table, hands clasping *Moonraker* down in front of his groin. A white-faced wooden ruler lay on a single sheet of graph paper on the table near him. I tried to see what was on the paper, but the marks meant nothing.

Every few seconds, Kenny's fingers twitched in behind the book and came out again. His *phizog* showed sheet-white: the after-effect, maybe, of seeing us. The longer he stood there, the more his hands shook; face tics went out in waves from his eyes. Was the fellow really that relieved to see us? When I asked him, in a whisper, if his nuts and nodules were still intact, he grimaced in a way that said my remark was untoward – an indication, I liked to think, that he hadn't been meddled with: mission accomplished.

Sounding like his usual disdainful self, Loan squared up to your man. 'Thanks for inviting us up, Father,' says he. 'For where he goes, I go; we always share and share alike, don't we, Kenny?'

Once he was out of his garb, Reggie commandeered less reverence than, say, Salty Burke, whose routine after making a gaffe was to place his elbows on the counter and cover his face: no such compunction here.

'Kenny says you let him read raunchy books and listen to Mozart,' goes Loan. 'Ah, Wolfgang Amadeus Mozart, the main man; I do like a little Wolfgang. I don't know what I would do, Father, if anything ever happened to my best pal here; sure, I'd swing for whoever laid a hand on him. Hey Father, have you any banned books? The likes of *Lady Chatterley's Lover* – I do hear that's a right juicy yarn, all the same.'

'Keep any Beatles records, Father?' says I. 'Don't mind all the classical junk.'

'Not that Mozart stuff anyway,' goes Codlotin. 'My mother says he's a bit much on the eardrums. She allows he put too many notes across the width of a page.' How many frigging mink, though, did it take to get the makings of a fur coat for her? 'My mother loves Bing Crosby singing 'White Christmas',' says he. 'Have you got that, Father?'

'Father, do you happen to have a calendar handy?' says Nick Loan. 'I want to teach this student the seasons of the year. Jimmy, my friend, Christmas falls in December. We don't usually play Christmas tunes in May, though in your case, we can make an exception. If you have it, Father, put on "White Christmas", especially for James here.'

From the look on his face, you could see that Reggie, in spite of his brass neck, hadn't regained poise quickly enough. Inhabiting a lumpen carcass unfit to impose control, he really had funked it when faced with our year's leanest specimens of young manhood. His flesh mass was as waxen as Mae's upper legs, exposed on the bench in our bar on a Sunday evening – from an age that seemed so distant.

Also gone was the finger-and-thumb grip Reggie had used to pinch the underarms of his pets along the cloisters, making them both squirm and laugh; each fair-haired little goof who, flattered by the adult attention, then had to undergo from his classmates such a scalding as taught him the indignity of his situation. If such a hard learning had saved other gullible mites from a fate far worse, then Kenny D. was in for some sore tutelage.

And I had long before thought that stories about the *bawman* were all only a cod, which old ones had concocted to frighten children in from the streets at dusk: *You had better get in here quick before Mister Bawman comes to take you off.* But there really was such a fucken fiend; this for a sudden morsel of news would shiver your timbers, boy.

'I'll tell you what, Father,' says I. 'The next time you get Kenny to bring up the copies, we will all come along to do a spot of reading. Ian Fleming is the one for the yarns, and you'll maybe have a Lennon and McCartney disc – so we can all do the Twist right here together, like this. *Come on, let's do the Twist . . . and we'll do it next summer.*

But when I stooped to swivel my hips one way, and my feet the other, to the twang of guitars in my head, and tried to get Codlotin to dance, he pulled away. Dance how are you? I wondered if his Ma was good for the Twist, or the tango.

'Come on, lads,' says he. 'Let's get out of here and go twenty thousand laps round the field before first-study bell' – he knew neither the seasons nor how to count. 'Are you right there, Kenny, boy?' he adds.

'Is that OK, Father?' says Nick Loan, still squaring up to your man. 'Do you want to come for a walk with us? You won't feel lonesome if we leave you up here on your own-io? And don't throw away the waistcoat when you're done with it; give it to the Boy, so he can wear it chasing the middle-aged floozies he's always on about.'

'Might even wear it while listening to shagging Mozart,' says I, 'or reading *Lady Chotterlay*. Ah do happen to like a little Wolfgang, you know.'

He poised an arm to feign a punch at me, while biting back a smile.

It was hard to tell if Kenny was grateful for being rescued; he didn't quite come out with it. Instead, he got narky with us, giving the impression we had messed up his afternoon's reading – well, the fecking little fibber. His mood had gone fierce flat.

The rest of us felt flat, too; we were at a loss for more adventure. Our old friends, the clouds of routine, were back, jam-packed with a lack of purpose, swaying, back and forth, to fill every space throughout the U-shaped arrangement of cloisters.

At the top of the left where that U-shape began, a glass-roofed corridor of eleven window embrasures ran alongside the big study hall – inside which twelve great windows rattled; two pillars and one hundred and sixty-nine full-width boards of scumbled wainscoting stood deadly rigid. Ahead of the hall, a straight flight of twenty-three steps raked up to a half-landing in the wooden stairs that wound up to first- and second-floor dorms, and then into an eerie garret – where, heaven help them, boys, too, had to sleep.

The next corridor, also eight quarries wide, held its ten window embrasures more or less in a straight run from the previous one, a line broken by the chapel entrance, which seemed to be all arches – big neo-Gothic feckers. The first right angle turned left into the third corridor – the main one, beside the tower – and held twenty window embrasures. To complete the U-shape, the next right-angle bend held a door, and swung into the long corridor, with its twenty-six embrasures and, most importantly, the refectory entrance.

As they gathered in closer around us, the wispy mountain-wave clouds turned to heavy stratus, and we inhaled them so much, we farted out big vapour 'O's of blandness, oodles of them slow-rising – *pop, pop, pop* – for each of us to gulp down and recycle as balloons of purer methane yet, being re-emitted from alimentary canals. As all about the place boys' sphincters clapped more thunder in each other's faces, and we took to this bubbles-of-puff recycling-boredom business, boy, like it was going out of fashion – or before the Beatles could turn out another number one hit. Well that's an end to verve, says you.

Nobody from our year again brought up copies to the lumpen man; instead, he was let collect them himself: his black-soutane-covered hairiness, sphincter-muscle-like, lovingly wrapped around them, the way a poodle is brought off to the vet for neutering or to be put down. Let Father Reggie do that job, with his tape and graph paper.

But to give the Reggie man his due, he remained the best teacher we had in 1C – and riddle me that now.

Another lesson on survival which we learned there was that safety lay in numbers; never to get isolated – for fear that Mister Bawman might want to do the tango. At least I knew what he looked like: Mister Bawman was one big black corpulent fucker, like your man on the port bottle.

Not that it mattered much. For the long summer was almost upon us: holidays, boy, holidays.

16

As time passes, a fledgling's feathers will grow and its claws widen, and almost before your very eyes, its neck and peck for deeds of daring will lengthen.

From the day that the joint had closed, our holidays had passed in a mad whirl round to yet another September; for us to be doomed again to months of confinement ahead.

Sultry days, and Tanyard Lane warm evenings, into which I had from early June gone belly-up basking, were drawing further behind in a sea of hankering and memories whose on-and-off afterglow of stark recall secreted a tang of something like freshly baked apple strudel topped with ice cream – flashes of fucken deliciousness, boy. Amid that bag of regrets and yens common to all boarders was a second-year's bleary relief to be out of first year: we had all, including Jimmy Codlotin, somehow made it through.

While September was a bragging month, with the chance to treat my mates to a few spicy holiday yarns – even educate them – it was also the time for planning: like how to arrange another little get-together with Rose. Let old acquaintances be renewed, boy, if not indeed nurtured and developed.

But would she recognise me in my coal-black mop-top, new chisel-toes from Cullen's, and just a hint of kohl filched from the top drawer of the Doll's dressing table to bring out my lashes. I had even got myself a black portable Philishave to raze the, by then, pervasive sprout. Its whirr on the chin was my moment of ritz sublime against the busy quiet of an early-morning dorm where few others yet shaved, let alone thought of owning such a gadget. And what's more, there in my locker, for occasions and private showings only, hung this most exquisite piece of gear, a dark-grey collarless jacket I had got in Dublin, the same type as Pierre Cardin had designed for the Beatles. My grey pants, too, were an exact cut, barely touching the tops of the chisels, where-as those of my cohorts billowed high like brigs under sail. The year before, they had been miles too long for them, and come next year, their new ones would be the same. You could tell from the length of his trousers what year a boarder was in.

At last, as Rose passed me in the main corridor, I discreetly got to drop a note in her bucket, suggesting that on her next night off we meet in the laneway outside the back gate after sup-per. Two days later, we locked eyes and smiles, before she veered towards me with a piece of paper naming the evening she was free. And so we were due to get back in action once more.

I chafed my hands from the snap tingle of thrill.

But I had barely read the message, and the girl had gone scarcely twenty yards past, when Billy Curry's big mauler landed on my shoulder. 'I saw that,' says he. 'What did she give you: a great billet-doux, was it?'

'A great Billy Curry,' says I. 'What business is it of yours?'

Making it his business, a fist to the solar plexus bent me over into a carpenter's square, and for a good two minutes I couldn't open my mouth but to gasp. If only those chisel toes on which my eyes were locked could be made to rise and swing round, describing an arc, to split mine enemy's crown and every last nib – not least his scrotum.

'Well?' says he. 'Don't keep me waiting: hand it up.'

Still bent over, I stuffed the paper in my mouth and swallowed it whole.

'You know it's vulgar and against all laws of plain decency for students to be consorting with skivvies; it lowers the tone of the college uniform. But we will help you become a more gallant youth, and to have better taste. Let me see now where to start.'

His accent carried the klaxon-tootle of hooligan supporters who had swarmed off the bus outside the park up the road ahead of our school's football match with Drimnagh Castle the week before, at which all students were expected to attend and cheer for our side and to out-shout our rival followers' dire, endless ribaldry. It was a twang of accent that, among others, would stay in your ear for ages after.

Some drastic idea was called for if I was to worm my way out of the wholesale hammering Curry was, with ribbons on, about to present me with.

'''Tis not for me,' says I. ''Tis for Martin Doran; I'm just taking a message.'

Curry was bound to have had enough regard for Doran's strength and presence not to confront him, I thought, and so at that the matter would surely rest. I might have given him Nick Loan's name too, except that they were on good terms – which was at odds with the savage way they laid into each other out on the sports field: the more intense their aggro, the more evenly composed Loan's temperament afterwards became, almost sedated. Aggression was hard to understand. It had to be a hormonal thing produced by a fellow's tetchy tickly gland located in the final section of his large intestine, switched on by the waste bulk his bowels in one go discharged, or by hunger. From whatever devil's coach-horse-ridden Dublin street basement he had escaped, this grotesque, overgrown guttersnipe here was glowering down at me like he would turn on the institution itself and tear down its walls stone by stone in a King Kong-filled frustr-ation, or from the non-stop gnawing of an empty stomach.

Not allowing for Curry being such a bad-intentioned moth-er flitch of a swine, I weighed up little else but how to save myself. I certainly never thought my words might set anything further in motion – ah, well.

'Is that right now?' says he, before leaving me with another carpenter's-square-shaping reminder.

Again, the air all at once went scarce. I stayed bent over, and dallied with pain till long after both he and it had gone. Holy fuck, that was rough – on pride and bone. Still, a fellow had something to look forward to; it helped getting him onto the vertical.

Our little get-togethers, when they came about, didn't amount to more than modest set-to sessions of fondling and pecking, during which our hands might as well have been tied: the sort of pristine activity that agony aunt Angela McNamara, in her *Sunday Press* column, would have approved of as suitable for couples. Herself, our own Jerry Rev and the bigwigs of morality at large were the only gurus capable of marking out the rights and wrongs for a nation's toad-horny youth: girls full of go were expected to don chastity belts, and fellows to handcuff themselves, through all romantic assignations and set-tos. Otherwise, our generation would go round jumping each other and filling orphanages, causing those poor Mercy Sisters to put on extensions to their sweatshop laundries. So, maybe they had got it right. At least Rose seemed to think so: *Now, now, pry-vaat; keep your paws off.*

We met weekly, sometimes once a fortnight, in a quiet nook up the lane outside the back gate, and occasionally by the rear wall of the ball alley during first-study period – in provision for which I dodged inside a cubicle of the outdoor jacks to let the place dampen down and the last loiterer withdraw to his study hall. Then, and only then, did I scuttle low by the walls of the nearby tennis court towards our hardball alley of love's sweet bower – oh, huh, huh, huh, boy.

Afterwards, I went to my study hall, looked the prefect dead in the eye, and gave him any one of a dozen dodgy reasons for being late: the dentist I was with downtown had run over with his surgery; I'd been visiting my mother's sister, who was in a bad way in the hospital; I got delayed when my father rang to ask me how to mix a piña colada and a horse's neck for people in from out-foreign. All excuses were given in the optimistic hope that our prefect wouldn't be bothered to check; though it meant having to stay low-key for the remainder of his watch. Once, I dared to walk in with a dripping hairbrush and say: 'Sir, when this fell down the loo, it took me ages to fish it out. I went up to the dormitory to wash it, but couldn't because the dorm was locked and when— '

'Stop,' says he.

The trick was to behave sheepishly towards the future Friar Tuck of some luscious mid-county parish; to hold the brush forward to prime his disdain, and rile him so much he would have no choice but to let out an imperious fecking: 'Well? What do you expect me to do about it?'

The fit of low-key tittering from nearby meant my effort to entertain had worked.

'Remove your article. Sit down, boy, unless you want to be sent to the dean.'

I retreated coyly to fantasise myself goggle-eyed into a cat-nap till suppertime, elbows over a Latin primer. Every last bit of diversion on offer there had to be availed of, for a fellow to keep from going who-uaa, wholesale zombie.

After supper most evenings this term, my pal Martin Doran and I lapped the field to take in the free air that floated over the wall from some breathtaking world beyond. Of late though, just in case, I stopped to peek outside the back gate, and when on the appointed evening Rose's shape ambled on ahead up the lane, I took my leave of Martin till the bell went for second study. At first, he believed his pal had slipped down to the nearest shop for fags. If a fellow was caught smoking, he got twelve of the best from Baldy; if downtown, it meant a long march to the president's room to be expelled – that execution word again. So with one leg propped against the wall behind him, Martin was happy to keep nix till I returned.

Most recently, he had taken to warning me about the risks: *Fellows have been thrown out of here for less, you know.*

'Like what?' I snapped, while picturing the president's austere old face, which was crinkled with indifference. 'Who gives a fat fiddler's tinkle? I'm not on a scholarship or under a compliment to anyone else for being here; I'm not some gimp who sticks slavishly to the rules. If that shower of soutanes wants to throw me out, let them. Here I am: the one and only Johnny Boy Piss-on-Your-Grave Ryan at your service, Your Reverence.'

Petulance was of late becoming an affliction, and so, lest it irk my old pal, I had to temper my outburst. And since there was only so much that one friend ought to keep from another, I told Martin of my dalliance with Rose, making him swear not to whisper a word of it to a breathing sinner: a precaution which was, in his case, hardly necessary to take.

But didn't he stop me in my tracks when, in a wistful voice, he came out with: 'Johnny Boy, you are one born-lucky bastard. I knew you were up to something. Can I let you in on a confidence of my own?'

'Sure, I'm all ears.'

'There's this girl I know who also works in the kitchen.'

'Upon my soul, I won't whisper a word of it to another of our species, I swear.'

'She's only just arrived here, and she's up from my end of the county. A real dazzler, with legs under her as graceful as a flamingo's. She wears white bobby socks – sometimes pink, that match the flesh of her calves; has a pair of fantastic-looking boobs.'

'Pink calves and fabulous tits! Sweet divine, boy, what would old Jerry Rev say if he knew what was in your head? Are you telling me you'd like to get off with Bobby Socks, or better still get the socks off her, feel her tits and run the paws up her calves?'

'Yeah, that's about it,' says he. 'But she's no calf.'

'A bit of a heifer then. Well, which girl is she?'

'Her name is Minnie.'

'Oh ho, Minnie my darling. How do you happen to be acquainted with her?'

'She's a sister of the girl you know. They're from my parish at the foot of the mountains. They used to prance along the sideline and watch us play in the school's league, except they never supported our team; it was always the opposition. When their heels got stuck and their legs wobbled, our mentors joked: *It's the dry season and the Nile flamingos have landed.* She cheered whenever I won a ball; I think she likes me.'

'*I think she likes me,*' I mocked. 'Sure you're only interested in books and sport. Now it's bobby socks, books and sport, is it?'

He laughed that rare Martin Doran, open laugh: 'Sure girls *are* sport.'

'You hit the nail on the head there, old son.'

To keep his brain focused, I went on: 'Now that you mention

it, I have seen this girl' – even though I hadn't. 'Got gorgeous cheeks that I wouldn't mind getting a grip on.'

'Yes indeed,' says he, 'she does have a lovely fresh complexion.'

'I mean the other cheeks. What's wrong with you, boy; why would you grip a girl by the face like you were hanging from the dewlaps of an ass in a derby up that airy mountain of yours, or the way Baldy jowl-winches first-years off the ground?'

'If you can manage to meet a girl while you're in this place, why can't I?' says he.

'Why can't you is right.'

By taking up a hobby that entirely bucked the rules, he would change our bond of friendship to one of kinship. Anyways, it seemed only natural that Martin Doran should dip his inclination towards the ladies, and continue the journey he had begun the previous term, when he had emerged from his shell to enjoy a diversion other than games – one which had become available to us. The problem was that he could seldom afford it.

I used to loan him a few bob on occasion. He had never spoken of his lack of money; no, he'd had his pride. You just knew by the way he'd hesitated the previous year, held back Spartan-style, and then declined to have a flutter on the big one, the Grand National.

It was at the telling moment on the Friday before the race, when Mack the Gabbard, the only day-boy in our class who would smuggle for us, came round to collect our bets for the bookies'. Martin Doran stepped back and put his head against the cloister wall, even though earlier he had gone through the list and squabbled over likely winners. On a whim, I handed Mack a shilling and told him to stick it on Ayala for Martin. That damned nag – a tip Jimmy Codlotin's old one had given him – must have got the whiff of a bucket of oats downwind four furlongs out at Aintree. If it had fallen, Martin might not have taken to the gee-gees, or begun his journey.

With a head for stats and shite, he had become such a dab hand at picking winners that by mid-term of second year he was as flush with moolah as I was. That he'd become one of Mack the Gabbard's most important must-spend-time-talking-to clients also had to count for something; for our merchant prince gave his customers chat-time only to match the value of their trade, and scarcely knew the names of those in our class who didn't truck with him. And Mack knew the ins and outs of life beyond the college.

When the Gabbard talked shop, Martin heard about the high-street stores where the day-boy, like a frugal old one after bargains, wound his way: Woolworth's for torches and batteries, Finnegan's and Murphy's for fags, Johnnie's for socks and jocks; and whichever huckster-shop owner, or barman, did business without squealing to the college authorities, and from whom he had dickered out at least a week's credit.

Mack had been christened in first year. Noses pasted against the front window of the pre-prep classroom one morning, we had been waiting for him to wind his bike up the sweep of the front-avenue, when Wally Furlong came out with: *He's as slow as a coal gabbard of long ago, snaking its way upriver on the tide.* Wally had likely heard it from his old lad, who, while riffling through a magazine, waited for an opened beast in its last spasms to jerk to a standstill on a hook, as the yard gutter carried gore onto the street in a rite of redress to some mad-dog god of butchery and naughty pictures. We slagged him and roared at him to hurry up: 'Mack, you're as slow as a shagging gabbard.' And the name stuck.

The great grey coat Mack wore, on even the warmest days, had pockets stitched into the lining for carrying contraband. He was liable to charge fifty percent on top of the cost price; while bullies, if they paid him anything, got away at cost. The way he plucked a pencil stub from his ear and licked his thumb to flick through a dog-eared notebook slid out from beside the Elementary Algebra book reminded me of the Gunner. But he didn't have the same chiselled good looks. Like my old lad, too, Mack had the right mix of horse sense and palaver as befitted his type, a knotty breed of baulky merchant man.

No fear either that his mammy might get to make a priest of him. It was just as well, or else he'd end up selling the last candlestick to invest the proceeds on the stock market and spend his days following the Hang Seng Index; the sort who at the door of the confessional would slap a levy on penitents.

'Bless me father, for I have sinned.'

'That's all right, my child; no need to waste time confessing. For your penance: that'll be seven shillings and sixpence, please; either that, or go on the sackcloth and ashes for a while. And do make a more regular habit of coming to confession.

'To you, my dear brethren at the back of the church, I say, cease the practice of tearing outside for a smoke, the minute our long-handled collection boxes strike holy terror in your miserable souls. I am now issuing a bull to my flock: from henceforth our collectors will advance beyond the church door to gather from those who stand outside or lean across the graveyard wall scratching their unwashed groins. Even if you run off up the street, mark my words, you will be followed by a box. As you fork out for all other entertainment, so shall you pay to come here of a Sunday. Upon these blessed hands, I will not be deprived of my dues: Christmas, Easter, for the harvest, and whenever else, as I may deem fit. Amen, and bless you my children.'

As business increased and his payload grew heavier, Mack's journey to school slowed; till one day Baldy nabbed him handing over sardine tins to a client, and after the flaking he got, his method of operating changed. Instead of prancing up the front avenue in impersonation of the Sheik of Araby's fine white stud stallion in dressage, he sneaked in through the back gate to reconnoitre before dealing with his customers, every so often going back outside for fresh stocks. But Mack faced automatic expulsion if caught again.

Concerned about his friend, Martin Doran regularly warned him to be careful – in the same way as he had been edgy when I had disappeared outside the back gate. Doran was the type who looked out for and worried about his pals, and this quality was what made him into the glue of our year, quietly linking all the odds and sods.

As well as that, he was coming out of himself. And when a group of second-years choose to take the law into their own hands to deal with a certain maths teacher, Martin Doran was there in the thick of the action.

Something had to be done about Alfie Bra; the man had too much mucous choler coursing through his blood. The latest battering he gave Jimmy Codlotin was, as he again bashed his brains against the blackboard, over not being able to show how the square on a bloody hypotenuse equalled the sum of the squares on the other two damned sides. It was through Mack's friendship with Martin Doran that we were able to plan our revenge. He persuaded Mack to make a sketch of where Alfie's aunt lived downtown. Mack had said she liked to brag about her nephew being a priest who taught mathematics above in the college, and how she spoiled him rotten with platefuls of English-mustard-coated ham sandwiches, along with tomatoes stuffed with mackerel-and-onion pâté, when he visited her for tea most

Sunday evenings; how he loved to play a spot of piano for her in the front room, just inside the curtains. Nick Loan warned Mack that unless the sketch was spot on, he would fling him and his bike into the harbour. Of course, Loan had to take charge of the operation. It was he who hatched the plot.

We took precautions going downtown: if we were spotted in a group out loose, we would likely get reported to the school authorities: townspeople knew that boarders weren't allowed out except for walks on free days and to school matches in the park. One Sunday night after supper, we paired off and walked well apart in the dark; each pair had a copy of the sketch. Mack was to bring along his old lad's car jack, and meet us nearby. We would remove the wheels from Alfie's car and leave the vehicle sitting up on blocks, which we hoped to find in lanes and gardens thereabouts.

We came across the priest's new black Ford Anglia, but there was no sign of Mack. Despondent, we heard Alfie chopping ivory inside a front window. When the music stopped, Loan allowed that the little man had gone over to prop his legs on a footstool and luxuriate in front of a big fire, to be fussed over like a full-blooded for-breeding-purposes Pomeranian, squelching out mackerel-and-onion-flavoured methane, to leave the aunt flummoxed over whether or not the gas mains was leaking.

But then, from his pocket, Wally Furlong produced a raw potato he had gone into the college farmyard for, in order to jam the exhaust pipe: he was the only one to think of it. He handed it to Martin Doran, telling him that the engine wouldn't start if the exhaust pipe was well blocked.

Jimmy Codlotin scratched right-angled triangles, and ABCs marking the points, onto the bonnet. 'Now triangulate that, you hoor you,' says he, as if Alfie was listening.

'You thick horse's arse,' Loan said. 'Jimmy, you fool. Put your name and address on it as well, why don't you?'

We had to take ourselves out of there before loud convulsions of guffaws brought people onto the street. Too flushed with the success of having appeased some of our outrage to be bothered about Mack having let us down, we carelessly returned to base in one big group.

We would deal with Mack again. And I knew a way.

Despite any concern over Mack, Martin Doran, you'd know by the look on his face, had enjoyed this venture every bit as much as the one we had made to Reggie's room when rescuing Kenny D.

His taste for the good life was coming along just nicely, thank you very much.

17

Moments may come and go, but that first bewildering clinch of the heart is an experience so once-off particular that it's impossible to even begin to make sense of the event; all other passions, however personal or eventful, are thereby measured.

Wally Furlong kept flicking the light at every last twig in the lane. It was hard to blame him: he had only recently got that torch, one of Woolworth's silvery-shiny best – bought through Mack the Gabbard, of course.

'Keep it down, Wal,' says Shamie Doyle. 'Or someone will spot us.'

'Sure, Shay, whatever you say.'

We went up beyond my meeting place with Rose as far as the tumbledown shed, whose gable wall, when caught in the beam, stood spooky and made us jumpy. They hesitated as I turned in right beside the ruin, where, earlier in the day while shadowing him, I had seen Mack veer off and go round to the back.

After poking through a wasteland-full of scrap and discards, in particular rusted car doors that were eerily accessing a nether-world beyond even the dark of this one, we finally came across the only things not being ingested by an intense scrub: a bundle of tyres, under which one or two patches of white-enamel light blinked back at us. We dragged off the tyres: it was not nearly as old and bockety a fridge as the one in use in our backyard. We opened the door and found what we wanted: the stockpile that Shamie Doyle under his breath a few days after our trip downtown had suggested was being kept hidden near the back gate – at which point the idea of tailing Mack up the lane had come to me. Finally, in over the horizon sails our ship of chance, to even the score with that merchant piker and savour the spoils, while causing just the right amount of blip to his business. So the pilgrim had been correct about the location of Mack's stash.

It would have been better to bring along Martin Doran instead of those two yolk sacs, but I had decided not to mention the matter to him till later, when we had skipped our usual after-supper walk in favour of this caper.

'Let's take the whole lot with us now,' Wally said.

'No, Wal, no,' Shamie objected. 'If we grab it all at once, Mack's sure to find a hiding place we'll never find. If we pick, say, two items each, he might think he's misplaced them, and we can come here again. Isn't that right, Johnny Boy? Don't you agree?'

I hadn't agreed with the pilgrim since the entrance exams in first-year. The cogs of that brain rotated so fast in opposite directions, it made him impossible to fathom. He was too logtable exact for my taste, and the tedious rigour he applied to each plan went way beyond his usual obsession with wanting to be right. It turned him fecking sessile-eyed, like he was on eyedrops – maniacal, boy, maniacal. Dismayed at even having to loan an item, he froze in mortal dread entirely at not being able to exact more than his fair whack from whatever gainful enterprise he had undertaken. The chances were, the pilgrim would return there later to swipe the entire loot for himself.

Not that Wally was a mountain of trust either, mind, but he didn't seem quite so deviously capable that you couldn't anticipate his moves – except of course when he'd got pranks in mind. It appeared a safer bet to go with Wally's suggestion – but not before I whispered in his ear that this was a favour he would in future be called upon to return.

'No,' I said, 'Wally's right. Let's take the whole lot now. Since he writes everything down, Mack will miss the least item and won't come back here again in a hurry. We've got one chance; one chance only.'

We set about cleaning the place out, and loaded up tins, bottles, chocolate bars and fags as would surely do each of us for a fortnight's gorging. Already with enough beans in my dorm locker to blow up half the college (no shortage of tinned salmon either), I haggled a swap for their share of the Powers' whiskey take – as regards which, anyway, those two hadn't yet fledged out enough to appreciate it, if ever they would.

Their next caper floored me. Without a word, Wally pulled his stockings over the trouser legs, shamelessly took down his trousers, and slotted in not just his own share of the spoils but the other fellow's as well, starting with narrow-width items at the bottom. I had to look away, even though this was happening on the verge of darkness behind the torchlight – a penumbra shadow, according to our dodgy-eyed science teacher.

From the corner of my eye, I saw it happen. The pilgrim's hand, as if by its own volition, reached in towards the exposed jocks and gave Wally's tinkler bauble a wee tug. The next step, according to the funny paper manual on how to lift pirates' plunder, was for Wally to catch the pilgrim's paw and hold it in position, for an entire second of time: *But not now, love. Not while there's company present.*

They must have thought it was too dark for them to be spotted. I had never suspected anything unusual between those two, but there, right in front of me, was yet another of Salty Burke's prophetic mysteries coming to pass.

From now on, a fellow could have no doubts about their friendship. It was more one of dalliance than alliance: no hesitation, no doubt in the wide-earthly world, about saying it. How had they managed for so long to keep it under wraps? I dared not imagine the below-deck funniosities and chigger-bug tangoing that had gone on between them. But, sweet divine, had the tide of husband-and-wife-like experience turned and left them so marooned in their state of mutuality that one partner was obliged to be compliant enough to drop his trousers without question and convert it to a common holdall? Sweet divine is right.

Wife: *You carry my yokes there for me now, like a good man.*

Husband: *Of course, darling. Here I am, honeybunch, trousers and all, at your disposal. You just put your things in nice and close next to mine, dear.*

For fuck sake, what was the world coming to? The shock seemed all the greater because I had supposed Shamie, though shrewd, to be more priggishly innocent than most other pilgrims along the viaduct we were all on.

At once, I recalled a balmy evening in early September, when Shamie had got sick from smoking his first Woodbine, and Wally had pushed his bulk in close over the yellow-faced one's shoulder – an action that at the time I had taken to be one of Wally's tricks, his feeble attempt at a foul travesty of sympathy. Besides, he'd always found it hard to park his carcass without blundering across someone's space. Although it had seemed a little peculiar that Shamie didn't flinch, giving instead a jaunty little flutter of the eyelids. Hell, I ought to have offered him a splash of the kohl I had nicked from the Doll at home – she hardly had any more use for it.

A dainty pair of chicks those two would make, farting and feasting on beans and chocolate up close for the next two weeks. Had they no sense of propriety?

I wanted to puke before taking off like chain fucken lightning out of there. But when shock fades, you're left with having to think. I didn't understand them. Such frightening tenderness between males was unnatural; it left a mark inside my head. Yet it happened to be what each of them wanted, and lacked the least sign of either lad taking advantage. Without any of Reggie's manipulation or Billy Curry belting fellows about, this was the opposite of bullying. And sure, what harm were they doing anyway?

At that remove too, the more I recalled how Salty Burke had explained humankind's inclinations – those that were too improper to be spoken of – the wackier the old man seemed to be. What matter if clumsy Wally and sly Shamie had a mutual thing going? Their fondness for each other, innocent or not, seemed to be the most redeeming trait either of them held, and made them human. I had never seen Wally carry things or lift a hand to help anyone else. Besides, they were welcome to each other.

Finding this tasty discovery was more satisfying than having come across Mack's stash in the first place. Boy, would I enjoy telling the rest of my cohorts. Wait; perhaps not; must hold on; think. Maybe I had been dealt a fistful of trumps: four for the future, and one for there and then. *Of course, dear boy, I will hold my whist about your secret. Now let's do a deal: one tin of beans, say, in exchange for two Baby Powers, all right?*

I pulled my sleeve down over my hand, plucked a nettle, and dropped it into the pudding bowl of Wally's trousers, which were already filling up round his haunches, but it got caught between the items. The spoils were divided, and the two fellows left together. I lingered behind, wondering if the nettle might soon find its target.

Martin Doran was waiting inside the gate for me, with one leg against the wall behind. 'The shops are doing a roaring trade this evening,' says he. So he had seen the lads laden down. But let him think what he wanted, I wasn't going to make him any the wiser.

'Here, you big duffer, give us a hand to smuggle this stuff up to the dorm, which should be open by now.'

We managed to bring the goods up without being caught. But on opening my locker, I thought better of stashing away the whiskey, fags and chocolate.

'Let's go make a feast of it this evening,' I said.

'What about second study period?' says he.

'What about it? Bring this out to the ball alley, and wait for me. Mind the bottles: it's liquid gold you're holding. You'll have a treat this night, boy; got a fucken great idea.'

So down the stairs I ran, and slipped in through the side door of the refectory – which outside of mealtimes was also off-limits for us. The area inside the door was in semi-darkness, but at the far end, outlined against the blistering light from the kitchen glass, a long-limbed new girl was laying tables for the next morning. It had to be her: Martin's taste in girls was spot on. Her every shape had been sculpted by some august artist – and not by the same geezer who had knocked up the old statue on the stairs to our dorm: the baulk of chalk I had found standing in my sink one morning the week before and which had on my precious new jacket, along with a cleaning mop over its head; with shoe-polished eyebrows and a face all tarted up in red crayon, it had a page strung across its chest saying *I wants to hold your hand*. It had taken three of us to lift and plonk the old saint on a pot inside the dorm jacks for the skivvies to deal with it.

I coughed to get her attention, and the gorgeous one came

over. I asked her where Rose was. Rose arrived and was down-right mortified over my lack of discretion in contacting her like this. She only relented when the new girl pursed her lips, winked at her and, in a pout of appeal, half-nodded towards me. At once ole king bald-as-a-coot ding-a-ling reacted at base midriff, telling me he would forego his right of support from the main trunk for twenty minutes in a cubicle with this hot-looking thing – he said that a lot lately whenever any half-decent good looker come to mind.

The girls smiled in cahoots, before Minnie turned and pranced away in a strut that reminded me of how proud Ayala must have felt while heading into the winner's enclosure at Aintree on a certain Saturday in April the previous year. When Rose agreed to meet me in the alley in fifteen minutes, I told her about my friend's interest in the other girl. But she wouldn't make any promises about convincing Minnie to come along.

In the alley, Martin had become queasy in case Baldy arrived on top of us and over missing study; that lad always had a rea-son to be fretting. At last when the outline of the first shadow appeared at the entrance, then a second, I knew we were in busi-ness.

Without need for formalities, I decided even so to introduce Martin and Minnie by the light of my chrome Zippo, which I kept flicking on to allow me gawk at the new girl. We gorged on chocolate, sipped whiskey, smoked cigarettes, and chatted for a while. I had to elbow my friend into action: 'Martin, you might like some privacy to get to know your new friend.'

They eventually went into the dark at the other end of the alley. I had no means of knowing what they were doing other than from the sounds coming across.

'Go easy,' says she. 'Not that way, pet. It's like this. Let me show you.'

It was enough to taunt a saint. For once, Martin was the born-lucky bastard who got to step into the breach and breathe the distant must smell as it grew into a full whiff of old nirvana in a café down in Buenos Aires, where a crinoline doll danced out from a shaded corner to raise her knee and tingle him with her thigh. It was he who felt the heat of danger in fingering smoke-buffed ivories, whose tinkled notes mysteriously stayed suspended overhead till the tall Latin beauty before him became denuded of her burnt-orange satin décolletage. Although the stored music at last burst over their heads, in picture as well as in sound, to reveal the combined sum of their past hillside experiences, it also gave off shadowy premonitions of all their future passions, which, because of this same lack of carefree danger, could never again hold for them such erotic fury. It was he, the fucker, and not me, who did a full-frenzied mounting tango that night.

The sound of Elvis's old *uh-huh-huh* had never made sense till the very moment that those same moans, with maybe a slight variation in their tone, echoed around the hollow space there. I just knew that this, their delirious pleasuring when tied in with that once-off first-time mutual urgency, would over time mould itself into a lovely delicate memory-fragment for each of them . . . while I had Rose Morals Morales to contend with. Martin was the one who had got to do the tango, and I a courtly minuet, or a morris dance. Because of the dark, my ears had been extended to take it all in, in their distinct way.

I could all but hear a radiogram wobble round, churning out my mother's one and only Carlos Gardel record, and see her smudged-rouge face in the dressing-table mirror, haughtily holding back her passions behind conjured-up sulky pouts of stoical heartache. With a hint of Latin-like vendetta added, she might be a dancer from San Juan or Guadalajara, mourning the loss of a limp-dead lover from Lima stretched on the bed behind her – except no bullfighter, either gored or bored, ever snored half as hard as the Gunner after a quick romp with his missus on the holy-hour break of a Sunday. Only here, and all at once, did it dawn on me that the Doll must have imagined herself as a bit of a leg-flinger doing the tango – a dancer whose searing sense of neglect I could at last identify with, strangely. No doubt we had the one Latin blood in our veins; the same ache.

After the girls had gone, Martin Doran and I waited there, smoking and imbibing, till the end of study period, when we just about managed to join the rest of our cohorts on their way up to the stairs after a night of noses stuck in quadratic equations.

I winked at the old saint, again in his niche after a trip up my end of the dorm – but winking back at me, his face began to look like the pilgrim's.

Despite the night's outcomes, it was good to see Martin Doran's extra-curricular activities come along in leaps and bounds. On that evening alone, they had taken one almighty shot in the arm, let me tell you.

You know, I think I'd make a good teacher.

18

Despite long days of drawn-out drudgery, the course of a life can all at once hinge on a single happening. At least that's the way it is in my case.

We got a day's break in that joint every once in a while. The senior of the house and his assistant dared to go out of bounds beyond the stained-glass door at the head of the cloisters and march side by side into the hallway curving past Sister Polyps' surgery, then up that fecking great Mount Olympus of a priests' stairs to knock on the president's door. Grovelling before old Crinkly Face, the great Zeus of days off and digger-humped-up pitches, they pleaded with him to look favourably on their request for a free day: that in his divine munificence he possibly might even deign to grant it upon the entire college, lay side and seminary alike.

If a free day was seldom asked for, it was far more seldom given – except maybe to mark the occasion of a college team having won some title, after which anyway the mood was too loose and dizzy for work without teachers resorting to the heavy hand. Then, out of the blue, for no reason other than that the place would benefit from a day's break, old god Crinkly blew kindly upon us. And on that Monday in April of second year, the news came as the most astounding, warm, delectable marvel: free from classes, we would have nothing but hours on our hands till first study at five o'clock – a whole day's haven, one great goose-summer unit of time.

It was the morning after a night of soft rain, the kind that noticeably greened the lay-boys' field – after which you all but heard shoots burgeon on branches up the back lane. Rays of eastern shimmer bounced up to our eyes from the tops of waves and narrow patches of water elsewhere in the harbour beyond as proof of the rule, according to the sleek-haired dodgy-eyed one, that the angle of reflection was, after all, equal to the angle of incidence. To get here, the morning silver used the water as a mirror to bypass an anvil of nimbus in front of the sun, while farther out, towards the horizon, where I then longed to be, a line of non-stop breaking surf pinpointed the perilous lie of a shoal that crossed the mouth of the harbour to link two spits.

Then just before the bell went for class, a cat's paw spread in from the offing and crossed the entire fluid pan to break the spell, so that no sooner had our lateral fellowship with the veiled sun begun than it was over. This same breeze soughed through the boundary mesh, to peal loose wires against metal stays as chimes of feeble caution for craft approaching beyond. But as the bell clanked out, we wistfully retreated from the scene and towards the cloisters – and the start of another ball-breaking long grind.

English was first. Any minute, the Shed would either rollick into our room in the best of high spirits, or more than likely lumber through the door in an oafish bluster, late again, having had the whale of a wild weekend; or just nauseated, as he had often said, by the thought of facing us as his first class of the week – a pity about him.

In such a surly mood, he was certain to bang open our prose at the very first essay in the book, 'The Vision of Mirzah' by Joseph Addison. It was as drab a piece as any second-year ever came across: 'Man is but a shadow and life a dream.' Give us a shagging break. The more of this horse manure we had to

rhyme off for him, the more tempted I was to stand up and sing
'I want to hold your hand' and to drum the lard out of a desk lid
like I was Ringo fucken Starr: 'I wants to hold your hand to
tango with ya, baby; proceed to do the Twist and with a flick of
my wrist . . .'

Let you miss a word while reciting a passage about the story's
broken bridge being comprised of seventy arches as blind gob-
shites dropped through trapdoors: the Shed would wheel round
and whip out a limp leather strap from the inside pocket of his
fawn wool overcoat, flung across the back of his chair. In a spate
of controlled vehemence – even if it was an open-and-honest
one – he flaked hands with the might of Desperate Dan come
alive from Shamie Doyle's *Dandy*.

This was what we sat there anticipating on that morning.
And as if to herald a turnabout in the day's fortune – or else the
tension was getting to him – Nick Loan broke the silence by
banging his desk lid, as was his wont in fits of folly, and shouting out a recitation that Kenny D. and himself had concocted
the previous year:

> Full well we know the day that lies ahead:
> this morning is nothing if not Hades.
> As Charon ferries us across the Styx,
> Baldy Klops will slash us through to the quick,
> and Gorgon's humour is that of the Shed's –
> I wish old Polyps would send me to bed.
> Then last we've Afie Bra for algebra:
> be damned to hell, it's double algebra –
> please, Sister Polyps, I'm not very well:
> I've got *ging gang gully gully gully*
> *wooly wash wash, ging gang goo, ging gang goo.*
> Three horse pills, Sister, please, and a glass of water.

The rest of us joined in till the room was filled with a hum that sounded like an incantation of Gregorian chant from High Mass on Sunday morning at eleven. The louder and more irreverent the chant rose – till a roar of mock solemnity was hit – the more redress thorough light relief we got to help ward off the morning's anxiety. With Nick Loan again acting as bandleader, the desk-lid banging started. When this was added to the falset-to-and-bass voice-part variation of fellows in counterpoint competition with their different lines creating a magic madrigal, the sound got amplified beyond harmony to a crescendo of yowling and desk-lid furore, before the entire commotion collapsed into an outbreak of viciousness against all authority. The class of 2C, boy: we were the only true rebels left in the place. The pure-brute madness was uplifting, and pride-infusing in the face of dread.

Again, the room fell silent. Each head bowed in a last-ditch attempt to learn our latest underlined passage, while listening out for that nearing knell of tan brogues. But on that day we didn't get to hear the Shed's heel-plates clip the quarries. Instead, an almighty roar erupted through the cloisters. Everyone knew what it meant without having to wait for the shout of 'Free day'. But, still distrustful, we held the silence for a moment before letting rip in one almighty holler. The room exploded into wholesale pandemonium. Wally Furlong hopped from one desk to the next, up and down.

Several minutes passed before Ken D., all delighted, came running in from his 2A classroom two doors up. Shamie Doyle stuck his nose round the corner, carrying a Monopoly set with a bundle of comics on top. The pilgrim ran over and jumped up on Wally Furlong's lap. *Not here, you pair of shaggers!* I kept myself from shouting.

'Go and play that stupid game of tiddlywinks someplace

else,' Codlotin said when Shamie had plonked his wares on Jimmy's desk. 'Me and the boy here want to find out if there's a walk leaving the college. If so, we are going on it. When the group reaches the garage corner, we'll sneak off to see what birds are about the main street. We might even get off with a couple; isn't that so, Ryan? We'll bring them into this old ware-house I know of along the quay, and lay them on grain sacks to shag the knickers off them the day long. Had I known, I could have sent word to my sister in the convent to fix us up with a pair of her big-booby pals. Hey, boy, are you listening to me, or are you deaf?'

'Lads,' says Jimmy, 'will youse come here quick to see the size of Shamie Doyle's horn from hearing me talk about girls. And he always struck me as being a bit . . . bent.'

'It's not talk of girls that's doing it,' says I. 'It's your sweaty body he has the hots for, Codlotin. He wants to lift the tail of your shirt and play Monopoly on the cheeks of your fat greasy butt.'

Codlotin's face turned tomato and the hair, long again, col-lapsed as he took off after me round the desks. Nothing about him that way had changed since first year.

When I called in next door to see if he would come on the walk, Martin Doran made excuses about being behind in his work.

'Look,' says he, 'it's all right for you, Johnny Boy: your par-ents pay for you here. And because we have football training in the afternoon, I must work all morning.'

Since that night in the ball alley, he had gone crabby with me, as if I was to blame for leading him astray. He hadn't said a word to me, either, about how he'd gone on meeting Minnie till the end of that first term in second year – Rose, too, had told me nothing. On our return after Christmas, Minnie had disappeared:

probably landed a better job. Although Martin had looked bereft, it was no longer my place to go poking my nose. He'd seemed to draw more into himself; to look sallow round the eyes – some of which must have been caused by all the training for colleges' championships.

But on this morning, he downright declined to step outside the walls to freshen his brain the way we used to after supper, and refused my offer on a plate to resume our friendship. I regretted having made the effort.

Later that morning, Codlotin, Kenny D. and I lined up with about twenty others to go on a walk, which was led by two cassocks-on-coat-hangers seminarians. I was looking forward to sneaking off at the garage, but at the last minute Codlotin funked it.

'Ryan,' says he in a whisper, 'one of them prefects has his eye on you. He thinks you're up to no good. Don't risk it, boy. And it wouldn't be fair to leave Kenny continue on his own. You know what he's like: won't take up with anyone who's not from our year. He's gone into a right fecking odd sod lately. Did you notice that, Ryan?'

Not one glimpse of a girl to whistle at along the entire way, our highlight was a stopover at a shop near the old bridge way beyond the town, where we gorged on Tayto crisps and eclairs ahead of the return leg. When I showed Jimmy how to shoplift, the hag behind the counter took a sweeping broom and tore out and crossed the bridge after us, leaving her old man to serve the scamps who all at once saw their chance to pile into the shop. When I turned to face her, she flung the twig at me as if tossing the caber. The thing bounced twice along the tarmac before somersaulting over the side and into the current with the zeal of an eel headed for the Sargasso Sea. Jimmy wrapped his arms about his gut to laugh. Her rasher-angry face changed to a look of desperation.

The real lark, though, was going on back inside. The crone returned to see fellows, with pockets loaded, run out without paying; she clipped the last lad on the ear as he left. Once the brown narrow doors were shut, a yell came out from the empty hollow: 'Thieves! I am going to report this to the college authorities.'

With their noses in the air, our fag-puffing prefects sat on the wall farther back the road, too taken up with theology and their future missionary destinations, off in Savannah and San Antonio, to be aware of our cutting up.

Kenny D. then came out with the queerest spake: 'Look at the brush the way it floats off; it's happier out there than stuck in a corner waiting for a crusty old hand to tug it by the handle across the floor.'

How could he envy a broom, or connect it with things like freedom and happiness? Codlotin had him well taped: the lad was turning into a right odd sod.

Our walk came in through the back gate. A gust had got up to bob some red sails about in the harbour. It whined dirges in the high mesh to make the stay bars peal out their unease far louder than they had done earlier that morning. Something else was up.

Boys raced towards the entrance at the top of the field. Most of us on the walk at once broke off. We rushed across the rise of the lower pitch, over the spine, and tore along the top, a million wildebeest in the Serengeti, to funnel through the entrance.

Between the locker rooms and the toilet block, we heard a rasping voice ahead. I got nobbled in the ribs by an elbow from a brute going past. He mentioned Martin Doran's name. But that wasn't Martin Doran's voice we heard shouting. The uproar had all the stirrings of a fight about it. My unease grew much more definite.

Around the corner, we got a shot-blasting full visual of the commotion. The crowd had not bunched or crushed forward on their toes, as they would during a fight. Everyone was standing back; it was easy to make a throughway. The shouting came from a raised-up position: actors were rehearsing an open-air play. The stage, though, was too small for the cast. The only play I would recognise was Shakespeare's *As You Like It*, which the Shed was doing with us for the following year's public exam. But this wasn't it: probably some other year's play instead, or a skit. One which Martin Doran knew – since he happened to be taking part. So that's what had been eating into his spare time.

The actors jostled on the half-landing of a galvanised-iron fire escape outside the first-year dorm. And Billy Curry held the stage with his ceremonial bellowing of a monologue. Those jackals in his gang stood close by admiringly; the minor members lined the steps back to the ground, forming a train. Curry played the part of some fantastic ungulate – the strut of a satyr from a Greek fable suited him. Previously shown only in single deeds of intimidation or havoc, here his true nature through the spectacle of an acting role was able to let rip in full torrid flow. His speech, though, was hardly from Shakespeare.

'Look at here,' he called. 'We can't have people thinking they are above everyone else. It is a crime for a student to see himself as being better than everybody else, and he must be made to understand that this is just not so. From the moment a boy dons this blazer, he is just one of many students here. And let him step out of line: then he must get his comeuppance. No boy ought to think he is superior to anybody else. The creature we have here stands accused of seeing himself as superior. Superior? In fact, he is of a lesser species than the rest of us. He is non-human, and is not even worthy to be compared to the most miserable wretch among you; doesn't belong with us. He just doesn't fit in here, or anywhere else either. How can boys go near this foul thing? Yuck, dirty, get the smell away from me. The animal doesn't deserve to live. Scumbag of second year, you are found guilty as charged. And what will we sentence him to? What will we do with him? Look at here, I am asking youse all a question. Do youse want me to go down and help youse morons to answer?'

Although addressing my old pal, Curry's face sneered at us, eyes scanning back and forth. Since he couldn't get round to everyone, he'd chosen Martin Doran to be our stand-in as the fool in the play. There again was that unmistakable trademark: terror peddled through the act of mockery. With a straight face, he fed us his brand of hard, cynical amusement. For Curry was not given to smiling broadly, or to outbreaks of honest belly laughter: we were meant to take him at once both gravely and jokingly. But that mix of jocose threatening with the one or two beatings-up he dished out per day was only a minor detail, a mere warning of how much worse he would, if he wanted to, make life there for us. But this scene here had more to it than that, and certainly gave off the power of the stage.

Martin Doran's hands were tied behind his back and his neck was tilted by a noosed rope that draped by his side, eventually reaching Billy Curry's hands. Boys' faces showed expressions which I had only ever seen in bad dreams. His eye picked me out. I felt my blood cool to a chill.

'I'll ask youse one last time: what will we do with him?'

A loud call of 'Hang him!' was answered in unison by Curry's cronies on the stairs. The crowd about me murmured something. Although I tried to swallow, I felt obliged to join in the answer: my mesmerised lips began to mime.

Curry shouted again: 'The culprit was tried and found guilty. I now condemn you to hang by the neck. It's time to carry out the sentence. Has the condemned one got any last request?'

Had the acting caper finally finished and reality taken over? What if all this was actual, and the terrible deed was about to be done? Could one feeling human do such a thing to another, even as part of an act? Pure Weatherman-terrorist stuff, it was, like what we'd heard went on in America – and I didn't know which way the wind blew. The true gods of oddity were at work here.

My brain couldn't take it in, or sense what was going on. That picture I'd had of how things were no longer seemed to fit the changing situation. The play lacked a story – even if it need-ed one to qualify as a play. This unbidden performance without a plot was going on before our eyes. Each boy stood on the spot, as petrified as a relic. I could only speculate on where this piece of drama was headed. I searched Martin Doran's face for an answer.

But his shamed chin hung low, scarcely defying the sisal. I tried to imagine what might be going on in the head of a fellow who was alone, with nobody to stand up for him. Was there not one person in the entire place who could stop this? All the sen-ior class were in their study hall, doing whatever it was that sen-iors did. Curry and his mob must have crept into the 2A study hall and overpowered my old pal from behind his desk.

'Have you no word of warning for the rest of these farts?' Curry called out. 'No last message either for Mama and Dada, no? If not, let's get this over and done with.'

The crowd's hush allowed us to hear our only friend, the wind, whistle through the metal fire escape. And far from being a mackerel sky, the dome overhead was so full of heavy stratus that had mushroomed from the previous nimbus, which had blocked the morning sun, it almost seated itself on our heads. The heavens looked ready to lash down spears and lightning in anger over our wanton carry-on. Like their protégé on the stage, those queer gods of oddity above were having one whale of a free day. Far from play-acting, this here was a thorough dose of reality.

Where was Nick Loan when we needed him? I tore through the spaces in the crowd, across the open yard and into the cloisters.

It was Jerry Rev, our spiritual director, I found, and demanded that he follow me out. I smiled at Rose, who passed and turned towards the stairs of the senior dorm. If only matters had been less pressing . . .

'Quick; do something before it's too late,' I insisted.

Jerry Rev followed. The moment his eyes took in the scene, his great limbs burst through the crowd and bound up the fire escape, clobbering Curry's cronies out of the way. He went on to the stage to flail the main dogsbodies down the steps. Serfs and minions from the realm of Flunkeydom at once changed allegiance. I climbed up in Jerry Rev's slipstream. But was it too late?

Even if he wanted to, could the bully stop? It seemed that Curry no longer held a rein on his own actions; that a force of darkness from the cataclysmic black in the abyss beyond the edge of our unseen viaduct was driving him onward. And if Curry didn't see it through, he'd never live it down.

Drunk in a frenzy of fury, his gang had hoisted the helpless mass of Martin Doran over the rail and left him to cling from the outside, his wax-white knuckles clenched to the rail behind. Both wrist-bound and ankle-bound, his heels on the metal deck took his weight. The lad's body hung forward and outward in a limp, a crucified limp. And the rope from Curry's hands was still about the captive's neck.

When Jerry Rev reached the platform, the piston of his elbow flew back, nearly taking my head off. His fist landed full in Curry's face. Good old Jer. Your pulpit zeal might have been a scream, but when all's said and done you proved to be a real man of the cloth, a genuine holy man, not just another hollowed-out bluffer in a soutane. Let your holy rage burn on, boy, burn and shine.

'Hold fast,' I told Martin Doran. 'Don't let go.'

I lopped the noose from his neck, but the wrists weren't as easily undone. There was that Zippo lighter in my pocket. It burned through the rag, searing his flesh; then the lace about his ankles, singeing his trousers. Though free to turn around and climb inside, Martin stayed fixed, unable to move. He was in a stupor beyond being distraught, as if resigned to his previous fate.

Jerry Rev had to pull him over. And while Martin Doran was the one who had been rescued, it seemed to me that his archrival too had somehow been saved.

Billy Curry would surely have to account to someone for what had happened. Equations had to be fecking well worked out. You know how it is, boy: that old equals sign rules everything and is not there for nothing.

19

A streaky-brown tit-lark perched inside my head keeps pipping out that my flight feathers are beyond repair, beyond repair. So what? All dreams must end, sooner or later.

Right now, though, my friend's need for new experience takes him into forbidden crannies and beyond, which few of our peers here even know exist. Although such a wilful fledgling is bound to draw down on his head the wrath of the powers that be.

Rose might very well be on the senior dormitory, I thought: not yet finished her chores. Anyways, some sort of diversion was called for to help offset the trauma of the previous half-hour.

Having made sure the coast was clear, I turned the corner and bounded up the stairs to make my way down the centre aisle between the cubicles. There was no need for her to know what had happened to Martin, and the only reason why I might tell her was to spur her on to say what had gone on between her sister, Minnie, and my old friend.

I reached the recess where the jacks were. She was there with her back to me, exactly like the first time we'd met; so I plonked one foot over the other, leaned against the side wall and waited, like I had done before. But just to see how she would take it, I decided to clasp her about the waist. She might at once think it was Baldy Klops, out of control from all that celibacy, gone stark staring mad for some female flesh in the round.

Rose writhed in shock and turned to face me; her annoyance came on fiercely as she thumped her fists against my chest. Then with a fair amount of intensity, but not vehemence, she flung her hands tightly about my neck. I could not figure out these two opposite reactions, or how quickly one followed the other.

'Did you think it was someone else?' says I. 'Your new boyfriend, maybe?'

It was said for devilment. But she pulled away without answering, and I had to wait while she got on with her work. Eventually, Rose picked up her buckets and mop and beckoned me to follow: the girl had free pass to each and every black hole there at the world's end. We walked through the secret door and down the steps, then out onto the half-landing on the priests' stairs. But instead of going down, she headed up towards the first-floor landing and the priests' rooms. I hesitated, even though I was past caring about being caught.

'Look,' says she, 'are you coming or not? Just follow me. It's quite safe. Doctor Quigley is gone away, and so are all the others. I know because I've already cleaned their rooms. When he goes, the others grab their chance and get out too; everyone here lives in dread of that man; he has this effect.'

One after the other, two pairs of feet tiptoed along the bright red carpet: it was strange being back in the heartland of Bawman territory. After motioning me to stop, Rose moved in close to the first door, knocked and waited for a reply, and then strode on inside as if the room was hers. A few seconds later, she re-emerged and signalled with her hand. It felt like I was being beckoned to a terrible reckoning.

Inside was a different world, a palace chamber, where the arrangement of well-spaced objects of taste was suitably eye-catching to divert attention from the room's work area of reference tomes and corrected, as well as uncorrected, stacks of foolscap paper on the floor at either side of an immaculate bureau centred on its wall. The main fixture was a flecked and faintly veined marble fireplace that also contained a red-flower pattern of taupe-coloured tiles, at an angle, to frame the grate core of matt black – in keeping with the colour of its owner's heart – within which a rick of coal lumps and kindling was ready to take a lighted match.

On a silent winter's evening, the sparkle of firelight off the brass companion set and coal scuttle was sure to match the shine on the back of a perusing bonce tilted slightly sideways, as usual. And in the same way, the plush claret-red velveteen on those carved-handle chairs and on the kneeler of a polished-pine prie-dieu picked up the predominant burgundy swaths of carpet. Only the best shag was to be had on a presbytery floor, as the Doll had once said, with exquisite timing, to put the kibosh on a vulgar barstool conversation. Two mahogany bookcases, full to high heaven and cornice, indicated how much learning their owner had got through in order to be tagged as a doctor, even if the afflictions he dealt out were in inverse proportion to the healing you would expect at the hands of a physician – or of anybody else who'd ever devoured such a mound of volumes. No matter, it was just another one of that joint's mysteries: the more letters after his name each member of staff had, the less he seemed to know and care. Once again, you could see the queer gods of oddity at work.

But the piece of furniture that most aptly reflected its owner's disposition was also the one most out of place in that room. A cross between a hallstand and cabinet, this strange pur-pose-made unit at the left of the entrance belonged more to a quartermaster's cabin where the door had been eerily left on the latch and abandoned, *Marie Celeste*-like – and where you would expect to see three stuffed shags, wings to the wind on a Bakelite crag. The pair of shotguns, some fly-fishing rods and a rifle sparkled as spotlessly as the knives in Wally Furlong's backyard abattoir.

'Come here,' Rose called. 'I want to show you something.'

I followed her into his bedroom on the right. The golden silk counterpane across a double bed uncannily looked so much like the ones in the dream I'd had when Billy Curry clobbered me on our second day of first year that I felt the hairs on the back of my neck tingle. The doors of a large wardrobe were open, showing so many items of clothing for one macho cleric with a passion for blood sports – even let him be a doctor.

'Will you look at that?' says she.

'What?' says I.

'He has more clothes than the queen.'

And dead right she was: he had enough clobber to last him two lifetimes. 'I wonder,' says I, 'if he keeps a flower-decorated enamel chamber pot under the bed. Let's take a look.'

There wasn't, thank heaven. I didn't fancy having to share my space with such an ornament, should the need arise for me to get down there and hide.

'I hear footsteps,' says I. 'Quick, get under the bed.'

She closed the wardrobe doors and got down beside me. I let on to be shivering, and put my arms about her. 'Here he is,' says I.

'Stop laughing,' she whispered. 'I can't hear.'

'Whatever happened to Minnie?' I asked.

The way she stared at me: it was best not to pursue the matter.

Rose got out from under the bed, saying stiffly: 'You didn't see what I wanted to show you.'

'I'm afraid to come out. What?'

But she insisted, and placed her hand on the shoulder of a fur coat in the wardrobe.

As soon as I jumped to my feet and searched the pockets, the impressions I had got of him in furs at once changed. For there, among a rosary beads heavy with medals and four half-crowns, was a scrunched-up envelope with no letter inside. The outside was addressed to a Mrs Codlotin. I recognised the scrawl as Jimmy's attempt at handwriting. The penny dropped. Not letting on to know anything, I said: 'Who is she?'

'You mean,' says Rose in her matter-of-fact way, 'whose coat is it? It belongs to Doctor Quigley's girlfriend, of course. Everyone knows about her. And it is said, too, that her youngest son, now boarding here in the college, is really the son of the good doctor. And let me show you something else that's hers.'

In a show of wait-for-it sham, dad-dah, surely rehearsed, she swished items to one side on the rail, whipped out a hanger and dangled a lace negligee before me: get 'em off you, Mrs Codlotin. She then placed the black article against herself and swayed in a fanciful dream of wearing it on her wedding night for her dreamboat Hercules, ready for action, boy. Too much shocked response, or indeed my sudden appetite to see her in this thing rather than sway behind it, might have spoiled Rose's moment of exuberance, her dream. But a glib word of tongue-in-cheek was called for to make the moment zing along towards that unlikely magic happening between us which the swing of her hips conjured up; even any sort of word, by heaven, to keep this thing going.

'Why don't you try it on?' says I, attempting to sound casual.

'Right you are,' says she. 'Turn around.'

Sweet jeepers. It took her less than a minute to change her clothing and become a real doll.

'Well?' says she. 'Now you can look.'

And look I did. Not as she gave me much time, mind, to take in the picture; for she was under the counterpane of Baldy's bed before my brain could relish the eyeful of delight. Strangely, my first thought was to turn the key in the bedroom door.

'You're not getting in with your clothes on, surely?' says she mockingly.

Again the brain had to figure things out slowly: what was the next step? I felt like an awkward, cumbersome fucker, and not at all the suave guy I had imagined I would be in this situation. Since there was too much light in the room, or because I had no control over what was happening, I felt obliged to ask her to look away.

This was the business, boy, the situation I had always wanted to be in from the first time I had clapped eyes on the girl down the cloisters, and in the dorm cubicle when the tips of my fingers had slid down to her right breast like a pack of five mules crossing the Sierras on an expedition to a goldfield. Then, she had rewarded me with a sharp whack of well-practised surprise, showing how well-schooled she was in anticipating such advances.

But at this moment, when my wishes were about to come true, I was suddenly unsure, and hesitated about it being what I really wanted. And this here was a different Rose. Had she planned her course of action? Why the change of mind about paws not being allowed near what was supposed to be kept under lock and key for the one who would lead her down the aisle: her special dowry for Mr Dreamboat on their wedding night? It seemed that I had no say in matters of close quarters with her.

Sweet divine, though, didn't she look good. Unbeknownst to myself, I must have fulfilled certain expectations, by chance pleasurably pressing the sequence of buttons to hit upon the right formula and become the aisle-stomping Hercules of her dreams – or at least his appointed deputy. Maybe she had changed her goals, or even dropped them altogether; perhaps left them on the shelf, for just this once. But jeepers creepers, I had better get on with business before she changed her mind again.

Startled by my own scrawny nakedness – hardly fucken Hercules' body, this – I slipped in under the counterpane and, like a seal pup, flumped over close to her. Where to pick up was the next thing: a long course of lip-smacking at first, her favourite. And that negligee must be got rid of: the circus-tent coverings winched from the Sierras to allow my teams of mules manipulate the passes – slowly, of course, lest they get swiped off – and then to remove that soft little article of gossamer below. My imagined desires were at last recovering their old powers to operate freely. Long John Silver would take over, steer the craft out beyond the harbour reef before raising the Jolly Roger, tack a southern course and catch the trade winds to the equator . . . But Silver wasn't really the captain here, was he?

Again, she was as blunt as was her wont: 'Don't block me now, boy. I don't want to be up the pole, and have to go to England to get it out, like what happened my sister Minnie.'

Jeepers.

And yet again, she had managed to put the kibosh on the course of our romance when it was just about to hit the heights.

No longer could I get the whiff of café must that only a moment before had promised to grow into the full aroma of nirvana away down Buenos Aires way, which was supposed to overpower and change my life. The brief outline of a crinoline doll remained steadfastly over in her shaded corner, only leg-flinging her shapes to tease. But it was all proving to be no more than that: a tease. Rose Morales, my Latin beauty, didn't raise a knee along my body or touch me with her thigh. And the only heated danger present was brought about by the thought of a bald bonce trying the handle of his bedroom door. Plenty of ivory was touched, but the notes remained suspended; the music didn't burst over our heads to fall confetti-like about her lovely naked shoulders. All too soon, the time came for us to get up and hightail it out of there.

That was it, then. Back to the kitchen and the chores, it was, for Rose, and the cloisters for me. Down to the corridors, where oodles of big vapour 'O's of blandness drifted slowly upwards – *pop, pop, pop* – for each boy to gulp down and re-emit as methane balloons, recycled puffballs of an even denser cyclical boredom. Where all that was left for amusement was the permanent clowns, who, with their sad white-painted faces and grey baggy costumes flying at half-mast, still didn't wear proper pointed hats like they should have. The same Joxers who moped round and hung out of window embrasures were ever on the lookout for unfortunates to mock and play havoc with their dreams, and, if nothing else, thought little of landing you in the middle of next week with a thump.

And it grieved a fellow to realise that such a blow to his dignity would go un-remedied. He would never get to overtake the size of his opponent's muscles and be able to redress the shame by walloping shite out of him; his circumstances of an innate lack of strength and age difference had bound him. And so the equation would not get balanced, even though there had to be a law, either inside our outside the universe, for levelling out such injustices, as well as all other inequalities.

It was different for the authorities in the joint. One way or another, by the end of school year they got to sort out their outstanding matters. Deeds we had almost forgotten about, or which we had put to rest and were sure we'd got away with, were chillingly resurrected; as the dean duly plonked our offences before us. And boy, did it make the bastard smile to dole out wholesale from his stash of retribution in balancing the school's ledger of waywardness.

With just a few more days left, Baldy came in one evening during the five o'clock study period. I was first on his list; next, Codlotin, Wally Furlong and the others who had done the job on Alfie Bra's car were called to the front of the hall. The dean pulled out his cane, swished the air and told us off about the sinfulness of vandalising property, not to mind the enormity of breaking that rule which forbade boys leaving the college grounds. For me, it was no longer a big deal: your hands kind of got used to the cane. But when he ordered us up to his room, where boys had already grouped outside the door, we knew something else was going on. Each one was called in separately to be quizzed and then flogged. Still no great concern: it was just a change in procedure.

Left till last, Codlotin and I were called in together. Baldy warned Jimmy: if there was any indication that he'd been involved in going downtown, damaging the car or robbing items from that shop on the day of the walk, he would expel the boy. Of course, seeing as how he already had so much fecking tidings on us, the dean knew only too well that his son had been implicated in these incidents up to his neck. When Jimmy got six of the best on each hand, along with six more for good measure, he was sent back to his study hall. Left to the very end, I was alone facing the dean. It had to be serious.

But not so much as a finger of anger did he raise, not even that look of cold contempt, except to grab my jacket lapel and march me from the room and up the next flight of stairs. When he knocked on a door, old Crinkly Face's voice invited us to come in.

They spoke to each other about me as if I was an object, a piece of farmland in need of a 'dozer to shelve it into two playing pitches; a double flat-backed thing about as fertile as a bald eunuch in charge of a honky-tonk of curved-flesh fresh concubines. The intensity of cold wrath given off in that room would freeze the gametes of a polar bear.

'Because of his negative influence on . . . leading boys astray . . .'

Eventually, Old Crinkly got round to making his final decree, issuing a mighty infallible bull.

Later, after supper, when a crowd of second-years had gathered amid the shrill mania of the cloisters to tease through what had happened, I felt sullen and at a remove from the heart of their confab. As they squabbled over who might have squealed to the dean, their intensity didn't rub off on me at all; none of it mattered any more.

One lad said it was Mack the Gabbard, seeing as how he hadn't turned up on the night to do the business on Alfie's car. Another lad, whose family knew the Codlotin family, was sure, but wouldn't say why, that Jimmy was the snitch.

'Nonsense, sure Jimmy got the most slaps.'

'Did you get slogged, Johnny boy?'

'No,' I answered. Since the reason why I hadn't been slogged was no longer important, they could grow frantic all they wanted to, before I would announce my news.

'So was it you, then, that snitched?' a voice came. They all turned and slowly drew in round me.

I hadn't expected them to be so frenetic over it; *rope* seemed to be written across their intentions. It was time to save myself, or the bastards might string me up. Lynching was getting too popular round here, for fuck's sake.

'I didn't get as much as one slap from Baldy,' I announced. 'But he did lead me up to the president. I've been expelled . . .'

That quietened them. The circle drew back. I left their company for good – and good riddance. I never spoke to that other stupid gobshite, Codlotin, again either.

Instead of going in for our second study period – and besides, there was too much nervous energy going on to allow me to sit cooped up in a desk – I made my way towards the refectory in search of Rose Brien. She told me where to go and wait for her. Then up to my dorm locker to get the last noggin of hooch, and the end of my fags and chocolate, before going through the college farmyard and into the storeroom where I was supposed to meet Rose.

In there, I had time to think of how, the first time we'd met, Jimmy Codlotin had been so full of baloney about savoury sausages concocted from pigs' blood and doodles, and stringy white bread made of lamb's wool and gut. It was hard to believe there was this other side to him: that he could squeal to Baldy about us, or even that the dean was really his daddy. Talk about a cleric being celibate: for feck's sake, that guy would copulate with a midge going through a skylight. If I had not been expelled, I would for certain never trust Jimmy again. But could I give his identity away to the others? It was hard to say. What I wouldn't do to his guts, though, if he was here present . . .

When Rose arrived, I told her about my news, and she was full of sympathy. We cried together, and our touching took on its own life – a sort of anxious desperation. She lowered her defences as the hour passed, and she didn't mind when I stripped her naked on the sacks. The desperation grew more urgent as she yielded to me; we did the business together for the first time – a little awkwardly, maybe forced, but it was done. Afterwards, the nervous energy in my head went and I felt calm. She told me that this was the place where her sister used to meet Martin Doran. 'Heaven help her,' she said.

But full of new-found affection, she stayed the night. In such glow off the yard lamp as came in through the fanlight, I watched her sleep and felt the cold sweat of moppy hair at the back of her head, but my hand and arm might stay numb, for I didn't want to wake her. At some stage in the night when she moved, I got to pull away and shake off the pins and needles.

Early the next morning, I went up to the dorm, packed my best bits of gear, and walked out the front door and up the road to hitch for home, just as I had always wanted to.

20

Only a week has gone by since his expulsion from the school for rooks, but Johnny is back there again, this time in style and with a purpose – because he is free to do so.

The place was empty, the Sunday morning serene. I was an untouchable old boy, at last, on a saunter down the main corridor, pulling on a John Player cigarette, and I felt suave enough in that new George Harrison look to clip a defiant ring off the quarry tiles, which were beginning to fade; as with a life of their own, almost, my raised-heel chisel toes trod out and onward. More than suave, it was fecking sweet: that pure mulled-wine delight of sweet warmth on a Christmas morning.

Never once in my two years there as a boarder had I experienced the cloisters devoid of boys and their jarring burble, which on wet days had increased to a stunning blare briefly checked by the arrival of a priest or prefect passing through to the seminary. Of course, it had ever taken the appearance of a certain burnished pate, breviary in hand, at the top of the steps for any real semblance of order to befall. His white eyeballs flashing among the shadows, the mouth set midway between smirk and sullen, he had put a dampener on the freedom to be noisy and defiant, but once this warm sweet wine of youth got soured, a student no longer held the urge to be imaginative or to fashion new ways to play. And just as Christmas comes but once a year, it takes such a fecking long while, too, for a fellow to begin again to invent.

But on this morning, all sense of the dean's presence, as well as that muddled menace in not knowing of his whereabouts, had gone, scattered like wisps of high clouds downwind, and of itself alone this felt good, really good. Not a soul to be seen, or the bound of one leather instep on a distant quarry heard; the place when still was seductive – beautiful, boy, beautiful.

Yet this thrill, too, like all others, lasted for just a jiffy. For the familiarity of yammering students, along with their quivering commotions – and aside from which I had been set so as not to experience them again – came back as old ghosts to haunt and scorn a fellow for getting himself expelled. *'Will youse look at the cut of him, eh, the boy.'* There as well, to gatecrash my empty corridor with their frequent flurries of splayed kicking and mock fisticuffs, came the gangs who were overly familiar with each other from being cooped up together for so long, and I all but heard a Dublin twang, from around the corner, shout: 'Out of my way, you stupid-looking fart.'

No, it wasn't easy to credit the joint with a tranquillity so all-consuming that even the distant jingle-clink ding of kitchenware and occasional slam of a door scarcely impinged. Those echoes gave a background enhancement that was as set apart as the hollow sound of an accompanying piano, or that distant saxophone's warble, on the Doll's record of Frank Sinatra singing 'One for My Baby' – the memory of which by then had lost its edge. But I was compelled to stand awhile and wait for the full flavour of this Sunday-morning-serenity experience to seep through the follicles of my mop-top and into the bowels of a brain whose space for such follies was limited, especially on this day's visit.

But growing all wistful at the breathtaking amount of cloistral freedom, I began to imagine the institution that this joint might be if only it was managed differently: without stifling rules and fear – especially the fear. Its buff-and-maroon walls and arches did hold the makings of a hub of enlightenment for the bright sparks and chancers of my generation to open out, in keeping with the burgeoning shoots on branches up the back lane – a place where a young lad's trust, that jewel of a thing, would be nurtured and properly honoured by mentors whose hands were safe for him to be near. I rightly turned pissed-off irate under the mop-top to think that we, a whole swath of cohorts, were being mucked about by a regime which belonged in the age of some medieval inquisition: that's not the way things were meant to be, or how Creation had intended our brains to grow. Of course, we'd heard stories of well-run boarding schools where lads didn't have to learn their *mensa*s on empty stomachs, but they were in far-off places.

Yet even here, on occasion, we'd found room to discover. One night during the previous February, our dorm prefect, Ahab, had allowed us to stay up and crouch in the cold by his transistor radio as Cassius Clay went seven rounds with Sonny Liston to take the world heavyweight title. Afterwards, we chased with a wily zest facts and titbits on all matters boxing – till the Easter break anyways. Had more gestures been made, who knows the paths we might have gone along? Even highfalutin shite like Latin, Greek and their queer old gods and myths could have become subjects of serious interest for some geezers, had they been fed to them with the right blend of free choice, help and fire.

Maybe, under some benign regime during the century before, this joint had been an eminent northern outpost in the revival of classical influence spreading up from way down south, a centre for the gracious babble of old languages to echo with no small meaning, and where the nosh too was good: with lashings of olives, figs, spices, great strips of wurst on the refectory tables, and maybe the odd tankard of ale for the senior years – scarcely the kind of fare we got for breakfast. Really, had this hole ever been a place where the business of learning was a genial way of life? Well maybe, in the future.

Besides, we could but dream of sucking olives in Arcady, as we tasted a main course of eau-de-cologne seeping spuds, three seared slivers of boot-leather beef à la mode and vintage carrots mildly sautéed in chef's ordure. Our dessert, as a final piece of gut-blockage, then steamed gloriously on trolleys from the kitchen: a slather of rice pud and, on occasion, pannikins of fabulous frogspawn that winked hello-how's-your-mickey. All downed to the tune of a whey-faced theologian at his refectory lectern non-stop gibbering from his book of collations; sure, a fellow might as well have been seated next to Hercules and left to chew on his two-and-a-half-thousand-year-old scrotum for sustenance. Starving Arcadians and centaurs seated by their troughs got so frustrated as to kick the knackers off each other under the tables, so much that metal-lined jockstraps to safeguard a lad's gems of lineage ought to have been standard first-day issue.

If indeed a golden age had ever come this way, it was long over by the time we had arrived in first year. You could smell the must damp of old books long-gathering on ceiling-high shelves behind glazed doors at the back of the big study hall, and from the great tomes that clogged up the two lofty entresols of the college tower: I had sneaked up there at Hallowe'en to meet Rose, but the place had spooked her and she wouldn't stay. The last days of the guardians of hidebound books had been tolled out by the Beatles twanging 'I Want to Hold Your Hand', and other sounds in four-four time coming at us from over a wall about to collapse. But that was then; this was a new, other day.

Of course, I was back there to meet Rose – why else? And on hearing the stained-glass door in the distance at the head of the cloisters squeak, I stepped aside into an open classroom to peer out from behind the reveal. For once, luck was with me: it was Rose, and on her own, coming this way. Not expecting to see me, she almost dropped her bundle of laundered sheets when I stepped out in front of her.

'Give me a minute and I'll be with you,' says she.

'Oh fair enough,' says I.

Carrying her bundle, she went back the way she had come. I strutted up to my old perch in the fifth window, plonked my heels on the heating pipes, and arched myself back into the embrasure nook. Fifteen minutes passed before she returned; it was then that the magic began.

With not another soul around, we had no reason to be inhibited. Yet from the way the glass door reluctantly squeaked this time and a chink of vertical light slowly appeared sharp-cut on the wall beside the opening jamb, Rose must indeed have felt hesitant, uneasy. I tried to guess why. Maybe it was because she was all done up, having swapped the blue Terylene work-coat for a scrumptious saffron A-shaped minidress, and wore raised-heel penny loafers instead of moccasin lace-ups. Her hair even more bouffant, the new Rose cautiously stepped forward from the shadows and click-clacked down the steps and along the corridor. At last, I had a wide-eyed chance to take in the picture.

My yellow rose of early summer moved as if swaying in a breeze. A pure delight, the perfect pattern of her type from Creation: one, two, three steps along towards me. As she passed the first classroom door, where the sunlight was already splayed across the quarries and skewed up the wall opposite, she was at once wrapped in a sublime aureole of gold, a hallowed moment. Would the chapel organ not blast out *Gloria in excelsis . . .* in celebration, and a full choir descend from a nimbus cloud to sing *Et in terra pax hominibus, bonae voluntatis . . .*

With a strut that changed to unselfconscious flight with each hip movement, and a smile that shone, she had become a walking contradiction of every word in Joseph Addison's drab story 'The Vision of Mirzah', and her loveliness defied Father Jerry Rev's pronouncement that life on earth was a passage through a valley of tears. Really? For her new presence in it, the world had become a strikingly beautiful place.

It was an odd thing then, so, to experience a return of those twinges, first felt when more than a year before I had gawped after her on the dormitory and noticed a loss of poise and a droop of her shoulders. But those misgivings had been mine all along; the worm of agitation was in me, and not in her: that much I had since learned.

The sight of Rose, her figure, arriving down the steps this time swamped a fellow. That striking shape of a fully fledged woman overwhelmed him; he believed himself to be incapable of matching it with this thin stripe of a male cadaver, complete with a great boil on the back of its neck, he had to offer. In heaven's name, why would such a full-on female come to meet the Boy? If only she still had that work-coat on, he at least might have regained a pinch of that vim from before and felt able to handle her – that girl, rather than this new woman. Dressed like this, she had become just too much for him. But a fellow must soldier on with some bit of gumption and put his misgivings aside. Anyways, under this day's circumstances, he would not tolerate any stabbing of himself in the craw.

Without seeing another soul, we left the cloisters behind and went up the tower, climbing the narrow dog-leg staircase to the top entresol. To make room, I heaved a number of musty volumes over the railing; they landed in a thud on the main floor below. Fixing some larger tomes into a raised plinth on which to sit, or lie back, I wiped off the loose dust with my white linen handkerchief.

As Rose parked her posterior, the hem of her dress slipped up about her hips, and I had to look away from such intimate roundness. Under the bow of a lancet window, familiar rollers beyond still brushed white against the sandbar, which from this vantage point seemed nearer than from the one in the lay-boys' field. It somehow seemed easier to fix on the curved shapes out where freedom had flown to than on those fornenst me.

But my eyes were drawn back to the businesslike ritual with which Rose undid her flesh-coloured suspenders, and how, on release, the darker rims to her stocking tops tended to roll up of their own accord. She slid an undergarment down her long slender white thighs, below white knees and off, along with her raised-heel shoes. We gazed at each other, but said nothing. Her look showed understanding, of allowances being made for a fellow's panic; so my urges changed to something else no less compelling. Without getting hung up on a rigmarole tracery of sensation and romance, having recently been through it all anyway, we both had a sense that the sun was up, the sky blue and the sea green. It was enough to know that an alignment of planets was taking place; how two internal worlds were conjoining to eclipse all the rest of creation. Slowly and gently, she allowed me to lay her back on the old tomes of ancient knowledge. *Gloria in excelsis* . . .

And that, too, was then, a glorious time when berries got ripe for the plucking. But things and seasons change, and each round of a romantic bout, with its dog days of high humidity, must fade into its own equivalent of the fall of a year. Yeah, boy, the year must begin to turn in on itself.

Over the summer, I called there several times to see Rose. But then, one Sunday shortly before the school reopened, she had news for me. She would have to go across to England for a few days, to the same place as her sister, Minnie, had gone.

She looked at a fellow with a fervour which only females have the knack of conveying; her eyes went through me for answers.

'Well?' says she.

Rose obviously wanted to know what I had to say, even though she hadn't asked me a direct question. Or maybe she required more: some sort of solution to her quadratic equation worked out. What she meant was all implied, as if I was supposed to have an intuitive way, some sixth sense or other, of tuning in to gather information and be able at once to understand the situation.

But in spite of the life-and-death intensity in her face, I did not quite manage to get the measure of what she meant. I couldn't even begin to guess what her question was, not to mind knowing the correct reply or be able to tell her what she needed to hear. It was like being back doing the entrance exam at the start of first year: I hadn't a clue what to do or say, with no means this time to cog or bluff my way out of it.

Without saying so, Rose then began to blame me for more than being unable to answer her unasked questions.

'Go back home to your way of life,' says she at last. 'I'll know where to contact you when I need you.'

The dismissal meant I couldn't bring myself to ask if this was the end for us. But even if it wasn't, something or other had come to an end. I didn't know what that might turn out to be.

A few months passed till we met again. Rose came into our front bar one Sunday night ahead of a dance in the Athenaeum. I took her out that night, and our meetings from then on continued: we often went to dances and to the picture house. But I tended to avoid making an exhibition of our liaison, and didn't bring her along when I'd got invites to sing at functions. It's easier on a performer when his steady isn't there to watch him ogle back at the intent looks of female fans whose legs throb on every beat of his song.

Indeed, since stealth, with its mood of defiance, which had ever spiced up our get-togethers, was no longer necessary, and we were also free of rules and restrictions, the intrigue of our liaison had been on the wane for some time; that vital ingredient of fun had gone out of the fling. What was the smack and thrill to walking out arms-linked under a parasol along the street in broad daylight? For feck sake. If it was with some other geezer's bird, then maybe. No, this was not quite my thing: it hinted too much of ownership – the distaste of which, no doubt, Rose understood in me.

We had definitely changed; maybe grown a little bit older. Yeah, that was it.

21

Although long gone from our place of confinement, my good pal is not yet finished in his dealings with the bald fowl; he seems destined to be haunted by that pest.

To be haunted is right, Sputnik, old son. I thought the black-hearted so-and-so would hound me to kingdom come. My breath went sharply at the sight of him once more; it was despairing to think I might never get to shake him off.

Outside, the still of a late-November evening, along with the lambent light off old street lamps, was proof, if proof was needed, that the year had well and truly turned in on itself; not the scratch of a mouse could be heard coming from Tanyard Lane nearby. Inside, where the usual few early-Monday-night customers were nursing their measly shillings, salting away all they could for Christmas, the wooden draught handles stood so idly by as countertop sentinels that the Doll and I seemed to be providing more by way of a facility for local news, curio-interest and chat, than the usual services a licensed public house has to offer. Where had all the hard drinkers gone, eh? Only one old lad, elbows on the counter, defied this general go-slow on liquor: true to form, he was throwing back the sup like tomorrow might never come. He, at least, kept the taps from rightly seizing up.

The sudden swirl of a breeze then meant that the front door had been opened. Although at once glimpsing his familiar bare pate, my brain needed a double take to register the identity of the new arrival, and longer still to credit it possible that my old arch-enemy actually had presented himself here on our premises. Along with an overwhelming drop in self-assurance, there swamped across my soul once more the chill of someone not just walking, but dancing a tango, on my grave; as well as the urge to get the hell out of there, or duck under the counter.

Even the Doll recognised him without having ever before set eyes on his *phizog*: such an instinct in women is so incisive, it's uncanny to behold. She scowled and looked at me, and then turned on her heels to stomp from the bar before she might commit a crime. What did that bastard want with coming in here, or, for that matter, anywhere else up this neck of the woods?

With no dog collar on, none whatsoever, he was the real dandy of a layman: dressed in the perfectly cut, faintly napped black suit of an undertaker, showing up here like a bad penny. You might even mistake him for a bank manager – bless the mark – a Joe Mac-like *solistor*, or a civil-service primper all the way down from Dublin. (Vatican II had driven the clergy stark staring fecking mad for fashion.) The last I had seen of him was on that day more than two years before when, after attaching his pincers to my jacket lapel, he hoisted me up before old Crinkly Face to be expelled. But what business had he in coming in here?

His head, as ever, was tilted, with an expression stuck non-stop between a smile and a sneer, that usual no man's land of a thing. Not the least hint did he leak of the unease you'd expect from a man of the cloth who has taken a wrong turn in off the street to find himself and his chaste loins suddenly standing on the spit and sawdust of a bawdy-barroom floor. As self-possessed as you like, Baldy Klops approached an empty space at the counter. What was it he wanted?

'Mr Ryan,' says he, 'seeing as the title "Master" is one that no longer becomes you, it would seem. Or else what form of address shall I use, huuh? Your compeers, I believe, used to hang the moniker Johnny Boy on you. Shall I simply address you as "the Boy" – huuh? Well, Boy, is the boss on the premises at the moment, or have I missed him?'

Was I supposed to feel privileged over his concern about what to call me, or flattered that he should know how my old cohorts had referred to me? The rising blend of a lump in the throat and of loathing in the chest kept me from answering him right away. And in the event that, as I was half-expecting, he should reach out with a clean-and-jerk to one of my sideburns – which were coming along nicely, thank you – my eye automatically fixed itself on an upturned half-pint glass within reach and then flicked upwards to pick an appropriate spot atop his polished crown on which to plant it. That same tremble of trepidation as I'd had on our first jostle at the entrance to the lay-boys' field again overtook me: you never forget a shit feeling. What did he want with the boss? The unwelcome caller would be made none the wiser by me of where my father, the Gunner Ryan, was.

'That's right, sir,' says I. The loud 'sir' came belatedly, a jousting stroke of genius, maybe, which gets depicted in comics as a bulb glowing over an inventor's head alongside the word 'eureka' printed inside a blimp trailing off from the cartoon character's mouth. Even if it had been more deliberate, the 'sir' moment could not have tasted more delicious.

But ignoring my impudence, the enemy continued to whine out in that high-handed tone of old: 'I don't understand what you mean, Boy. Would you kindly . . . '

Well, shag that for a yarn. As a mark of disgust for that voice of pretension, I swung my back on him to pick up and wipe an age-old tankard from the lower shelf. His collar may have been missing, but not the dogmatic manner ingrained in his bowels since he'd come down from the mountain and gone to Rome for tuition in how to strike an attitude; as though for the sake of a little extra ornamentation, creation in all her majesty needed the bombast of yet another pompous cleric. But here on our floor, my realm, without his Superman's soutane on as a mantle of muscle, he appeared no different from any of our town's dapper cadgers on the make. Adding to this quandary, his poise showed a marked lack of awareness that the place on which he stood was barbarian territory, a pure fucken abomination to men of his calling – or at least, it had been up till that time. And the longer he was left there standing-waiting, the more I got to recover my composure.

With as much fusty-barman-like pose as could be mustered, I turned to give him another shot at showing that he'd amended his approach enough to warrant my attention; and with lips pouted in the shape of a duck's arse about to discharge its bowels, I spoke slowly from the front of my mouth: 'What you said was correct, sir.'

His look of puzzlement had endured long enough for my liking. So I went on: 'Yes, you have missed him.'

The way those eyebrows flicked up and shoulders shrank back meant he was confused about whether I was being serious, or just as mindless as ever and disrespectful of him and his status – but anybody's approach of trying to pull rank on our floor always, as an unwritten rule, called for a scant response. Whatever he chose to believe, it no longer mattered: his power of dominion over me had vanished on the day of my expulsion. But again I froze, as, with that same motion from the past of reaching inside for the cane, he stuck his hand under the jacket. Instead, this time, he pulled out, wait for it, a thick Sellotaped envelope, a brown one, and curtly said: 'Please ensure that he gets this.'

In a reactionary twitch provoked by his old fear-foisting gesture, I rashly snapped the envelope from him, lobbed it below
the countertop and sidled off to deal with a matter more pressing. It was time to replenish, with the instant smile I had been
trained to show, the glass of our long-time stable regular, who
had been trying to get my attention for the previous five minutes
and whose tongue lolled out in want before turning an apoplectic purple. Old Salty Burke's alcoholic brain had become too
sodden to appreciate how uncanny it was that, though I badly
wanted to tell him, he should be seated next to a top dog from
the very institution about which he had once made such effort
to warn me. Not another glance did I throw Baldy till he had
turned his back to leave.

The Doll, too, was nearly apoplectic as a result of the dean's
visit, but was she not as entitled to her bias as the next person?
She had blamed him outright for ruining her dreams of magnificence, in which a pious mother aptly wrapped in fur kneels
before her only son for a conferral of that newly ordained
priest's especially potent first blessing, and all other attendant
endowments remitted along rays beaming down upon her head
from the fluffy high heavens. Then to be denied her great wish:
she was not only free to feel piqued and pained, but to be entirely possessed by a full-on outbreak of contempt.

'I just don't like his manner.' She fired out the words. 'Priest
or no priest, his presence is more unsettling than that of any
other customer who's crossed our floor.'

'But he's not a customer,' says I. 'He didn't ask to be served.'

'And he won't be served either,' says she. 'Not while I'm
here.'

I relished the aroma of her spite, seeing as she was blaming
him rather than me for snuffing out her aspirations. But whether
or not the Klops had picked up a hint of this denunciation, it

didn't stop him from showing his face on the premises again ahead of the following Thursday night's racing above at the dog track. And didn't the Gunner launch himself out from behind the counter to greet the bald one with a display of grovelling not seen from him before for priests, whom he had often referred to as 'sky pilots' and 'natural-born foes of your plain drinking man'. Then, just as the two cronies, old boy-like, were headed out the door, the Doll, her mouth open, looked at me quizzically, as if I could provide her with an explanation of this new phenomenon.

All the same, your man didn't put a foot inside our door again. Not because it was still unacceptable for well-fed clerical haunches to be seen girdling barroom high stools – a curb which hardly bothered Baldy much – but more likely because the Gunner had warned him off with the story of my mother's broken dreams and changed attitude towards men of the cloth. Yet such an effort as it took to keep their friendship off our premises had to entail a fair whack of furtive plotting. Theirs must have been the one approach which our town's middle-aged, open-shirted and medallion-wearing gut buckets, for whom golf was too strenuous, indulged in during their wild-night sessions at large in other towns to sow the last of their hairy-chested seeds of wild vigour before the dilemma of drooping willy set in. They would meet for a quick one in our bar before setting off. Sure, as soon as the Doll had gone out from behind the counter, you'd hear their defiant catchphrase: '*When man has mind to, he must thresh well away from home.* Old Chinese proverb, haw haw.'

The touch of shadiness no doubt helped Baldy and the Gunner to buttress their camaraderie with a deal of spice.

The next time I saw them together was on a mid-morning after Christmas below in the Corner House Hotel. Leaving the Doll in charge of the shop, I had gone down the street with a spring in my step to slip into the foyer on a little bit of business of my own.

Since only the receptionist's head and shoulders were visible above the curved parapet of the desk, I had to stretch across to whisper my latest naughty little suggestions into her ear while keeping an eye out in case old Magsie, the manageress, popped her giant perm and hammerhead chin around a corner to let out her usual fair-day buck-ass roar at me. Old fuzzy-head was not my keenest fan, not even when I was invited there to sing a few numbers at weddings and do's. On the other hand, the receptionist was securely on my side, and kept me in the know about all the goings-on thereabouts. Angie would tell me the floor on which Rose happened to be cleaning.

'Go on up, she's waiting for you, ay-eh-eh, heh.'

'Where's the Big Fuzz?'

'Below in the kitchen, so you're safe enough. Don't forget to lift the phone to tell me the room youse are in, so I can buzz you back if the boss goes up that way.'

Angie's code of warning was: 'Chocolate moose in the hoose.' Although wearing an engagement ring, she had hinted at how she only needed a beck from me to abandon her post for a romp in the nearest vacant bedroom. I planned to take her up on the offer sometime, but for the moment Rose and I were in the clouds with each other. Rose Brien was showing no ill effects from her trip across the water, after which she had got a job here in the hotel – to be near me, no doubt. One of these days, I might surprise her with a monstrous rock – well maybe in a year, or two, when I'd have got Angie out of my hair.

On that morning, as I reached over the desk to supply her with a fix of smutty insinuations and peek down her blouse as an aperitif before meeting Rose, Angie said: 'Before you go upstairs, take a look round the corner of the front lounge. It might interest you to see who's inside.'

The lounge door stood open, leaving enough space between the doorpost and hanging stile for me to spot a group of two women in fur coats, and two men – one of whom had gone bald. That scene contained the jolliness of a Frans Hals painting – a postcard of which one of the drinks reps, back from a holiday out foreign, had left on our counter. Each scene gave off a sense of being viewed through two windows, one smaller than the other, at once. This double-mounted picture, come to life before my eyes, held the cuttlefish-brown, homespun charms of another age, and allowed me to witness the immediacy of a scene in which some moment of glorious conviviality was being lived to the full. I shuddered in wonder at the allure of this fleeting vision, whose characters reclined in a winter-softened sunburst distilled further by the leaching effect of opaque-glass brick in the wall overhead. For sure, here was a shaving of perfect bliss filched from eternity, linked to the divine – and it demanded that a fellow ought to go on his knees in awe. The eyeful I still have of the Gunner smiling away to his heart's content in the corner of that front lounge has through the years turned into a right keepsake of memory. It was the last time I saw him ooze that old gaiety – such picture-postcard glee. Let me tell you, as well, the low table before them held more than four spirit glasses.

I wondered if one of the fur coats turned away from me was Mrs Codlotin's – for I might have gone in there, Baldy or no Baldy, to enquire about my old pal, Jimmy. Not that he had need of my asking, for over the following years he managed to go on for the priesthood and get himself ordained – a day on which the good dame's fur coat and shapely legs surely got a fine airing; and on that night, she no doubt wound her way up the priests' stairs towards Jimmy's daddy's room to complete the ritual. It was written in the stars that Jimmy would become the Friar Tuck of some luscious mid-county curacy and lay his hands on the warmest buxom belle of a housekeeper for going to town shopping with him on Fridays and to fend off the loneliness of winter nights in a shadowy presbytery. Anyways, the waster deserved some jollity lifted from the hereafter.

In this framed picture here, however, his mother was not one of the raddled old dolls present. I felt a tinge of regret.

When I went back to the desk, Angie made a point of informing me that your man inside was a big-nob of a priest who lectured to seminarians below in the college.

'Tell me about it,' says I. 'The bare shell of that josser's pate is as well known to me as the pretty round of your chin.'

'Imagine taking Communion from him in the morning,' says she, 'not knowing where those hands have been the night before.'

'Hey, gorgeous, I know where my hands would like to be right now. Give us a kiss, will you, you little nibble of scampi?'

'Stop,' says she. 'Certainly not here on my desk, anyways, or I'll lose my good job. Can you believe it though, Johnny? He comes in here wearing no collar, tootling on his arms two old tassies *slaumed* with lipstick who think they're film stars and who, I'll bet, half the time don't even wear any knickers under them fancy coats.'

'How would you know, Angie dearest? Is it because you don't wear any yourself, especially when you know I'll be coming here to see you?'

With more caress than reproach, she spanked my hand, and waited for me to make the next move before she responded in kind, to raise the stakes yet further in this single-file game of teasing. But content to let the hare sit, I stayed lackadaisically stretching across the parapet of her desk, as Baldy Klops passed by on his way to the hotel jacks.

'Good morning Mr Ryan,' says he. 'Feeling a little listless today, I gather. Would you mind, awfully, stepping into the lounge with me for a moment when I return?'

Though expressed as a request, his call still smacked of strictness so much that it was hard to resist. Angie looked up at me and whispered: 'Uh, very well got there, aren't we? Would you mind awfully doing without that nibble of scampi I was about to offer you?' She collapsed her head in her hands and held back the throbs of mockery hissing through her teeth. Then it dawned on me that she had only ever been clowning with my sensibilities. That place was a real circus.

I followed Baldy into the front lounge. The Gunner wanted to know what the hell I was doing out gallivanting. The nerves that should have beset me on seeing Baldy reach for his inside pocket were no longer any bother. This time he pulled out another thick envelope: what deep pockets the man had. Silently he glanced sideways, as if asking the Gunner for some kind of a say-so – a deference you would not have expected from him.

I felt obliged to reassure the Gunner that everything was A1 back on the ranch.

Before I could pick another pause in prattle to find out why he had summoned me, Baldy asked if I had ever been to Pete's bookies or knew how to place a wager. He wondered if I might be trusted to show discretion about his foible of having the odd flutter on the races, since it was not the done thing for clergymen to express such an interest. He wanted to know if I possessed the subtlety to carry out this message for him.

Before I could ask what he was on about, the Gunner blurted out with a laugh: 'Of course he can be trusted. He's my son, ain't he? The lad has got trust bred into him. He already goes up there twice a day with slips to beat the band. It's part of the service our establishment provides for its customers. And we will extend this courtesy to you – just throw the lad a few bob to help with his pocket money.'

Pocket money is right: a fellow could scarcely take a girl to the pictures on the fiver a week he paid me; my extra bit of earnings had to be snaffled from the till. Since the Gunner no longer checked the overall stocks, I accounted for my topped-up wages by sneaking in bottles from the crates outside to keep up the numbers on the bar shelves. When the discrepancy showed up in our end-of-year accounts, the Gunner passed it off by assuring the auditor: 'We'll have to be more diligent about things, eh.'

Besides, our accountant didn't seem too pushed that the figures for purchases and opening stocks were so close to those of sales and closing stocks, or about any of the other figures he got from us, as long as he could make some stab at a trial balance. In his musty office, he sat across a file-laden desk from the Gunner; they gurned at each other, then hummed and hawed without giving away much. Something for sure, a mischief that was greater than my petty diddling, needed to be covered up. Anyway, I would replace my share as soon as I made a killing in Pete's bookies, after which I might even have the price left of a sparkler to go on Rose's finger. Things were bound to work out.

And if all other fruit failed, I would work on my repertoire of cover versions, and go on the road as the singer in a show-band – might have a word with Paddy Joyce of the Herdsmen the next time he called into the bar. Eventually, I would get my own band together, Val Ryan and the Rhinestones, and make the big time; well, big enough for female fans to fling undergarments galore at me on stage, and to find a fresh poke every night. Imagine: being able to scan the dance floor for the best bit of tush and tenderly beguile her with a smoochy warble. Having hooked her attention, I would discreetly tap my gold wristwatch, hold up five fingers, one for each minute, and point to the door. Besides, my absence offstage while the band played on would only leave the dancers more appreciative of my performance. Hell, the fecking life, boy.

But as regards doing a run to the bookies for Baldy: I knew more about that business than either of those two behind the counter. Pete himself had offered me a job: 'If you ever grow tired of the bar-and-grocery trade,' says he, 'you can come and work for me.'

I had often thought of opening a book on the side, with the intention of eventually getting a permit for a change of usage for the grocery part of our shop, the takings from which already had all but been put paid to by the new supermarket down the street. When I floated the idea to the Gunner, he just laughed: 'We will to be sure,' says he. 'We will to be sure.'

My old dean of discipline held out the envelope. 'Can I trust you, for certain? There are five hundred smackers and a list inside. You will hand it to Pete; to no one else.'

Imagine that: five hundred smackeroonies, boy, in one job lot, and all to go on the nags. What would that amount to if a treble came good at odds of, say, ten to one: the price of two houses? Sweet divine, the man had money to burn. Some of it probably belonged to the pair of old dolls, and some to the Gunner – the right old chancer, anyway. Yes, I will have to admit, I was tempted.

What a fecking circus life was turning into. The Gunner and Baldy show had hit town running.

22

When bother comes knocking, a tidings of magpies stands alongside on the threshold, and by the time those hungry friars are done feasting, courage and resolve get pecked to the bone.

The Doll was less than happy about my former dean of discipline's ongoing association with the Gunner – and not just because he was the one who had ruined her designs on life by expelling her only son. There was too much extra mucus in her choler for it to be just that.

So, unlike the woman I had known of old, she got tetchy over every bit of bother – for certain towards customers who were inclined to be awkward anyway – and threw a wobbly when the wholesaler delivered the wrong brand of flour, or the milkman hadn't collected all the empties. Her reactions at times were hardly a million miles from the state that Alfie Bra used to work himself into back in geometry class, steam coming out of his ears when faced with our grasp of Euclid – that git. She also had his nose for picking up the least whiff of shenanigans that went on behind her back, and was, too, the older she got, a great one for the premonitions.

'The hold which that cursed priest has over your father will be the ruination of us yet,' says she. 'I don't like this set-up. It certainly doesn't augur well for the judgements your father is capable of making.'

Then one weekday morning, my mother rose early, did herself up and marched down to the bus stop at the bridge. She went through this same routine for months, once a week catching the first bus to the town where I had gone to boarding school, and made it back before the Gunner was out of bed: knackered out from the night before, he seldom managed of late to see daylight before noon.

'That man is gone off the rails altogether now,' she insisted. 'The company he keeps along with that so-called priest will be his undoing, if not the downfall of us all.'

Not only were her predictions not open to question, she was as infallible on matters of the heart as the blooming pope in Rome was about dogma and papal bulls; even as she spoke, her prophesies were being met. So damned well right, she was, about the Gunner. I had seen for myself the man in action below in the lounge of the Corner House Hotel, and then one night when he'd got out of a big Zodiac and slipped round to the back room of the Bootleg Inn in narrow River Place, a house of debauchery where, before an inferno razed it to the ground, high-stakes poker games were known to last till dawn – not to mind the raunchy women who hung out there, and the fights. On the two occasions he went with his new-found friends to the Cheltenham three-day race event, the Doll's haunted brow furrowed yet deeper as she muttered something about Cheltenham wives.

'Where I'm lead to believe,' says she, 'as much high-stakes rutting as racing goes on. He has gone and lost the run of himself now entirely.'

At the same time, it should have been clear to my mother that the Gunner's antics were less influenced by Baldy Klops and Co. than by the effect on him of the changing state of the bar-and-grocery trade – a pressure he'd never before had to undergo.

One after the other, supermarkets were hitting town, and

grocery shops unable to match them in either price or product range suddenly became old hat. As well as that, our bar business had begun to fall. Newfangled ballad-singing lounge bars, carpeted up the bloody walls, nearly, with Paraná pine-sheeted counters and leatherette seats plush enough to take full tilt the butt-end of a sultan, were robbing us of our younger customers: spit and sawdust were no match for PVC-backed carpet.

'Come here till I tell you. We went out for drinks last night.'

'In Ryans', I suppose.'

'Not at all: go 'way will you. Me fella brought me into the Lounge *bor* of the Corner House. Such luxury: *korpet* everywhere, even as far as the loos, and you should see the panelling round the counter area, oh.'

The things my father had got up to were as a *consequence* of our predicament, I tried to tell the Doll, and not at all the cause of it. The picture was bigger than just being about us; times were changing horrid fast – too fast.

The memory of how the house of Ryan finally went to the wall is now hazy. It happened all in a slap. One day, I was serving customers; the next, we were out of business – for good. Along with the Gunner and my mother, I stayed indoors till the yacking on that topic about town had turned into yesterday's news.

With a head on him that resembled a fish up a weir, sucking on his meerschaum pipe and only occasionally puffing it, this lanky old galoot, sent by the bank and followed everywhere by his tool, landed with his bag of tricks onto our floor one evening, saying: 'Well, that's that then, folks.' My eyes, as I recall, could only fix themselves in pure and helpless ire on an upturned glass as he waved a piece of paper in our faces telling us we could live upstairs over the premises for the moment, but that from then on we had no more to do with the shop except at his bidding till he sorted out the business and saw what could be salvaged – savaged, more like.

We ended up, anyway, losing the whole fucking shebang ship. Between them, the big two banks were bullying the country.

The sickly-sweet smell of the receiver's special-mix tobacco, along with whatever other substance he had in that bowl, seeped into the walls and up the stairs; I can get it in my nostrils yet. The business and premises were eventually sold as a going concern.

We had to move to a two-up two-down in a small street close to the dog track, near where the black pearl of Boley had lived before she'd taken the cattle boat to England for good.

The entire caper happened within the space of a few years from the time Baldy's head had at first appeared on the shop floor and the Gunner's habits began to change: it took the Doll, of course, to point up that link.

I was still seeing Rose, though less often. But I couldn't bring myself to confide in her about my family's straits; not before she got to hear of them from elsewhere. Because our trysts were meant to be fun, with the toils of the world left outside, what was the point in going on about the bar-and-grocery trade, especially when she didn't understand its ins and outs? By the time I told her, however, she had already got her own version of events – a warped one in which she wasn't shy about letting me know that what had happened was my father's doing. But bluntness was hardly what I most needed there and then. Oh all right, she was peeved because of my lack of trust in her.

To mistrust her once in such a serious matter may have been a gaffe, but to do so twice was simply one clanger too many for her to take. I should have gone to Rose for a shoulder to cry on when the Gunner upped and kicked the bucket for himself. Yet the inside of my head was too fraught for putting up with the same crisp stance as she'd offered when our business had gone wallop, with no idea of what the whirlpool of ferment was like for a person in mourning.

And not just her: most people had little grasp of how isolated the spot was where the Doll and I were left washed up; how unstuck we had become. No sooner had the town's pompous asses, panjandrums, upstarts, and even that crowd from the bank – the neck of them, anyway – paid us a few words of pity at the graveside than they were shifting on their uppers to be away from our spectacle of woe-begotten faces. The public's interest in bereavement has the lifespan of a blowfly on a supermarket sausage.

The good had gone out of him. What with losing both home and livelihood, especially after the way he'd been pushing out the boat, the Gunner couldn't help but fall into the pits of misery. But at no time did we suspect that his heart was weak. One day, he just dropped dead on the kitchen floor at our new address.

I still can't forget that face, with its blend of slate and purple against the cream-coloured lino, and the Doll in terror. It was surreal staring at his face in the coffin, expecting his eyes to open any moment; hard to take, in that the pipe dreams beneath those black tufts of eyebrows were over. I expected them to wiggle, and that a smile would appear before he would say: 'I fooled youse all there right well for a while, and why are youse two sitting around gawping at me?' Then he would sit up and place a hand on the Doll's forearm and squeeze it firmly for a full sixty seconds in a bare-faced exchange of some uh-huh-huh how's-your-father lust. Then the hair on his head would go back to the colour it had been, only beginning to lighten at the temples, on that day outside Mrs Maguire's house. The man could be the devil and all when wanted to be.

'So there you are, my good woman,' he would say.

There was no stir. And when they lowered him into the earth without protest, all expectation ended. We were left in shadow to recall the past from behind curtains of filmy gauze – a feat we managed without faulting him. Not once from the day he died did she blame him.

Neither at the removal of the remains nor during the burial, even though I kept a sharp eye out for her, was Rose to be seen. In a way it didn't matter . . .

A few weeks later, when I called down to the hotel, Angie told me that my girlfriend was very busy that morning. The receptionist wasn't a great liar; something hadn't set right into her expression: in a mix of unease and knowing, she reeked of excuses. And as things stood, I was up to my chin in a commotion of internal sensation, without the bother of sweetheart angst being added to the mix. As far as what Rose and I had going, it seemed best to let the hare sit for a while.

One morning months later, while getting the Sunday paper uphill from the church, I spotted Rose, all got up, passing by the shop window. She was not alone. They were down along the pavement among the other mass-goers before I made it out to the shop door. I still managed to glimpse the lumpy rump of the goon she was linking, and recognised his shuffle, the feet turned in. So she had met the mule-stomping, musk-bag-hanging Hercules of her dreams – and this was he? And that was that over then, too – the season for endings. We managed to avoid each other over the following years.

Finally, the word was out. Rose Brien and Wally Furlong were throwing a spread for their engagement, and had booked the services of a certain newly ordained priest, a lovely young man. Father William Curry, a native of Dublin, they said, would perform the upcoming nuptials before he headed off for South

America to take up a missionary position: hooray for fucken missionary positions in South America! And they wouldn't be asking me to do any spot of singing at that gig either. Ah well, you know yourself.

But the world had to go on, and the years pass. What with my new job in the slaughterhouse, adding more squealy-pigs guts and red spill to the pipe into the river for gulls to shriek over, and one job then following another, there was no choice but to stop thinking about Rose. And to help numb the senses and lust nodules alike, I underwent with an all-out dedication the only treatment known to man for this ailment: large measures of undiluted grog taken orally as often as possible. And my lifestyle had to adapt to suit the medication.

After bumping into each other again one day at the bookies, my old pal Martin Doran and I took to the drink professionally; he also had his woes to ease. And whenever he had no place to stay, I left the back door on the latch for him to come in after the Doll had gone up to bed. Of course, she said little when she found out. She didn't need to: the sharpness of her glances sideways at me was enough, her nostrils sniffing at the fetid morning air for a familiar cocktail of methane and hops.

It became easier to stay out all night, sleeping here and there under high heaven in fine weather, than to face my mother's dismay – no matter how much I had imbibed. And on rainy nights, my friend Angie, before she went home, unlocked the side door to the hotel boiler room for me – a spot from which the bottle store was easily accessed. But mine wasn't the only lifestyle in flux.

Almost in sync with the wheel-spin of the seasons, my mother was ageing. She spent more time in the bedroom living life by proxy, stuck in her temple of memories and dog-eared photos, and probably prayed there too. The radiogram by her bed, used only as a table for memorabilia: racecards from the dog track, faded receipts for clobber bought for me in boarding school, the fees marked *Paid*, even the prospectus itself . . . that fucking thing.

Because she had never actually come out straight and faulted me – instead blaming the good Doctor Baldy – the strain between us had grown too complicated for me handle: all that guilt for breakfast wasn't worth it. And at some point I stopped going home.

We bumped into each other one day on the street. She smiled when telling me the news about Baldy Klops. Doctor Quigley had finally got his comeuppance and been shagged off to some place nice and hot on the foreign missions. Her persistence with all those bus trips to the bishop's palace whilst the Gunner slept, she said, to complain about the errant priest's ways had paid off. Fed up of listening to her gripes, the old *bish* must have decided that Brazil was the best place for your man – heaven help South America.

From then till they day she died, I saw precious little of my mother. Mrs Maguire, an old family friend, found her lying in a puddle of blood and vomit on the kitchen floor lino near the same patch as where the Gunner had collapsed: the coincidence was too spooky for a fellow to read into for signs of significance or chance. The season for endings was not yet over.

'Poor thing,' Mrs Maguire said. 'She's been complaining of that condition for a long time.'

'What condition?' I asked.

'The worst one of all,' says she: 'the big C. Didn't she tell you?'

On the day the Doll was to be brought to the church, I lit a fire in a barrel in the back yard and burned most of my family's belongings and mementos. The Ryan collection, it seemed only fitting, should be cremated in a Viking-style rite of disposal. It was supposed to mean something, but what? The last item on the pyre was that wood-veneered radiogram, and her one Carlos Gardel record. With this odd desire to view my handiwork through a frame, I went back inside next to the kitchen window, leaned my cheek against the lace curtain and longed for fingers of old to tousle my unkempt hair. The flames and swirling smoke were mesmerising; I instinctively called her to come and see the spectacle for herself. But no reply; none was permitted in response to such vulgarity. And amid the white noise of silence that beset my ears, the only sensual trace that she had recently been alive was a faint whiff of pee.

Yet, from her bier in the stark front room, the Doll's tacit sway still pervaded the house, in a whirl, congealing. My fist thumped its owner's craw to breathe, and again. My breathing went back to normal. I knew that Dolly the Barmaid just had to be bigger than any idea of dying.

A few people – mostly her old friends – had dropped in earlier in the day to pay their respects, but their dribble had died off, and for the last two hours the front-door knocker had stayed silent. Then all at once, as if the gods of oddity would deny me this last bit of peace with her, iron battered down on blasted iron.

Rose stood on the step. She removed a black glove to sympathise.

I invited her in; she followed, hesitantly. I led her into the front room and left her alone with the corpse. Within minutes, she appeared on the kitchen floor lino. I turned to face her hostility. There was none; something else. Pity, possibly; yet not that either. Maybe the old embers had not entirely died. Anyway, we embraced; it lingered. And what was meant to be an apt gesture of sympathy became something else; neither of us spoke.

Maybe I held her for too long, a liberty she might not take too kindly to; so I stood back. For no reason under high heaven, other than to get her going, I did an Elvis number, *uh-uh-uh, uh-uh-uh, uh-uh-huhuu*. One song led to another. It was easier than talking: no need for unease or fudging excuses.

'I do so much prefer your voice to his,' says she, 'and you're *live*. You're the devil of a shaman, you know.'

It didn't matter that she was saying it through gritted teeth; I would have played along with her anyway. What else was there to be doing?

'I ain't no shaman,' says I. 'This here is your regular Mr Bawman, or, if you like: the Maharishi, Yogi Ryan, here at your service, ma'am.' My voice sounded dissonant, almost bogus. It hardly mattered, though. All the effort was coming from Rose.

'Oh, lovely,' says she.

I hummed a slow song as we danced close. Then up the stairs we went, and climbed under the sheets.

The Doll in her coffin down in the front room had no objections; at least none that I could hear.

It felt comforting to be able to put Rose in a trance and unlock her passion cache, and to see that the ties between us went further than my robust itch for any hot-blooded touch or her hankering after security and status, and to live in the right neighbourhood. Such links could not be pinned down – at least not on the day that was in it.

We met again and again, mostly by night, out the mill road, in the wood below the scrub road, down by the river, and here under the bridge. When a full moon caught the white on the round of her stomach or the great pear shape of her arse as she rolled over, the world once more held meaning. When she groaned underneath me – in reaction to which my splayed arms braced my torso off the ground in order to lever myself back and forward like a battering ram, and her hands in turn locked about the nape of my neck, the idea of time passing, or that any matter outside of us existed, was totally overlooked. I think she felt the same way. This was as good as anything about life could ever fucken well be.

Our little get-togethers had regained that vital essence of stealth, and this time we banged away against a different regime. But like water past the old rock factory, that was then.

And this is now – the moment that's in it right here. We now have a grasp of one another's needs, mutually allowing for the wants we can't satisfy in each other. I am the only one permitted to experience the outlandish side to Rose's nature; she knows it, and that I am grateful for the privilege. And I am, for sure: the facility for allowing someone close space in which to breathe and move comes hard-earned to a fellow. It can mean a lot; a quality not to be sniffed at.

From time to time, she will, amid her husband's cavernous snoring – sleep apnoea, she says, he has – arm herself with a blanket, make up a parcel of food, and slip out of the house. Here, under the bridge, she is free to rest her head on my shoulder till the early light; then free to go. And the food she brings keeps the other sozzlers from tittle-tattling too much about us around town: the security and status in her life oughtn't to be put at risk.

Lately, I learned one of Elivis's last songs for her: 'Moody Blue'. Take it away, Mr Presley, boy. You right one, you.

23

From the parapet above, a shrieking voice breaches the Sunday quiet under the arch of the bridge and interrupts our story. And I hoped we would reach the end before its owner arrived back. Now that he's here, I suppose, he has to become part of the account – but a small part only.

We all know the go-by-the-wall article who owns that screechy tone. The Louse has got above himself, if not gone entirely beyond redemption. He is back here to pester us.

'I have tickets for the circus!' he yells from overhead. 'Tickets for the lot of us!'

A few minutes later, he slip-slides down the mudbank and shuffles with bluster into the parlour, waving in each hand what from here look as much like coupons off a cornflake box as valid passes to a show under Duffy's big top. He does a jig for joy and hops up on a mound of paper – from which a groan rises above the sound of crunching cardboard. A hoary old tub of guts crawls out in distress from underneath that pile.

'Sorry, Salts,' the Louse mocks indifferently. He turns his back on him, to continue his victory dance in a belated attempt to belie the mean streak at the heart of the act, but only manages to wipe out whatever merit he has earned from us over finagling tickets off big Johnny Leary, the poster man for Duffy's. Well, that's the Louse for you, and if Salty Burke, the sailor, wasn't gone so feeble an old sot, he would get up and floor the little gouger – the likelihood of which at some level of awareness the Louse no doubt knows.

Quiet up to now, another vagrant leftover from last night's commune of quaffers is annoyed by the Louse's conduct: we, communards, do still have dignities to uphold. In a voice that sounds as if it has been drawn from under a plinth stone of the bridge pier there, he croaks at the Louse: 'You most likely nicked them tickets off Johnny Leary sooner than ask for them straight out. Take the clock from over Kerr's shop window beyond, you would, if you could reach it. Just a common crook, you are. Youse had all better mind, youse, your things: he'd pinch the sight out of your eye. He took two pounds on me the other day, which I had put by to get a Mass said for poor old Dolly Ryan; a pure lady, rest her soul, if ever a woman was.'

The vagrant's brain must be all-out perplexed; that incident happened a long while ago, not the other day. And why can't he leave the Doll out of it? She has got nothing to do with anything any more. How many years is it since?

Next month will see in another anniversary of my mother's too-early a-passing. Hers wasn't the only one, either.

The vagrant, who is as pie-eyed as Let-me-at-'em Larkin from the past ever was, has triggered my return to a dream movie-like state of mind, and the Louse's fanfare over tickets can do little to distract me further from this Sunday recollection.

The river, the bridge, and all else besides feels remote – even though a touch of remoteness is no harm with which to spin yarns. And moving by instinct to a place I've visualised before, a sultan's fuggy tent where belly dancers frowst about on beds, a secret hand brushes aside with an almost audible rustle the off-white gossamer curtains and damask. As every other picture fades now, I find my old familiar spectres, and the faces of people gone from us are more in focus than those of breathing beings; the past becomes more immediate than the present; extinct voices return to the crypt inside my head and ring through the silent white noise in my eardrums. Even the Doll still gives out to me: *Don't do this, don't do that, and bring your coat with you in case it rains.*

Although Rose Brien isn't dead, she too appears: that fresh young face she had before she hitched her carriage to the butcher's block comes right back to haunt me. But then again, so does her sister's – and maybe even more so. *Well, well, Minnie Brien, how d'ye do? How d'ye do, Miss Minnie O'Brien? How do you do?*

From the moment I introduced them to each other under the light of my chrome Zippo in the ball alley, all of fourteen years ago, my old friend here was tee-totally taken by Minnie Brien – or even from before, when he had seen her in a sports field near his home. My supplies of whiskey, fags and chocolate relaxed them; their intimacy came on easily. What's more, that fondness between them – a lovely thing – didn't last long enough to turn tart. Yet in the process, it changed my friend splendidly. He has since told me all about what happened, and has cleared the air between us: we are good old pals again. Aren't we, Sputnik?

The weight of urgency to excel at exams, games and shite was raised off his shoulders, mostly, as every other activity had to give quarter to an all-exacting desire to be near his dream fetish, his well-haunched, long-legged lovebird. On the night they walked across into the absolute dark at the other end of the ball alley, he was at once and for the very first time, the worst and best of times, rolled into one, beset by passion, with all its prickly burs – and it was so random. Well, that was my friend for you, who for no good reason hereabouts nowadays goes by the name of Sputnik; it falls off the tongue more easily than his real name, don't you think? Listen, which is easier to say: Martin Doran, or Sputnik?

In the alley, Sputnik probably assumed I wasn't wangling my big bird quite as well as he was Minnie – a set-up that belied the impression I had given him of how I was beyond compare at the fine art of making out with the ladies – and so he decided to keep their future trysts from me. Otherwise – as he thought – I might only bear him some sort of a grudge. Well, Sputnik, I never . . . But what on his part started out as a means to forestall begrudgery soon turned into something else: the need to avoid me altogether.

Right up to the Christmas holidays of second year, Sputnik and Minnie held their get-togethers in that warm, secreted corner of a jute-sack-filled storeroom off the college farmyard, where afterwards I, too, met Rose, to spend my last night as a boarder. But when Minnie told him he'd got her up the pole and that she had decided to take the boat to England and have herself seen to, their passion bus jerked to a sudden stop. And as he still puts it, whenever he gets carried away: 'The star left my night firmament.' Good on you Sputnik, boy – a romantic to the very end.

Months later, when you-know-who heard that the lady in question was working as an assistant housekeeper in a curate's residence near his home village and had found a new geezer with whom to amuse herself, the news tore him to shreds. The idea of her steamy sessions with him being replaced by those she was getting up to with this ploughshare – some randy git who had gone from shagging hogget ewes to doing it with his lady – kept eating him up inside. And when he again met her, she stuck her nose in the air and strutted past without a word. Not a day goes by now when he doesn't think of his slender girl: the sparkle of her airiness haunts both his head and his crotch. Around that time too, the hairspring in his brain went; he somehow got locked in time.

After those Christmas holidays, no five-minute period passed without him thinking of her. Class subjects lost their relevance; togging out for games became a chore he began to make a hash of: the hard graft on a muddy pitch offered him poor relief from desperation.

Then came the day when disaster rightly struck, and his mighty future got sheared off at the butt. It all started during football training when Billy Curry tripped him. Our friend here got to his feet in a rage and took a poke at his rival's chin. He should have known better though, and guessed how vindictive Curry's nature might be.

And there was another twist in the story. The previous fall of the year, Curry had gone into the farmyard to retrieve a ball and chanced upon our friend and Minnie coming out of their store-room rendezvous. It had been a mistake to presume that because Curry afterwards made no mention of his discovery, he'd forgotten the matter. The incident on the training field was what finally burst Billy Curry's locked trunk of fetid spite, but his reprisal exceeded what any specimen of vertebrate species was roguish enough to unleash upon a fellow member. As I guessed then, bubo-headed Curry and his mates crept through the open door of the study hall and came up on my friend from behind. Maybe that felon will meet his own ilk below in São Paulo.

Afterwards, the inner workings of my friend's head went on the blink. He ended up getting a breakdown, and was sent home to recover. Although he returned to class in September, the nerves were again at him, and he just about made it through the public exams at the end of third year. Indeed, neither Kenny D. nor himself here, the brightest of our year, got very good results.

On the other hand, of course, Shamie Doyle had no bother

doing well – and received a gold medal from the bishop for his efforts. Whenever I bump into any of my old cohorts and we, as ever, chew the rag over boarding school, the story I like to hear the most is the one about our pale-faced little pilgrim and the measures he took in order to do well in those public exams.

On the eve of the first examination, another wily cohort of ours, Neady Beird – Neady of the stocky build and crew-cut – got the job of carrying sealed boxes into the supervisor's room, and managed to leave on the latch a sash in one of the unused steel windows – unused, because it was mostly stuck. The exam supervisor returned later to open boxes, check the contents, and lay out papers in readiness for the next morning. When Neady climbed in through the window before daybreak, there ahead of him sat Shamie, with the top of his head visible behind a stack of papers, writing away under the light of a torch: Wally Furlong's, probably.

The doctor in the asylum recommended that our friend here take a break from school. Indeed, the lad gave up on his education altogether, and went to work on a farm. But the sizzle-cymbal sounds again started up inside his skull, as did the numbness. He made a stumer of even the simplest task, and didn't last in either that job or any of the others. Ever since, he has been in and out of the asylum below. But things are improving: the man has of late steadied himself, and remains on the outside for longer periods at a time. Of course, he checks himself in to update his certifiable state in order to stay the judge's hand over any breach of the peace or public-order offence he may occasionally commit.

Another old cohort of ours wasn't so lucky. Kenny D., ever the glum mix, began to get testy with anyone who went near him, eventually becoming so unhinged he had to be locked up. He is in there, shuffling sideways, zombie-like, along tiled floors, in mortal terror of the comic-book five-headed monster that is always after him. Never again, barring a miracle, will Ken D. get to see a full day's sunlight on the outside. Something serious befell the unfortunate. He still owes me a red fecking ten-shilling note from back in the old days.

Life has been less than kind to the brightest of our year – those with the greatest sensibility. Methinks the queer gods of oddity were seriously at work there.

All the same, we've made it here to this evening's show. Yes, all the cock-eyed hobos are at the circus. Away from the jibes of bullies and immune to sarcasm, we are truly part of an appreciative audience, and it's safe for a while up here on these perches. It feels heady looking down at those zany harlequins of the ring, all dickied out with diamond-patterned overalls and white pointy hats as they muck about to make fools of themselves and the world – but it takes one to spot one: they can't mock us. We already are the true jokers in the box; we have long since been the professional clowns on this slice of the planet; it's a certified right almost – if only a poorly paid one.

'One of them looks so much like Elvis, it's spooky,' says Sputnik.

'Elvis is dead, my friend,' the vagrant cuts in.

'He is not,' says Sputnik. 'A real king never dies.'

'Good on you, Sputnik.'

'And now, the main attraction of the evening!' the ring-master bawls out.

Out come the acrobats – mighty-limbed men and frilly ladies – they enter the ring and bow as the spotlight finds them. Sputnik's face is full of glee for his Frilly Lillies. We are back far enough, and at a safe distance, to watch with ease as they swing each other up to the crow's-nest in the shadows. The light catches them and, one after the other, they take off, in defiance of gravity, to fly wide and wild, and reach to where they can just about touch the underside of the canvas. Those spreadeagled birds' only desire is to escape from space restricted, confinement. We know that force of feeling and their predicament: how the need to fly outweighs all risk. Our dreams spiral with theirs: it shows on the faces of my companions.

'They're early-morning crows sidling on wires to scan for scraps,' says Sputnik.

'They're what?' says the vagrant.

'Get 'em off ya, Mrs Codlotin,' I shout. And my companions go: 'Whoopee!'

This is as good as things can ever be; there's only so much happiness to go round. And sure, isn't it good to be alive and part of things, and yet to be apart from them? And here comes the one and only Widow Flynn in full regalia hawking her basket of delicacies, timing each moment with a glorious knowing – an opportunist to the last. But opportunity is a two-way thing: who knows, I might not be sleeping under the bridge at all tonight. But first of all: how to lay my hands on a bottle of Blue Nun.

Bananas, apples, oranges and chocolates – only the last few left now. Anyone for oranges, apples or chocolates? Get yourself a nice ripe banana there, son, to put the colour back in your face.

*

I didn't mean to call them crows; they're lovely starlings, really. Look, will you. Look at them soar into the night heaven, swoop down again and then hook up: a murmuration of starlings just about ready to swoosh to ground and let the dusk settle. All is very well and quiet so, here under the stars.